FULL
IRISH

Copyright © 2014 Pete Morin and Susanne O'Leary

This book is a work of fiction. The names, characters, places and incidents either are products of the writer's imagination or are used fictitiously. Any resemblance to actual persons living or dead, actual events, locales, or organizations is entirely coincidental.

All rights reserved. With the exception of quotes used in reviews, no portion of this book may be reproduced, used, stored, introduced into a retrieval system or transmitted in any form or by any means without written permission from the copyright owners.

Cover design by J.D. Smith Design

McAvoy might be Irish, today.

PETE MORIN & SUSANNE O'LEARY
FULL IRISH

Pete Morin

Dedication

To men and women of Irish heritage, the world over.

Acknowledgements

We would like to express our appreciation to Dara Rochlin, book doctor, for her deft and efficient treatment of our manuscript, and Jane Smith, for her outstanding cover design and formatting. We are indebted to Rebecca Forster and Al Kuntz for their early feedback that put us on a corrected path; and also to Michael Strahm, a reader's reader whose searing analysis and pointed suggestions did as much for **Full Irish** as they did for **Diary of a Small Fish**.

We both deeply appreciate being members of the independent authors community. Having met (virtually) in the early days of Harper Collins' experiment, *Authonomy*, we have amassed a small army of writer friends around the world. They are enthusiastic and unhesitating in their willingness to support their fellow writers. It is an exhilarating time to be a fiction author.

Table of Contents

Dedication	iii
Acknowledgements	v
Chapter One	1
- **Meeting a train, a new client, and a day of mourning**	
Chapter Two	17
- **A success story, American tourists, and purloined evidence**	
Chapter Three	31
- **A man's castle, visiting relatives, and overtipping**	
Chapter Four	49
- **The bluest eyes, business class, and a coincidence**	
Chapter Five	61
- **A power nap, dinner banter, and the art of manipulation**	
Chapter Six	77
- **A stemwinder, biding time, and a right hook**	
Chapter Seven	91
- **A grudge match, comparing notes, playing in a dungeon**	
Chapter Eight	103
- **Playing for pride, an invitation to leave, a collaboration**	
Chapter Nine	120
- **Unauthorized pursuit, a turf war, and fighting dirty**	

Chapter Ten	133
- An exhortation, a heads up, and a sucker punch	
Chapter Eleven	144
- An identification, an accusation, and a phone that doesn't ring	
Chapter Twelve	157
- An insider, pouncing jackals, and a fetching photo	
Chapter Thirteen	171
- A monkey wrench, a chauffeur unmasked, a command performance	
Chapter Fourteen	185
- A breakfast ultimatum, front page news, and unlikely allies	
Chapter Fifteen	201
- A liar and a sissy, four 'ayes,' and a viral photograph	
Chapter Sixteen	217
- A dumpster, the undead, and a rat	
Chapter Seventeen	227
- An arrest, a brother, and another pint	
Chapter Eighteen	232
- Two confessions, attorney-client privilege, and a referral	
Epilogue	244
About the Authors	248

Chapter One

Meeting a train, a new client, and a day of mourning

Monasterevin Railway Station,
County Kildare, Ireland. May 2.

Rooftop security cameras recorded Eoin Ryan as he paced the length of the inbound train platform below the restored stone edifice of the old Victorian station building. Other commuters trickled in as the clock approached 9:00 am, until his pacing was confined to a short stretch at the lower end, where the last car always stopped. A cold drizzle came and went. He tightened the belt on his Burberry trench coat, and regretted leaving his umbrella in the boot of his Renault. A few constituents recognized him, and he returned their polite greetings and thanked them for their support. But his manners were forced. The train to Dublin would be crowded, humid and hot.

He reached into his pocket and fondled the item he was set to deliver. He looked around at the other commuters, then down the track.

The station clock showed two minutes to nine, the platform now full. Most would be commuting to Dublin for work, alone. Ryan looked at his watch, although the clock would be clearly visible from there. He pulled out his phone, looked at it and put it back again. A woman toting a suitcase behind her approached. She dropped the handle and the suitcase toppled over. Ryan bent over and helped her lift the suitcase. She spoke briefly to him. He nodded and said something.

The bright yellow face of the train appeared out of the bend.

Ryan gripped the item in his pocket again, put the tips of his shoes on the yellow safety line, and hoped the doors would open in front of him, so he might get a seat. He leaned forward, looking at the approaching train. The crowd behind him jostled for position, just like every other morning he'd traveled from home to Heuston Station, transferred to the 25 B bus and exited at Kildare Street, just outside Leinster House. But this morning, he had an important rendezvous at Temple Bar that would take him slightly out of his usual way, before he continued to Government Buildings. He looked around. The crowd seemed eager to get out of the drizzle.

The nose of the train approached. Eoin Ryan looked down the length of the yellow line, countless shoes and boots covering it. The crowd tightened. A surge from behind propelled someone into him. He pitched forward.

The Monasterevin commuters toeing the yellow line had a clear view of Eoin Ryan's body toppling into the face of the commuter train and onto the tracks as the train rolled over him.

* * *

Boston, Massachusetts, USA, early May.

Paul Forté sat in his spacious corner office in a rehabbed loft at the bend in Melcher Street, pining for a new case with panache. He looked out on the Fort Point Channel, watching the trickle of walking commuters cross the Summer Street Bridge, while he waited for his partner to show up for their twice-weekly 8:00 am "Partners Meeting," a routine they'd followed faithfully for the three years of Ford Forté LLP's existence.

Mickey Ford liked to call the law firm "the two-man wrecking crew," given their reputation for bringing down big people. Paul had to admit, it was apt. The story of his battle against a United States Attorney, especially how the man had been dragged out of the courtroom in handcuffs in the middle of Paul's trial, had become legendary in the time since Paul and Shannon had married and moved to California. In the meantime, Mickey Ford had taken down a judge and sent two probation officers and a state rep to Shirley State Prison. When Paul got back to town two years after he and Shannon had left, Ford invited him in, they quickly discovered they had common interests and opportunities, and a law firm was born. A law firm that didn't have to advertise.

The phone rang. Paul was alone in the office. It was only 7:45 am.

"Ford Forté."

"Paul Forté, please," a man's voice said.

"Speaking."

"Sorry, I didn't expect an answer at this hour."

"I didn't expect the phone to ring, so we're even. How can I help you?"

"My name is Francis Duggan. I'm the CEO of BosTech. I'd like you to represent my company in a contract procurement matter here in Massachusetts. May I come by to discuss it with you, at your earliest convenience?"

Paul hesitated. "You know I hate bureaucrats, on general principle?"

Duggan chuckled. "I don't care whether you hate them or bring them chocolates and roses on Mother's Day, I just want you to stop them from screwing the only local company on the bidder's list."

"Tell me a little about it."

Duggan's company was a product of the Massachusetts high tech boom. They manufactured software designed to track, control and predict state government spending. The Comptroller's Office was looking to replace some junk that had failed so badly, the state had lost track of close to two billion dollars.

"Initially, there were seven interested parties, but four dropped out because they couldn't qualify. Of the three remaining, we're the only American company. The others are from Toronto and Ireland. Royale is the Canadian firm. The Irish company is Chiar-Tech."

"There's a software company still in business in Ireland?"

Duggan laughed. "You're behind the times, Paul. Their banks are in the shit, but there is a resurgence of the tech sector. All the big companies are moving there because of the tax policy. Google, LinkedIn, PayPal, Amazon, Twitter, Dropbox, they've all snapped up locations down on Silicon Docks. A few of the indigenous start-ups have weathered the storm, if they didn't invest in real estate."

"And Chiar-Tech?"

"They were smart. Didn't put a dime into brick and mortar."

"Do either of the foreign entities have any local ownership?"

"Not that's disclosed."

"What do you think is going on?" It's always good to know the client's worst fear.

"I think this Irish company's wiring the contract, and I'll be damned if I'm gonna let it happen."

"Who's representing them here?"

"Some ex-rep named Boyle. Dennis Boyle."

Dennis Boyle. One of Paul's former colleagues from his days in the House. Another in the endless line of former committee chairmen who strode briskly through the revolving door and began to make hay like there was no tomorrow. Dennis Boyle, a man so oily, if he gave you a ten for a five you'd still feel like you got cheated. Another dark product from the Jesuit hosts at B.C. High, B.C. College and B.C. Law School.

Another fucking Triple Eagle. Another golfer who cheated. "Come on over, Francis. My calendar just opened up."

* * *

Finola McGee jumped off the bus from Ranelagh before it came to a full stop, slipped on the wet pavement, but managed to straighten up before twisting an ankle. No need to wobble into a pub so early in the day. She checked her watch. Shit, late again. Eoin was always punctual, and today, considering the urgency with which he asked to meet her, she was certain he'd already be waiting. Eoin had tracked her down the day before, to a book launch at The Arts Club, where one of Labour's sycophants was touting how their austerity measures were pulling the country from the ashes of the bankruptcy caused by Fianna Fáil's bailouts. While the man droned on, Ryan had pulled her aside and muttered in her ear about having some information to give her.

As political editor for *The Irish Telegraph*, Finola had to attend these tedious events, just as she had to endure the endless parade of politicians lying to her face or sticking their heads in the sand. But Finola had been surprised to see Eoin Ryan there. As Minister of State for Environment, he was singularly dedicated to his causes. He was one of few in the Dáil who publicly demanded jail time for the bankers that had practically ruined Ireland. If he tracked her down at a book launch, he had a good reason. Eoin was a crusader. If he had a crusade, it usually meant a good story.

She slowed to a walk as she approached the pedestrian crossing in front of Trinity College. The light drizzle turned to heavier rain and umbrellas snapped open all around her. Cursing herself for having forgotten hers, Finola ducked her head, turned up the collar of her raincoat and broke into a half-run when the lights changed.

The pub in Temple Bar was only a short, usually pleasant, stroll away, but in this weather, she only gave a passing glance at the beautiful façade of The Bank of Ireland. Thinking that at least the throngs of protestors were no longer clogging the pavement, she turned the corner into the narrow, cobbled alley, at the end of which lights glowed inside the entrance of the pub. She ran the last few yards, pushed open the door, and entered the warm, dry pub with a sigh of relief.

The pub was empty, the barman nowhere to be seen. Nor was Eoin. Strange that he'd be late. She expected him to be sitting in their usual place, pointing at his watch as she rushed in. She took off her dripping coat and took one of the empty stools, looking forward to teasing him for being late. She glanced at the huge flat screen TV over the bar as the news came on. She hadn't had time to check the newspapers online or listen to the latest broadcasts before she rushed out earlier this morning. Here was a chance to catch up, if only the telly wasn't muted.

"What can I get you, Finola?" The barman appeared behind the counter as she watched the first raft of ads before the news broadcast. "The usual?" he asked, his hand on the handle of the pump, ready to pull her a pint of Guinness.

Finola laughed. "Not at this time of day, Fergus. I'll have a mug of coffee."

"How about a cappuccino? We have a new espresso maker. I can make one of those for you, froth and all."

"Perfect. Thanks." On the TV screen, the weather map predicted the same. More rain, what else was new? She sighed. She'd be splurging on a taxi to work from there. What was it Eoin wanted to tell her? What was so important he couldn't have told her at the launch last night, or e-mailed her about it? Perhaps something he had discovered recently, yet another scam by some politician. Eoin had an uncanny nose for sniffing out bribery and corruption. And he was insistent and unapologetic about exposing it. So much so that he had few friends in the Dáil. Here was Ireland, struggling to get back on its feet after the banking crash and still so many politicians lining their pockets. It was a miracle there was any money left to run the country.

"One perfect Cappuccino." Fergus slid a cup on the table in front of her. "Must say I got it right first time. I even did a smiley face with the cocoa powder. Admit you're impressed."

But Finola hardly heard him. The somber face of the TV anchor hinted at trouble. The picture changed to a portrait photo. Eoin Ryan, looking at her. She shook her head trying to make out what the newsreader was saying.

"Fergus, turn up the volume, willya?"

Fergus grabbed the remote and soon the empty pub echoed with the speaker's voice.

"Eoin Ryan, TD for County Kildare and Minister of State for Environment, is dead."

* * *

From the moment he left the House of Representatives, Dennis Boyle took for granted where his lobbying business would come from. He knew because, by pure stroke of luck, he enjoyed life-long friendships with two well-placed state senators, one of who happened to be the Senate President.

Dennis Boyle had no reservations about making hay while the sun shone, and as one client followed another, the modest sense of ethics he'd learned at B.C. High dissolved into a murky pit. He hadn't crossed the line, at least not in his own mind.

Then the phone rang one day two months earlier, and he was asked to become the legislative and executive agent for an Irish software company called Chiar-Tech. He'd get ten grand a month, but he had to share that with someone else. He didn't ask who.

Boyle would be the first to admit, he was okay at math, but he was no computer geek. At B.C., the Jesuits rewarded his mathematical aptitude in a way only Jesuits would. They taught him how to count cards during his 3-credit "ethics" course. But his typical daily computer usage consisted of three blackjack sites and an almost obsessive viewing of an Internet camera that spied on his children's Brazilian nanny.

The client was only interested in his relationship with Charles Sligo, the Senate Chairman of the Committee on State Administration. *Fackin' Chah*-lie, as Boyle had dubbed him during his Sigma Zi rush.

Initially, this singular focus on his ability to "deliver" Sligo grated on Boyle, if he had to admit it. Sure, he had to feed a family, like anyone. But he was a lawyer and officer of the court. He had honor, for crissakes.

But ten grand a month bought a lot of honor, and paid a few K-6 private school tuitions as well.

It also bought (thanks to *Fackin' Chah*-lie) a skein of language in a "Request for Proposals" from the Office of the State Comptroller that virtually guaranteed that Chiar-Tech would be the highest ranked qualified bidder for a software contract worth about $27 million.

He also had Sligo's commitment to earmark the upcoming state budget with money to fund the contract. But anything can happen during a budget debate, and that's where Dennis Boyle earned his dough. If the Senate put it in their budget, he'd have to get the House to go along in the Conference Committee.

That he could do, he assured his buddy one more time, as they sat on barstools at "Temperance," a bar around the corner from the State House, named by a man with sly humor.

"I'm not feelin' it, Dennis," Sligo said. His head full of black curls hung between shoulders anchored to a bar by two elbows. "And what the hell? What am I gettin' out of this?"

"What do you mean, what are you getting out of this? We're

doing our jobs."

"Yah, and if someone starts squawking about the way I'm doing my job, it doesn't affect your sleep or sex life, does it, brother Dennis? You running for re-election?"

"Come on, Charlie."

"I'm taking all the risk here. I want some of the reward."

"Your reward comes on the other side, pal. You know that. You're not stopping at State Administration. Your reward is Ways and Means. Your reward is Senate President. You know we're grooming *you* for that, right? Don't tell me there's no reward."

Chairman Sligo sighed. "Dennis, you know what the tuition is at St. Mary's? It's seventeen-six. Times three." Sligo's wife had been unexpectedly fertile. He ran his fingers through his hair. "I can't afford to wait. I'll have three college tuitions by then and Janice is no buffalo squeezer. She just bought a new Land Rover, for crissakes."

Chip the bartender slipped down to their corner to refresh their drinks. He knew enough not to stick around. This was what Temperance was all about. A watering hole, a refuge from prying eyes, staffed with people who heard and saw nothing.

"You told me you were marrying over your head thirteen years ago, Charlie."

"And the chickens are coming home to roost." He picked up his fifth Guinness pint, toasted his pal, and took a slow pull, inhaling the woodiness. "What're you gettin', ten grand a month? That's a lot of cake, Dennis. You could share some of that with your pal."

"I'm not getting ten grand a month. More like six. I have to give the other four to someone else."

"Yah? Who? Who's earning the four grand more than I am, sticking my neck out like this?"

"You don't want to know." Boyle patted his buddy's shoulder. "Look, Charlie. I'll be happy to loan you some dough. I have a nice equity piece coming out of this when we pull it off."

Full Irish | 9

"Why don't I get equity? I want some fuckin' equity."

"We'll figure something out, don't worry about it. Let's just get that fucking money in the House budget. Your best friend will find a way to take care of you. Okay pal?"

* * *

"Who the fuck is BosTech?" Sligo barked into the telephone an hour later. Not angry, not ready to choke someone. Just emphatic, and perhaps a little peevish.

"BosTech is one of the other two bidders. The only one based in Massachusetts." The voice belonged to Teddy Price, a high-ranking staffer in the Comptroller's Office and the chairman of the bid committee for their biggest software overhaul since the Internet was turned on in the state office buildings.

"Some local start-up? You're not going to let a start-up bid on a project of this magnitude."

"Senator, they're not a start-up. Their product went through years of beta testing and has four patents. It's a very good product, it's done very well, and they have money behind them."

"Well I don't give a fuck who they are or where they're from. I don't want anybody making trouble for the biggest software company in Ireland. This is international economic development here. This is important shit."

Price took a few breaths to regain his patience. "Senator, I need to remind you that your candidate's financial statements were not, uh…inspirational. And if I disqualify BosTech from bidding, I might as well get a bullhorn and announce, 'we're bid rigging here!' Their legislators will holler from the rafters."

"Who are they?"

"Bill Toole and Ed Cook."

Sligo scoffed. "Nobodies. Biff Toole and 'Shortie' Cook? Back benchers."

"We have to let them bid. We'll take care of it on the scoring. I know what I'm doing on this. I *did* work at the MBTA for fifteen years, right? And yes, I am aware of the Senate President's personal interest in *this issue*."

"Of course you do, Teddy." Sligo felt his heart racing. "Okay, I gotta get the hell off the phone before I have a stroke." He glanced at his watch. "Jesus Christ, I've got to get over to St. Mary's for the girls' choir. Janice'll kill me if I'm late."

Charlie Sligo slammed the phone down, grabbed his suit jacket and charged out of his Chairman's corner office suite in the west wing of the State House, hesitating for just a few seconds to scope the rear end of a Suffolk University political science major.

* * *

Paul rummaged through one of a few boxes stacked against the unadorned, century-old brick wall of his office. He figured after three years it was time to hang the rest of the evidence of his career, maybe even the aerial picture of the State House. The sort of thing that potential clients might like to see, his partner suggested. But hanging more picture frames on brick might violate the lease restrictions on "defacing, painting, reconditioning, staining, repointing, moving, or otherwise altering the Historical architectural features of the leased premises." Even though he owned the building, he thought it was important to establish an example. Thus, a lot of his past remained in boxes, including the front page of the Boston Herald from a December day long ago: "Ex-rep cleared of federal corruption charge - U.S. Attorney arrested in courtroom during trial."

At the precise hour of his appointment with Francis Duggan, the outer office door opened, and a tall, dark haired gentleman struggled through the doorway pulling a two-wheel cart that held three boxes strapped to it with bungee cords. He wore an elegant, dark blue chalk stripe suit that hung on him like a da Vinci at the Louvre, a playful foulard tie and matching pocket square, and shoes that cost more than Paul's Saab.

Paul wasn't one to notice such things ordinarily, but Francis Duggan was the epitome of tall, dark and handsome. Black hair, combed back to show off a sharp widow's peak above thick black eyebrows. Rugged Irish nose and mouth. Liquid blue eyes. Paul's first thought was to keep the man away from Shannon. Then he laughed to himself. He looked forward to her reaction.

Paul hustled out to greet him.

"Mr. Duggan." He extended his hand, and Duggan grasped it like it was a strength contest.

"Glad to meet you, Paul. Call me Frank, eh?" Duggan's eyes scanned the open office space, taking in the high ceilings and rough-hewn wooden beams. "I love offices like this. Didn't some of these used to belong to the British Crown?"

Paul nodded. "When the House of Windsor decided to liquidate, these old buildings went like free booze. We were lucky to grab this one. Come this way."

Paul led Duggan down the length of the open space past four cubicles, at which young men and women peered intensely at computer screens. "We run our operation lean and mean, Frank. We have the best law students in Boston working for us as interns, and we're in a growth mode."

"As long as you get the job done, I don't care if you work alone out of your car. Do you still have that Saab?"

"I didn't know the car was that famous." Then he remembered the stupid Boston Phoenix photo with him and the reporter, Cory Fitzpatrick, grinning in front of it. Paul had left town the following day.

They entered a long conference room, the outer wall brick, and windows looking out across the Fort Point Channel toward the U.S. Postal Annex.

"You don't review your press clippings then," he said. "One

of your puff pieces discussed your propensity to eschew the trappings of wealth, and quoted you referring affectionately to your 'shitbox Saab.'" Duggan wheeled his cart to the side of a conference chair and sat.

"That was Cory Fitzpatrick. He was part of our team."

"Is he still part of your team? Always helps to have a friend in the press."

"We stay in touch." Paul waved at the boxes next to Duggan. "Why don't you start from the beginning of the world and take me up to this morning. Try to omit the irrelevant parts."

Duggan chuckled. "You'll be sorry you asked." He flicked the bungee off the top box, removed the lid, and hefted four three-ring binders, each four inches thick, onto the conference table. "These contain every document you'll need to review. I'm going to give you the view from twenty thousand feet. You ask me what you want. Then you can spend a few days looking through this jungle of bureaucratic gobbledygook."

"Sounds like a plan. Tell me your story."

* * *

A weak sun penetrated the clouds and shone on the granite façade of the church. A crowd was gathered around the entrance, milling about, talking in hushed tones. Finola pulled her black raincoat tighter around her, lowered her head and walked swiftly past them. She hesitated at the door. She still couldn't quite grasp that Eoin was dead.

He had fallen under a train, the newspapers said. A tragic accident. But how was that possible? How could someone who took that very same train every morning fall onto the track just as the train arrived at the station? Was it intentional? Suicide? No. Not possible. He had seemed in very good form the night before, except that he was worried about something. He was on his way to meet her. He had something important he wanted to share with her, he said.

Someone touched her shoulder. "Finola."

She turned around and came face to face with Seamus Nolan, Deputy Secretary of the Department of Finance. Still as short as she remembered, when they worked together in Labor Party headquarters, taking orders from Aidan Fahey, before the banks were failing and Fianna Fáil was still in power. With his fair hair, boyish face and freckles, he looked younger than he was. But Finola knew that inside the boy-next-door was the mind of a shrewd political thinker. She had been fond of him, even after he'd been unwilling to confront Fahey over his misconduct. And his loyalty to Fahey had paid off, as his rise to the top of the civil service showed.

"Seamus," she said. "Hi."

"Dreary day."

Finola nodded. "Yes."

"Terrible business."

"Awful."

He put his hand on her arm. "I know he was a special friend. But we all liked him. Who wouldn't? Such a fine, honest man. It's a great loss. "

Finola shivered. "Yes."

"I suppose we'd better go inside. The family will be arriving shortly." Seamus took her hand. "Come on, we'll sit together. We can go to the back of the church. That way you don't have to look at—"

Finola sighed. "Thank you, Seamus. That's very kind."

"Not kind at all. I need a little comfort, too."

Together, they walked into the church and sat down in one of the pews at the back. The air smelled of candles and incense; an organ played softly as people filed in and chose a pew. Finola could see the corner of the coffin, draped in the Irish flag, and thought how apt that was. Eoin loved his country, and everything he did reflected that love.

The family arrived. Eoin's wife, Orla, walked down the aisle, hidden by a wide brimmed black hat and veil. She held her two youngest children by the hand. The bishop and two priests followed them.

During the mass, Finola barely heard the words of the sermon, the many readings or the hymns. All she could think of was the circumstances of Eoin's death and his urgent need to give her something. It didn't quite add up. Tears stung her eyes as she watched Eoin's brothers carry the coffin out on their shoulders. The despair in Orla's face and the bewildered eyes of the children as they walked out behind them was unbearable.

Seamus handed her a crisp, white lavender-scented handkerchief. "Here. Have a good blow."

Finola blew her nose and wiped her eyes. "Thank you, Seamus. Trust you to have a clean handkerchief in your pocket. Don't know many men who do these days."

"Ah, well, my mammy told me to always have a clean hanky on my person. You never know when a lady needs to wipe a tear or two."

Finola gave him a wobbly smile. "Your mammy was a wise woman."

"She was." He stuffed the sodden handkerchief into his pocket and peered at her. "Feeling better?"

She nodded. "Yes. Thank you."

"Good." He got up. "Come on, we have to go to the house. Orla would appreciate your support."

Finola nodded. "Of course. And everyone will be there. All wondering who'll win the by-election and take Eoin's seat. Like bloody vultures."

"Of course," Seamus agreed. "Kildare is an important constituency. Eoin's death was a tragic accident. But whoever takes his place will have a great influence on the balance of power in this government."

"Especially as there is a general election at the end of this year," Finola remarked, looking at Seamus and trying to figure out what was going on in that sharp mind. That by-election would be important to him, especially as a civil servant.

Eoin had been so worried about something. She had seen it in his eyes that last time they met. She had to find out what it was.

Chapter Two

A success story, American tourists, and purloined evidence

Francis Duggan laid out the story of his company like he had given the spiel a thousand times, and he probably had, given the amount of time he'd probably spent raising equity capital. Duggan was an economist and forensic accountant by training. Received a Ph.D. from Cornell, where he wrote his thesis on the effects of the contemporary electoral process on the accuracy and predictability of budget forecasting. This got him interested in creating financial accounting tools for government budgeting that eliminated many of the unpredictables inherent in agency spending, mostly caused by incompetence or political interference. He laid his algorithms and oversight tools on top of a state-of-the-art financial management information system design, essentially creating a second layer of oversight which not only flagged entries that fell outside of the algorithm's parameters, but also provided a traceable two-step authorization procedure tied to independent managers. Against the wager of the best intellectual property law firm in Washington, Duggan was granted four design and utility patents, which raised the interest of venture capitalists and enabled him to obtain a second round of funding for beta testing and design tweaking. More patent claims followed as the design was enhanced and perfected.

Duggan was raised in Lowell, and he remained a loyal native son. He started his company in one of the old mill buildings along the Merrimack River, before they were restored. He kept the company there when he could have moved ten miles north to New Hampshire and saved the company a bundle. He was something of a big shot in the City of Lowell, which made him a "friend" of his state senator, which he thought would be worth at least a meeting when he ventured into the public bidding field. How wrong he was.

Now, the Massachusetts Comptroller's Office was upgrading the financial management system for the entire Executive branch. Really, he said, what they were doing was stumbling out of the Stone Age, replacing systems that had been invented before Bill Gates had left Harvard.

"Seriously," Duggan said. "This is supposed to be one of America's technology Meccas. How can our own state government be so behind the times?"

"Compare the last names of people in charge with the state legislators. That's a good place to start," Paul said.

Duggan flipped open the first binder. "This is the RFP, the bid document. It's two hundred seventy-seven pages long. Single-spaced. I swear to God, Paul, I've never seen a more ridiculous procurement document in my life. And I spent two years at the Pentagon."

Paul cringed, recalling his days at the MBTA, where procurements were more of a sport than a selection process. "Do you know who Rex Barkley is?"

"Isn't he the financial investigator who uncovered the fraud involving the U.S. Attorney who was prosecuting you?"

"You've done your homework."

"Naturally. Do you plan to use him for this?"

"Quite possibly," Paul said. "Anyway, Rex had a simple statement - where there is a procurement, there is an opportunity."

Duggan winced. "That's why I'm here."

"It seems to be someone else's opportunity?"

"Yes. And it twists my knickers to think it's someone from the Old Country."

"You have family back there?"

Duggan nodded with eyes closed. "I have cousins in Kerry. They own several bars and inns in Cahersiveen and Waterville."

"Never been to Ireland."

Duggan gasped. "I thought you were an avid golfer. How could you live half your life and not have made at least one pilgrimage?"

Paul sighed. "I lied. I went to Ireland once. I had to attend to the return of my parents' remains to the U.S."

Duggan said nothing.

"They were involved in a fatal accident on the highway from Cork to Dublin."

"I'm sorry, Paul."

"No apology necessary. Anyway, it's been long enough now. I *should* go, while I still have a golf swing." Paul looked at the pile of binders. "Can you shortcut my review of this garbage and tell me what the main problem is?"

"It's simple. We're a relatively new company with a short, if impressive, track record. The 'qualifications' section of the RFP indicates that bidders will be scored on a number of factors. They have set the minimum parameters so high that we are at risk of being disqualified."

"So let me guess. Based on the factors and the scoring, Chiar-Tech might be the only qualified bidder."

"That's right."

"What about the rest of the RFP?"

Duggan let out a slow, long breath. "You know how these things go. They leave themselves enough wriggle room to score a bid any damn way they want." He gestured toward the stack of binders. "And as you will see when you get around to reading, some of the best features of our software aren't even counted in their requirements."

"There's no catch-all at the end?"

"Well, there is, but there's no obligation to count it for anything."

Paul muttered under his breath. "Jesus Christ, no wonder we're $17 trillion in debt."

"It's a travesty. We understood at the beginning that we might have to change the paradigm somewhat, but we've got a product that increases the utility of every public dollar spent, and we're treated with outright hostility."

"Well, this is Massachusetts. You might have begun in a state that was a bit redder. Like Texas."

Duggan scoffed. "They're no better. They talk a good game, but they've all got bread that needs buttering."

"One man's pork is another man's pride. Tell me about this Irish company."

Duggan raised his hands in surrender. "Afraid I can't tell you a whole lot. As you may be aware, Ireland has developed quite a thriving technology sector, thanks to their government's tax policy. Business was raging until the global recession and the government's near bankruptcy. They saw quite a contraction, but it's back on the upswing. This company's been around for about six years, and they've had quite a string of sales among the European Union countries."

"Who's behind it?"

"I'm afraid I don't have much information on the individuals. Their CEO, Seamus Nolan, is also Deputy Secretary of the Department of Finance. His boss, Aidan Fahey, is the Minister of Finance, TD for Kerry and a member of the Chiar-Tech board. I assume his political influence in Dublin is substantial."

"So, Fahey is a member of the Dáil, the Minister of Finance, *and* a board member of Chiar-Tech? Do they have conflict of interest laws over there?"

"In theory, but you wouldn't recognize them."

"Is Fahey a crook?" Paul eyed the binders, dreading the reading assignment.

"Put it this way," Duggan said. "He's never been convicted of anything."

"They might award points on the bid for that."

"The Faheys are sort of a political dynasty in Kerry. Aidan's the latest, and probably last. I don't know much about him."

"What's the timing?"

"I have no idea. We can't get a straight word out of anyone. It's maddening."

"Didn't you have counsel up to this point?"

"We do," Duggan said. "Former Raytheon counsel out of Worcester."

"Roger Lawrence?"

"Yes, you know him?"

"Went to school with him. Good lawyer."

"He is. Good enough to know when he's hit a wall. He's taken this as far as he can, but he's a procurement lawyer, not a brawler."

Paul sympathized with his old classmate. "Okay, here's what I think. Their lobbyist is capable of anything. I'm betting he's got a few of his pals in the State House running interference for him. We need to get some intelligence on these Irish birds. If they're connected well, I won't know who the hell to talk to without tipping them off. Why can't your cousins help you?"

Duggan shook his head. "I'm afraid my history with them is a little dodgy. If I were to ask them for help, they might be inclined to go the other way."

"Still, they could be helpful for information. They're in Kerry, right? Fahey's district? They must know something about him."

Duggan shook his head again and shrugged. "They run bars, Paul. They don't know this end of the game."

"Maybe I'll take my wife over for a little due diligence. I have a friend at the State Department who can help me set some things up."

"If you think it'll help. How much of a retainer do you need?"

"I'm not going to represent you, Mr. Duggan."

Duggan's face sagged. "What the hell are you talking about?"

"Don't panic, for crissakes. If you engage me, there are a lot of things I can't do, like talk to anyone from Chiar-Tech. If you don't hire me, I have no ethical constraints. At least, not the kind that the Board of Bar Overseers cares about."

Duggan eyed Paul with a crooked smile. "Oh, I don't think Dennis Boyle has anything on you, Paul Forté."

"Yeah, well…" Paul ruminated about his criminal trial, when he was convinced of his own culpability as his lawyer argued his innocence. "In politics and business, virtue is a relative concept."

* * *

"We're going to Ireland!" Shannon shouted from the rooftop. Literally.

Paul informed his wife of their imminent travel plans as they lounged in sweaters by the terra cotta chimnea stove on the secluded rooftop pergola of Shannon's penthouse condominium on Farragut Street in South Boston. They reclined in the same Adirondack chairs they'd occupied when he first had the courage to say, "I love you," nearly six years earlier.

Paul poured Shannon some more pinot noir. "I contacted an old friend at the State Department. He made a few calls to the American Embassy in Ireland. They're setting up a nice VIP tour of Leinster House, where the two houses of the Irish legislature meet."

"They don't call it that. It's not Parliament, either. What is it called?"

"The government is called the Oireachtas," he said, pronouncing it oy-*REEK*-tus. "The legislature is bi-cameral, like here. A

House and Senate, called the Dáil and the Seanad." He said *dale* and se-*NADE*.

"Same thing, different accent. They're all a bunch of crooks."

"Yes, the crooks in the Dáil are called TDs."

Shannon swirled the last of her glass. "And you're going to inform me what TD means."

"Yes, I am. This is important. We're traveling as Ambassadors without portfolio."

Shannon cackled. "You mean we're faking it."

"Yes, we are under cover."

"Okay, what does 'TD' mean, Ambassador Forté?"

"It's short for Teachta Dála." *TECK*-ta.

Shannon guffawed. "You bozo, it's CHOCK-ta. And Oireachtas is o-*ROCK*-tas. And it's dawl and she-*NAD*."

"I'll have to work on that."

Shannon frowned. "Do we have to spend a lot of time schmoozing with pols?"

"Just the intros, maybe lunch. Then you can hit the galleries. Maybe you should bring your portfolio and try to drum up some business among the Irish elites. They might like paintings on toilet seats, too."

"Not a bad idea," Shannon said. "My brand is a little faded here." She'd done well with her trompe l'oeil art in the U.S., but her prices were starting to drop. The toilet seat thorns had netted her ten thousand a mere five years ago. Now she'd be lucky to get five, so she'd turned back to canvases.

"And there is one government building you won't be reluctant to tour."

"What's that?"

"Castle Cormack."

"The government owns a castle?"

"Sort of. They used to own it. It's now a hotel. We're staying there."

"No shit? We're staying in a castle? Is it drafty? Does it have ghosts?"

"It's a five star hotel. They have heat and everything."

"Do they have a butler?"

"I bet they have several."

"How about a dungeon?"

"I doubt that."

Shannon sipped her wine and inspected her husband's face. "Why are we going to Ireland, Paul?"

"It's sort of work." He told her about Duggan, the Irish competitor and the nature of the V.I.P. event they were to attend at Castle Cormack.

"We're going there for a rubber chicken dinner? Do I have to go?"

"You'll have a blast," he said. "The Irish people will love you. You'll be a spectacular hit."

"I'll have to buy a dress," she said.

"Pack light."

"And new bags."

"Oh, shit."

"I have some kind of relative over there. Maybe I'll do some research and we can visit him and have a wee drop on the auld sod."

"Sounds like fun."

She smiled.

That's all she ever had to do. It was a perfect smile, set in the middle of a perfect face, with dark eyes and the mannish eyebrows of her Irish ancestors. As striking to him now as when he first saw them, when he was a witness in front of a grand jury and she, a grand juror, stared back at him.

"Let's go downstairs," he suggested.

"I dunno, I'm comfortable up here."

"But we can't do up here what we can do down there?"

"We can't, huh?" She stood up, unzipped her jeans and slid them down. The chimnea stove cast a golden glow on her thighs.

"It's kind of cold up here," he said.

"So keep your sweater on." She dropped down in front of Paul's chair.

* * *

Sipping tea and nibbling sandwiches at the widow's home, assorted TDs and higher civil servants paid their respects and then resumed their murmuring about what had happened and who was likely to win the by-election and take Eoin's seat and if it would affect Labour's majority. Like jackals, Finola thought yet again, as she moved through the queue to offer condolences to an ashen-faced Orla.

Finola gave her a warm hug. "I'm so terribly sorry," she whispered. "I know there's nothing I can do, but…"

Orla hugged her back. "Thank you, Finola. I'm so glad you're here. I need to see you in the study before you leave. Once I finish accepting condolences from all these…well-wishers."

Finola nodded. "Of course. Give me a nod and I'll sneak off." She squeezed Orla's shoulder and went to join a group of journalists from RTÉ, the Irish broadcasting service, in the living room. She greeted Paula Donnelly, their female anchor. "Sad day."

Paula nodded. "Such a shock. Poor Eoin. We'll miss him terribly. He was always great with the press, wasn't he? And such a great debater on *Prime Time*. He really made his opposition sweat, especially the Taoiseach in last month's showdown. We had to redo his make-up during every commercial break."

Finola laughed. "Eoin was a bulldog. He never let go."

Paula smiled wistfully. "He sure dug up stuff none of us wanted to touch."

Finola knew all about that. "He made the Labour party with their so-called social conscience look like the two-faced liars they are. Pay the bankers all their money, sure, but nothing for the farmer who can't get a loan."

"They'll have a hard time getting re-elected," Paula said. "But for the moment, the Taoiseach's department is rustling with the sound of nest feathering."

Finola looked at a group of men by the window, where Aidan Fahey, TD for south Kerry, was holding court, talking loudly and slapping people on the back. "Yes. I see one of them over there, networking like mad. Fucking slimeball."

Paula looked startled at Finola's sudden venom. "Aidan? Yeah, a bit of a lad with the women. Fancies himself big time. But why do you feel so strongly about him?"

Finola tried to hide the seething anger she felt every time she saw him. "Old story. Nothing I really want to go into." She glared at Fahey's back. "One day, he'll get what he deserves."

Paula followed Finola's gaze. "Oh, Aidan's not the worst of them. He's very popular in his constituency." She nodded at Seamus Nolan, just breaking away from the group. "I'm more interested in higher civil servants in the pockets of politicians. That's not right. But Nolan's too cute to let any mud stick, of course."

"Seamus is a very clever political operative, and he's gotten to the top with Fahey's support. I don't know how he can stand the man. He's a nice guy behind it all, even if his boss is a two-faced liar."

Paula smiled ironically. "Aren't they all?"

A young woman touched Finola's shoulder. "Orla wants to see you," she murmured. "She's in the study."

"Of course." Finola excused herself and walked to the study, where she found Orla sitting by the window, staring out at the garden.

Finola went to Orla's side. "Is there something I can do—?"

Orla squeezed her hand. "Thank you. I know how close you two were."

"He was my best friend." Finola pulled up a small petite pointe stool and sat down opposite Orla, so close their knees touched.

"You know Eoin was on his way to meet me?"

Orla didn't reply, but stared at Finola, twisting a sodden handkerchief. Small white linen, with little shamrocks embroidered around the edge, Finola saw, the way you notice tiny details in moments of great distress. Her frail blonde looks were a stark contrast to Finola's sturdy frame and unruly dark hair.

"For God's sake, Orla, don't hold something important back just because you think he still loved me," Finola pleaded. "He didn't, I swear. We were just friends. Good friends, but that's all."

"He was mad about you at college."

"And then he saw you and forgot all about me. Or anyone, actually. Never saw a man so carried away. He loved *you*, Orla, don't you ever forget that."

Orla's face lit up for a brief moment. "Yes. I know. I'm sorry. Shouldn't have said that."

"It's okay."

"I knew he was going to see you. But that's not what I wanted to tell you." Orla dabbed her red eyes with her handkerchief. "Eoin was murdered."

"Murdered?" Finola exclaimed. "Where did you hear this? It can't be true."

Orla nodded. "It is. The Guards were just here. They told me that the security cameras were unclear, but two witnesses have come forward. They both saw someone push Eoin forcibly onto the tracks just as the train arrived." She started to cry again.

"Could the witnesses identify this person?"

Orla blew her nose. "Not yet. They got a look, but not enough to make sense of. The man wore a hooded sweatshirt. Slightly different descriptions, too. You know how unreliable eye witnesses can be." Well, anyway they're making inquiries and searching the station. Just lip service, really."

"But who—?" Finola started. "I mean who would have wanted Eoin dead?"

Orla looked at Finola with red-rimmed eyes. "I can't imagine.

Full Irish | 27

Of course he had enemies. Some people who weren't too pleased with his whistleblowing. The Guards are asking around too. I knew there was something going on and that he was very upset and worried. I thought since he was on his way to see you…" Orla got up and walked to the desk nearby and pulled out a drawer. She took something out and showed it to Finola. "I think this is what he was going to give you. It was in his pocket."

"A flash drive? Do you know what's on it?"

"No. I didn't have the heart to look."

Finola shot up and took the flash drive. "You should probably give this to The Guards. I mean, it could be important evidence."

"Yes, but I got all of his belongings from the hospital before they knew he was… murdered. It wasn't evidence then, so I thought…" Orla sighed. "I prefer you to have it. I don't trust The Guards these days." She smiled ruefully. "Eoin was a troublemaker. If he's got something on someone, I don't want The Guards mucking it up. And who knows? You might find out who killed Eoin before they do."

"I hope I do." Orla's words prompted the memory of Finola's last words with Eoin, at the book launch. Just before she'd left, she'd seen Eoin in a tense exchange with Fahey, poking his finger at Fahey's chest as he leaned close to say something.

"But keep it safe," Orla warned. "You never know who might want what's on it."

Finola stuffed the flash drive into her bra. "It'll be very safe here."

"Are you sure?"

Finola grinned. "With my love life? Safest place in Ireland."

*   *   *

While checking off the to-do list before his trip to Ireland, Paul jumped on Skype for a chat with his old pal, the semi-retired private investigator Rex Barkley. With any luck, Paul would catch him in his "office," an outdoor lanai on a deck looming high above Kaneohe, on the island of Oahu. The "office" was part of the fruit of Rex's victory in exposing an insurance fraud scheme involving federal transportation funds. The same fraud scheme that, coincidentally, brought down Paul's prosecutor, the notorious Bernard Kilroy. Paul stayed out of jail; Rex collected $17.6 million in a whistleblower award.

"What do you want," Rex barked. "I'm about to go fishing."

Paul looked at his watch. "Sorry, I didn't realize it was so early out there. You're practically in China."

"Hawaii is not a foreign country. It's our fiftieth state."

"It was a sleepy little kingdom, until American businessmen overthrew it and bought its annexation from our government."

"Ancient history. Why are you bothering me?"

"I have a small job for you, of course."

"Small job. I don't do small jobs."

"You need more practice. Listen." Paul told him what little he knew about Chiar-Tech, where he was headed. "I need to know who owns Chiar-Tech, where they got their money, company structure, that kind of stuff. Their CEO is a guy named Seamus Nolan, also a Finance Minister of some kind. There's a TD named Aidan Fahey who's supposedly on the Board."

"TD?"

"Yes. TD stands for Teachta Dála, a member of the lower house of the Irish legislature, called the Dáil."

"Fascinating. If it's a private Irish company, it's not a small job."

"So? Call it a medium-sized job."

"When do you need it?"

"By the time I get back from Ireland. Eight days. Including weekends."

Paul heard muttering.

"What are you doing?" he asked.

"I'm going through my contacts, for crissakes, hold on... Iceland. India. Ireland. Yeah, okay."

"Okay what?"

"Okay, I got a guy in Ireland. Can I go fishing?"

"I'll email you whatever data I have. Not much."

"Goodbye." Click.

Good ol' Rex.

Chapter Three

A man's castle, visiting relatives, and over-tipping

Murdered. That word rang through Finola's mind. Someone hated Eoin Ryan so much they wanted him dead. Or he knew something that was so damaging that murder was the only option. And he was killed while delivering it to *her*.

The flash drive burned against her skin as she made her way home in late afternoon traffic. A few streets away from her flat, she remembered her laptop was in the office. There would be no flopping on the sofa in front of the early evening news. She reversed course and returned to the Telegraph building, rushed into her tiny cubicle of an office and slammed the door shut.

Finola's hand shook as she pulled the tiny device from her bra, inserted it into the USB port and opened the folder. Two files with png extensions. Screenshots of something. She clicked on both. Some sort of financial transaction records.

Her boss, Maureen Fitzgerald, editor-in-chief of The Irish Telegraph walked into the office. "I have something for you," she said, shaking her floppy, red fringe out her eyes. Tall and rangy, Maureen always reminded Finola of an Irish hunting horse, chomping at the bit, ready to tackle the roughest terrain.

Finola looked up. "What? News about the murder?"

"No. Something else. Rather important." Maureen handed Finola a steaming mug. "Here. Got you some coffee."

Finola minimized the document on her screen. She wanted to find out what it was before Maureen spotted it. She took the mug. "Thanks. Something else?"

Maureen sat on the edge of Finola's desk. "Not more important. Just different. Might be good for you take a break from the awful Eoin Ryan situation. In any case, Liam's the crime correspondent. I've assigned the murder story to him. What have you got there?" she asked, nodding to Finola's screen.

Finola met Maureen's gaze. "It's something on a flash drive Eoin's wife gave me. It was in his pocket the day he died. Something to do with government finances. I haven't figured it out yet, but it could be connected to his murder."

"If it is, Liam should handle it."

"I'd like to be in on this case, Maureen," Finola argued. "I know I'm not a crime reporter but crime and politics are synonymous these days. Liam's busy enough, he could use some help."

"Yes, he is. But Eoin's murder is top priority. I want him to handle it. You can chase down whatever you've got there, but I want you to share it with Liam."

"And you'll tell him to share with me, eh?"

"Okay," Maureen relented. "And there is an event I want you to cover."

Finola sipped her coffee, trying to be patient. "What kind of event? Not the state visit by the Queen of Denmark, I hope."

"No, of course not. That's something I'll give to one of the girls who handle the celebrity pages. Glitz and glamour and what are they wearing. I wouldn't insult you with stuff like that."

"Thank God for that. So what's up, then?"

Maureen looked at Finola with a strange expression. "You might like this assignment. Could be just what you need right now."

Finola frowned. "What are you talking about? Stop teasing

me, woman and tell me."

Maureen smiled. "Okay. How would you like to spend a weekend in a luxury hotel?"

Finola narrowed her eyes. "I smell a tough assignment. Something I won't like."

Maureen looked innocently back at Finola. "Oh, no, you'll love it. You're going to Castle Cormack for a weekend. All expenses paid."

Finola dropped her mug, sloshing coffee on her desk. "What? Castle Cormack? Did I hear you right? The most luxurious hotel in Ireland? Where government representatives schmooze European high-flyers to get grants and tax deals?"

Maureen nodded. "So the rumors go. But this time the ones being schmoozed are not from Europe."

Finola mopped her desk with a tissue. "Americans? Give them some Guinness and tell them a few jokes and they're happy. What's it all about?"

"Supposedly, getting more U.S. technology investment into Ireland. It's a joint event hosted by the government and Chiar-Tech, who, as most of Dublin knows, now own the castle."

"Yes, bought from our impoverished government for a fraction of its value."

"Naturally. There will be a bunch of TDs there, and the Taoiseach is going to helicopter in for one of his appearances. And the host is the Minister of Finance, Aidan Fahey. Great opportunity to gather material for the by-election.

"Aidan Fahey is the host?"

"Yes. Why do you look like you're going to be sick?"

Finola fought to control her breathing. "He's not one of my favorites."

Maureen shrugged. "Well, he's the Minister of Finance, and he is on Chiar-Tech's board of directors, so he's something of a big cheese for this event. You'll just have to suck it up and turn on the charm, like a good journalist does."

The thought of socializing with Aidan Fahey turned Finola's stomach, but then, perhaps there was something to be learned from him that might relate to Eoin's murder. She might learn more if she could only get a chance to look at those goddamn pictures. "A weekend in Castle Cormack sounds lovely, I have to say." Finola threw the tissue into the wastepaper basket. "But I'm not sure if I want to go. Sounds like one of those fluffy PR events, which I hate."

"I'm not asking you to go, Finola. It's an assignment. The paper's made all the arrangements." Maureen looked at her watch. "Anyway, I have a meeting. You'll have to leave tomorrow, so no need to come in, just go straight from home. And try to have a good time!"

"If I must."

As soon as Maureen closed the door, Finola returned to her laptop, opened the two screenshots and stared at them. One appeared to reflect a transfer of €5.7M from one of a half-dozen numbered accounts listed under the heading "MEA-LWP." She googled the acronym. Nothing relevant on the first two pages. On the third page, toward the bottom, she spied a link to a .pdf document from a government report. Ministry of Environmental Affairs, Liffey Water Project. No wonder Eoin had been agitated! He was the Minister of State for Environment. The Liffey Water Project had been his baby. His pride and joy. Yet someone had taken a large chunk of its budget. For what? Maybe that's why he was in Fahey's face at the book launch?

She examined the second picture. Another budget record, showing the arrival of the same amount into an undesignated numbered account. There was no title for the sub-account, like the DEA line item. Where had that money gone? What had Eoin found?

* * *

Paul piloted a rented Skoda Citigo at a brisk pace down the N21, on their way from Limerick to Waterville via Killarney. The countryside was a million shades of green, rolling and elegant, except for the occasional speckles of half-built commercial centers and housing developments.

"What's with all the abandoned developments?"

"Hangover from the banking crisis they had. A lot like ours, in many ways."

"Did the government end up saving the banks, like we did?"

"They did, and it's put them in quite a hole."

"Did any of the bankers go to jail?"

"Not enough of them. The ones still in business can hardly show their faces. They get heckled in the pubs, I heard."

"Oh that sounds like fun. Let's find some bankers and heckle them."

South of a town called Castleisland, the divided highway shrank to a two-lane road barely wide enough for the miniature box of steel they had stuffed themselves into, the shoulders bound on both sides by endless, ancient stone walls that seemed inches away. Yet another paneled truck roared by Paul's window as the nose of a tractor crept into the intersection ahead. Paul flicked the wheel left then right, slipped Shannon's window past the nose of the tractor by a few inches and, she covered her eyes and swore.

"I don't have a will!" she shrieked. "Stop the car, I need to write out a fucking will."

Paul chuckled. "They're not as close as they seem," he lied. "This is the smallest car we could get. Be thankful we didn't rent one of the big Audis."

"We're riding in a sardine can on a skateboard, Paul. We'd be demolished if we hit a goat, of which there are plenty." They whizzed past another farm where goats, lambs and cattle passed the time swishing their tails.

Less than a week after Paul's meeting with Francis Duggan, Paul and Shannon Forté landed in Dublin with letters of introduction from their congressman and the U.S. Ambassador to Ireland. The "American dignitaries" toured Leinster House, lunched with the Taoiseach, and met the Minister of Finance, Mr. Aidan Fahey. Fahey had extended Paul and Shannon an invitation (through the Ambassador, of course) to attend the weekend festivities (as "guests of honor") at "Castle Cormack." But they hadn't learned a thing about Chiar-Tech.

"You sure you want to hunt down your relatives? Where is it, Kilcummin?"

"Yes, Kilcummin. The Garden Valley Road. Sounds magical."

"Do they expect us?"

"Hell no, what's the fun in that?"

"Well at least it's on the way to Killarney."

They rode in silence for a while, scanning the countryside, counting cows, sheep, and unfinished, weed-choked subdivisions, evading tractors and beer trucks. Just north of Killarney, Shannon called up her GPS and played navigator.

"Take a left up there."

He turned onto a narrow dirt way, ditches on both sides. "I hope we don't meet someone on a corner."

"Just drive."

The country way took them past humble cracker box homes and sheep pens. A few miles up, the dirt road turned to two wheel tracks through grass. The road climbed and dipped and swung. Glimpses through the heavy roadside brush revealed fields beyond.

"Okay, at the top of this hill, there should be a farm on the left. The McGonigle farm."

The Skoda climbed with a soft whine. The roof of a dwelling poked over the wild roadside hedge. Paul stopped the car short of it.

"It looks like a thatched roof, how cool is that?" Shannon squeed.

"The roof has a hole in it."

"Go past, find the driveway."

Paul crept forward, spied the dirt driveway through a break in the hedge, not convinced he should take it.

"Turn in!"

He broke the wheel hard left and the Skoda skidded into a muddy patch and stopped.

It was a farmhouse, at one time. Now, it was a ruin. Ivy climbed up dirty, cracked whitewashed walls. The windows that weren't broken were dirt caked. Decrepit farm equipment littered the yard. A moped sat by a side door that lay open.

"This can't be it," Paul said, rolling his window down.

Shannon looked on, speechless. "I'd hate to think you're wrong."

A man appeared in the door, leaning on the frame. Dirty gray trousers held up by binder twine over a soiled tee shirt. He hadn't shaved in a while, or combed his hair. Or bathed.

"Ya lost, eh?" he slurred.

"He's hammered, Paul. Let's go."

"We're looking for the McGonigles," Paul called out. "They neighbors?"

The man meandered out the door, weaving his way toward the car. His eyes were glassy and dull. "Who's askin'?"

"A relative from America," Paul said.

The man stood still, taking that in. "From America, eh?"

"Yes, from Boston. We're looking for relatives of Darren McGonigle."

"Darren McGonigle? Never heard of 'im. He die? Leave me money?"

"You McGonigle?"

"I am. If you don't have money for me, then you're keepin' me from my drinkin'. G'wan, there'll be no family gatherin'."

"Come on, Paul. Get me out of here."

Paul put the car in reverse and backed out as the man glared at them.

They rode back to the main road in silence. Paul stole a glance at his wife, saw the sadness behind her eyes.

"It was a good idea," he said.

"It was a shitty idea," she muttered. After a bit more silence, she inhaled deeply and exhaled. "At least he wasn't in jail, like my father."

They reached the end of the way and headed south on the road to Killarney. Paul handed Shannon the Ireland guidebook. "Stop thinking about it and see what this says about Castle Cormack. It'll take your eyes off the oncoming traffic."

Shannon snatched the book, and after more muttering and page flipping, she read:

"Situated just outside Waterville, County Kerry, Castle Cormack was built in the seventeenth century by the Connolly-Smith family who were granted the estate by Charles II after the Cromwell wars. Situated on the remains of an 11th century castle, it had been in the Connolly-Smith family until the late nineteen nineties, when it was sold to one of Ireland's technology companies, which uses a portion of it for its corporate headquarters and leases the remainder as a semi-private hotel. It has been restored and refurbished by the new owners, and now stands as the most luxurious castle in Ireland. It boasts twenty-two sumptuous bedrooms, a dining room that seats forty, a drawing room, library, study, billiard room and gymnasium. Standing on a hill overlooking Waterville, Castle Cormack enjoys breathtaking views of the Atlantic to the west and MacGillycuddy's Reeks, the tallest mountains in Ireland, to the northeast. Apart from golf on the nearby Waterville golf course (considered by many to be Ireland's finest), it offers clay pigeon shooting, hiking and climbing, horse riding, surfing and other sports activities. The hotel is managed by Sir Alistair Connolly-Smith who, when he sold the property, reserved for himself a life estate and the right to manage the hotel for as long as he wanted."

"Ireland's finest, eh?"

"Twenty-two sumptuous bedrooms, Paul. Is that where the word 'sump' comes from?"

"I don't know, but I hope we'll have an opportunity to sumptuate."

"You can sumptuate on the links. I'm going to enjoy the breathtaking views of MacGillycuddy's Reeks. Who is this man, MacGillycuddy, and what makes his Reeks so special?"

For the ten millionth time since they'd wed following his victory in court years ago, his insides laughed at his dumb luck in finding this woman.

* * *

The country road crested a hill and the quilt of green pastures gave way to the picture postcard town of Killarney. The main street was lined on both sides with two story whitewash buildings end-to-end, each painted its own pastel hue, every window adorned with flower boxes dripping with geraniums and begonias.

"My God, Paul, this place is gorgeous. I want to live here."

"How about we settle for lunch and a nap?"

"Maybe we can drop into a real estate office and inquire. Sounds like a good time to be buying." She put her hand on his knee and squeezed.

"Let's see how lunch goes. I'm dying for a nice Irish cheeseburger and a pint of Guinness."

As if summoned by his desire, a pub appeared on the corner of the next block, a simple brown-on-white sign stating proudly, "MacGillycuddy's."

"I say, that has the look of a pub," Shannon said.

"Let's utilize it."

"And I shall ask him about his reeks."

Paul spied a looming empty parking space on the street and hit his brakes and blinker. A squeal of tires and lengthy horn blast came from behind him. He waved out of his window as he tried to find reverse. The car behind him swung out to pass and stopped parallel to Paul's open window. The driver, young woman with brown hair and a million freckles shouted, "Bollocks! Drive like that in this country, you end up in a box!" and up came her middle finger as she roared away. The car was some sort of European box like they were driving, with dents and dings.

"I didn't know the middle finger was an international sign," Shannon said.

With substantial concentration, Paul struggled to parallel-park the rolling shoebox without mistaking left from right, and the lovers were soon ensconced in a corner booth of MacGillycuddy's, devouring burgers that could have been made in Noank, Connecticut. The lunchtime crowd was thin but exuberant, possibly owing to the pints of Guinness standing before every patron.

"It seems that the custom here is to have at least two pints of Guinness with one's lunch," Shannon said, lowering her voice to conspiratorial level.

"When in Killarney," Paul said, and raised two fingers to catch the attention of the barman, an older fellow with a roadmap on his face and smile lines that ran from his eyes to his hairline. The barman nodded and soon delivered fresh pints to the booth.

"Say," Shannon said to him, "are you MacGillycuddy, the fella who owns the Reeks?"

He gave her an admiring smile. "I am MacGillycuddy, mam. The mountains were indeed named after my forefathers. You're Americans, eh? Where ye from?"

"We're from Boston," Paul said.

"Are ye then? You don't sound like it. We get a lot of Boston folks on their way to Tralee and Waterville. I can tell them from the other Yanks with the accent."

Paul looked at Shannon. "This woman was born and bred in Savin Hill, Boston. Her name is Shannon McGonigle Forté. She has a Boston accent that rivals anyone who's set foot in this pub."

MacGillycuddy grinned, dragged an empty chair to the end of the booth, and sat. "McGonigle, eh? Let's hear it then," he said. "Where do you park your car?"

Shannon grinned back. "I pa'ak my cah in Havud Ya'ad."

From under his eyebrows, MacGillycuddy nodded his respect. "That's awful good, mam. Awful good. So ye're headed to Waterville, then? On holiday?"

"Yes," Paul said. "Our first visit."

"We're going to Castle Cormack," Shannon said with pride.

The smile in MacGillycuddy's eyes vanished. "Ah. Would ye be attending the fancy shindig that'd be going on this weekend?"

"We would," Shannon said. "Guests of the Minister of Finance."

The old man's face hardened. "I see then." He paused a moment and stood. "Will ye be needin' anything else?"

"I get the sense that you're not a fan of the event," Paul said.

MacGillycuddy looked at Paul with a poker face. "You've never been there before."

"Nope. Don't know what to expect."

"Down this way, we don't like our government spendin' our money to be feedin' rich people. They let the banks run wild, then pay their debts, talk and talk about economic development and jobs and such, but we don't see much result. Except helicopters flying them no good politicians from Dublin to Waterville, to do…whatever it is they do in that damn place."

"You know anything about the people who own it?" Paul asked.

MacGillycuddy weighed his words before answering. "Our bloody TD, Fahey, and his fancy high tech people. They sure got their economic development money, but not us. And he says he's Labour Party. As far as I'm concerned, there's no difference between 'em, Labour, Fianna Fáil, Fine Gael. They're all in the same damn bed together." He glared at Paul. "Ya wouldn't be one of them American politicians would ya?"

"Hell no," Paul crowed. "I hate politicians of all kinds. They practically ruined my life. If it hadn't been for this woman here, I'd be in jail because of them."

MacGillycuddy's face softened. "Well, you better put on yer happy face then, because you'll be spendin' the weekend with the lot of them, Irish and American, or so the news told."

"Paul's a good faker," Shannon said. "He's full of the *blah*-ney."

MacGillycuddy's smile slowly crept back as he watched the corner of Shannon's mouth rise.

"I used to be a politician in Boston," Paul said. "But I've repented. I'm like a reformed smoker. Now I make sport of them. I'm a do-gooder."

The old man gave Paul a pitying stare. "You don't look broke."

Paul and Shannon guffawed, and the old smiling eyes returned.

"Say," Shannon said, "are there any bankers in your pub we can heckle?"

MacGillycuddy winced. "Afraid most bankers are still avoiding the pubs."

"Well, we'll go on down to Castle Cormack and heckle them there, then," Shannon said.

"I'll give you a warning, if I may?"

"Please do," Paul said.

He leaned forward, palms of his weathered hands on the table, and spoke without moving his lips. "Shake hands, but count yer fingers. And stay out of the basement."

He gave the couple a solemn nod and returned to the bar.

* * *

Undecided as to whether to prolong their rest or push on to Waterville, the American couple strolled the main street, admiring the quaint charm of the architecture, the pastel colors, the window boxes, the narrow, crowded streets. They stopped at the window of a local realtor and examined a number of listings posted in the window.

Two bedroom cottage, one bath on half acre, two miles outside of town, 450k euros.

"Holy shit," Shannon whispered.

"No worse than the Cape. Too hard to get to. Come on, before I go broke."

They continued their window shopping, exchanging brief pleasantries with shopkeepers. To a person, the locals were polite, friendly on the surface, but reserved, guarded in some indefinable way.

A dozen storefronts further, they came upon The Arbutus Hotel, an elegant early Victorian building, cream-colored stucco and antique brown trim, window boxes billowing with geraniums. Directly across the road, on the corner of an intersecting route, the McCaffrey Arms Hotel touted "hotel accommodations, bar, steak and sports pub" against a garish pink façade.

Paul and Shannon exchanged glances, entered the Arbutus, and felt as though they'd walked into a museum of Old World European elegance. They would have felt underdressed if it weren't for the group of American tourists clogging the lobby with their luggage while their travel mates bickered with the front desk.

"Let's visit the pub while these nice people say their goodbyes," Paul whispered.

They weaved through the Americans, none of them moving so much as a shoulder bag, and passed through an archway into Buckley's Pub. It was late afternoon when they crossed the threshold.

* * *

At twenty minutes to midnight, Paul Forté admitted he might be persuaded to have *just one mor*e, and Kevin McGinn, the barman and expert pint-puller, poured him another Guinness.

McGinn did not pour a twin for Shannon, as she was no longer present. Paul had escorted her to the hotel's front desk, begging for a room, any room.

"Please don't make me take this lovely woman to McCaffrey's," he'd wheedled. "Are McCaffrey's patrons even *allowed* in Buckley's, the finest pub in Ireland? I'll have to cross the street three times, in this condition!"

"Three times?" the patient young man had replied.

"Yes. I've a pint on the bar in there, and Kevin is waiting for me to finish a story."

So the front desk had relented, Paul poured Shannon into a comfy four poster bed that looked like it was made in the 17th century, kissed her as she mumbled, and returned to his Guinness before the head had lost one bubble.

"Ahh, I tell you Paul, you're a funny drunk."

"I'm funny all the time. I don't require intoxicants for comedic invention. Oh look, I used eleven syllables on four words."

McGinn had had a permanent grin on his face all night, but Paul hadn't yet determined if it was made for the patrons or genuine, although it felt genuine.

"You see a lot of funny drunks, I bet," Paul said.

McGinn picked his words. "Some funny. Some who think they're funny. And some who're just angry."

"Nobody likes an angry drunk." Paul raised his glass to his lips, with a slight wobbly detour.

"That's the bar business. What're ya gonna do?"

"I suppose in a recession like you've faced, your patrons might have things to say when the tongue is loosened."

"That's a fact. Fella from the Anglo-Irish Bank still won't come in. I don't blame 'im."

"I bet you see a lot of American men, like me, coming through on their way from one golf course to another."

McGinn wiped a spot on the bar. "I see 'em." He wiped too long.

Paul snickered. "Ah, Kevin, you're a politician. Let me tell you what I think you see. Stop me when I err."

McGinn's tight smile broadened but it was arms-length. "Okay, go on."

"They throw money around like confetti. They call you 'pal' after the second drink, and by last call, they think you're their best friend, and all they gotta do is 'call Kev' if they have any local difficulties."

McGinn's teeth flashed and his eyes winked a salute.

"They act worldly, but most of them are fakers who left angry wives behind because they really couldn't afford a vacation *together* if he went to Ireland with his buds, but he went anyway. He'll be paying for it the rest of the year, so what the hell, let's go wild. Right?"

McGinn actually chuckled, an extraordinary act of expression for him.

"On balance, they may be a big pain in the ass, but they tip their asses off," Paul said.

That got McGinn laughing. "So they do," he said. "They get drunk and want to buy your friendship. Your Irish Americans, they're too bleedin' sentimental, too forward about dumping their junk on ya. We all got problems, lad. But here we keep 'em to ourselves and our families."

"But you folks do love your gossip, and you love a good grudge, just like we do."

"We do like to hate our politicians. A contemptible lot, all of 'em."

"I'll get a chance to see my first Irish politician up close tomorrow night."

"How's that, then?"

"Shannon and I are on our way to Castle Cormack for the

weekend. Some big dinner party to promote Irish-American joint economic development. Sounds like a bad way to drink good wine, but we'll muddle."

McGinn's eyebrows flicked up and his mouth flicked down. "If you're talkin' about gossip and politicians in the same sentence, then Castle Cormack is gonna come up."

"What's the gossip?"

McGinn balked.

"Come on, Kev! I need to know what Shannon and I are in for. You saw that beautiful woman I'm married to. How could you risk putting her in harm's way?"

McGinn lowered his head as he laughed.

"MacGillycuddy up the street there? Good ol' MacGillycuddy. He was forthcoming, Kev. He gave me lots. He said five words to me. Give me five words, at least. Don't let MacGillycuddy outdo you."

"What were the five words?"

"Stay out of the basement." Paul sat still and watched McGinn. "Shannon and I had a blast speculating on what he meant, but we were being silly. You know what he meant? Stay out of the basement?"

McGinn smiled a big Irish smile for Paul. A friendly, confidential smile. A smile that told Paul all he needed to know.

"You'll be meeting Aidan Fahey, then? Our glorious TD? Leader of the Kingdom?"

"The Kingdom?"

"Ancient history, literally."

"Tell me about it. For the thousandth time, I assume."

McGinn sighed, and launched into a speech he must have had memorized for decades. "Kerry is the anglicised word for the Gaelic *Ciar raige*, or Ciar's Kingdom. Ciar was the progenitor of the O'Connor Kerry Clan. Around 65 AD he took possession of an area of land stretching from the river Maine in the south and the Shannon estuary in the north and included the peninsula of

Corca Duibhne or Dingle Peninsula. This territory at the time was known as Clar na Cliabh or The Plain of Swords. By the 6th century it was known as Ciarraige or Ciar's Kingdom. It is mentioned in a 6th century manuscript as Ciarraige of the Plain Swords a combination of the old and the new name at the time."

"Fascinating. Ciar must have been one ferocious fellow."

McGinn smiled. "There's a lot of ferocity bubblin' under the surface of Irish people, Paul."

"What about Aidan Fahey? Is he ferocious?"

McGinn leaned forward and spit into the sink. "Aidan Fahey's a snake, that one. A lyin' weasel. First his father, now him."

"His father held the seat before him?"

"Yes, yes, they've been holdin' it for years. Like the bleedin' Kennedys over your way. Like they fuckin' own it. Just like the family before them. I swear, these Kerry politicians must really think it is their kingdom, the way they clutch to their seats like thrones."

"Aw come on, Kev, tell me how you really feel."

McGinn shook his head and showed his teeth. "I don't resist speakin' my mind about a bollicks like that. He's a smarmy bastard, that one. He's got no friends in this village, I tell you that. Shake his hand, count your fingers."

"S'what MacGillycuddy said."

McGinn nodded. "Well, he's damn straight."

"What's this about Castle Cormack and some software company?"

McGinn's face turned red. "That one. Jesus, Paul, you're gonna give me a stroke. The government took the castle because the old man there–Connolly-Smith—couldn't afford the taxes. Then they turned around and sold it to Fahey's company, who leased it back to the government for their use. Fahey's old man pulled that one off."

"The government leased it back?"

"That's what I heard. From the drunken mouth of Fahey himself, sittin' right here in this bar. Proud of it, he was, the bastard. 'Open it for all the people,' he bragged. You know how many citizens of Killarney have been invited to Castle Cormack?"

"Precious few, I'm guessing." So, Chiar-Tech gets the castle but the government pays the upkeep. Slick.

"You'd be guessing right." McGinn slapped a damp towel down on the bar. "Now you got me worked up, ya prick. Go on, get some sleep and let me clean up and get home to the missus. Can I put the tab on your room for you?"

"Nah, s'okay." Paul shoved his hand in his pocket, pulled out a pile of loose bills, picked through them, and threw 150 euros on the bar. "Am I over-tipping enough, Kev?" He slid off his stool, extended his hand across the bar.

"That's a grand tip there, Paul." He clasped Paul's hand, a good, vigorous shake. "Be safe," he said. "And remember. Count yer fingers."

Chapter Four

The bluest eyes, business class, and a coincidence

Driving great distances while hung over was not on the Fortés' short list of fun things to do in a foreign country. Doing it in a car that whirred and whined like a model airplane did not improve the experience.

Doing it in a sideways rain was downright torturous.

Paul had thought it best to indulge in The Arbutus's legendary "full Irish" breakfast, of which they caught the very tail-end, approaching noon. As their eggbeater approached the outskirts of Cahersiveen, he regretted his decision.

"Who eats brown bread and fish for breakfast?" he groaned.

"Hung over Americans," Shannon muttered. "Where the fuck are MacGillycuddy's Reeks?"

"We could be driving right into them, we'd never see them." In fact, they had driven by the range on the road to Killorglin, and again when they turned south at Killorglin for the long run into Waterville. But the cloud ceiling was barely 500 feet.

Paul had heard from his golf friends about the notorious Irish weather. The incessant, dank, cold rain, blowing sideways across the exposed links. He'd come prepared for anything, at least equipment-wise. But he found it hard to believe anyone, even

American men on a stag golf holiday, would play golf in weather like this.

Shannon hunkered down in her seat and pulled her jacket snug around her. "Turn the heat up, for crissakes. I'm rattling like a…"

"Like a what?"

"I have no idea. Jesus, I feel awful."

Paul white-knuckled along the country road as vehicles zoomed past his right ear, blasting water against the windshield, reducing visibility to zero for heart-stopping seconds while the wipers struggled to catch up. The tires hissed on the wet tar, needles of rain pecked at his window and rumbled on the roof.

"What's with the basement, you think?" he asked.

No answer. More hissing and pecking and rumbling. A panel truck roared by, wheels on the centerline. Paul tweaked the wheel left for the extra inch of clearance, certain he and Shannon were about to meet the same fate as his parents.

"What's usually in the basement of a castle," croaked a voice from underneath the jacket.

He thought through the water racket. "Wine."

He heard a scoff. *Pfffff.*

"An ogre!" Paul raised his finger dramatically, but he had no audience. He pulled Shannon's jacket away from her head. "Have we read anything about dignitaries disappearing with no explanation?"

Shannon pulled the jacket back over her head. "A dungeon," the jacket said.

"A dungeon." The racket slackened in between sheets. The dull monotone gray of sky morphed to thick rolls of clouds in folds every shade of gray. The pecking ceased.

The car followed a slow bend and a body of water appeared on the right, the low clouds covering a hill across. The farmhouses receded, commercial building sprouted, and soon they were rolling slowly through a tunnel of buildings, some colored brightly, as in Killarney, others unpainted stucco, lacking the riots of color from flower boxes. Traffic slowed to a crawl.

"What sort of dungeon?" he asked the co-pilot.

The head emerged from under the jacket. "A dungeon of pleasure, of course."

"Get outta town."

"What else? A real dungeon? MacGillycuddy was warning us that we might be strapped to a rack?"

"Why didn't he say, 'stay out of the dungeon' then? He said 'basement,' not 'dungeon.' I'd have to guess that 'dungeon' and 'basement' aren't likely to be used interchangeably."

The pained look on Shannon's face required no emphasis. "I'm having violent thoughts."

Paul surveyed the storefronts while the traffic inched along.

"Gee, there sure are a lot of bars in this town." Every other door belonged to a pub. At a corner, a plain, white panel truck parked in front of a large establishment. Unlike the other one-door, storefront pubs, this one ran at least thirty feet along the main street and an equal distance down the side street. The building was a freshly painted tan, with a contrasting black trim. A large, carved signboard, black with gold lettering covered the entire length along the main street. *An Croi Dubh*. A stream of restaurant workers carried kitchen equipment, tray carts, boxes of liquor, to the truck as others loaded it.

Two men stood in the vestibule outside the doorway, smoking while they watched the workers. They were big men, over six feet, the same build, and the same head shape. Curly black hair, thick black eyebrows. Paul was on the opposite side of the street, looking across traffic at the men. One of them looked back at him, staring. His eyes were cold, distant, almost angry, Paul thought. And blue.

"The bluest eyes," he said to himself.

Shannon glanced at Paul, followed his eyes, and looked at the man. He nudged his friend, nodded toward Shannon. They both stared at her and smiled.

"Scary men," she said. She shrunk down into her seat. "Wake me up when we get there." The head dipped under the jacket.

Paul welcomed the loosening of the traffic snarl, and the car took him through more of the patchwork of greens, yellows, browns and grays, still wearing the thick gray blanket above it all. A drizzle began. It grew to a hard mist, but not rain. Still in this cold, gray air, the greens of the pastures were vibrant, vigorous.

He would have missed the sign for Castle Cormack if he hadn't been warned *and* had reliable GPS. The warnings were true. The sign was small, plain, two colors that did not contrast well. He took the turn a little fast, jostling Shannon awake as the car slid onto a gravel road and began to climb through dense woodland. He followed the road a half-mile or so, and wondered if he'd mistaken the sign or the turn. He stopped the car to consult his GPS. Correct road, it said. He remembered the words of the fellow who'd invited them, Fahey.

"If you think you've taken a wrong turn, you haven't," Fahey'd said, chuckling in a grating way.

Around one bend and up a hill, the trees fell away and the road passed through a great iron gate and crossed a sweeping vista of green hillsides dotted with sheep. At the top of the hill, exploding out of the thickets in a gaudy display of granite was Castle Cormack. Paul stopped the car. They stared up the hill, mouths agape.

Shannon gasped. "Are you serious? Paul freakin' Forté, do you see what I see?"

"Yeah, and we're still a mile away from it."

"Do you think it has a moat? I've never seen a real moat. I'm gonna swim in it."

"It doesn't have a moat, darling." Paul stepped on the gas, but he was in no hurry to rush the approach.

"What, you been here before?"

Paul followed the gravel road up the hill, curling left around dense bushes and back to the right, where the road emerged from a tunnel of brush and ran in a straight line toward the center of the edifice. Twin granite pillars framed the driveway. They were bookends to a wall that ran away into the hillsides. As the car passed between the pillars, Shannon gasped again. Between them and the castle, at least 1,000 feet of manicured gardens, sculptured shrubbery, fountains, which the gravel drive framed in a large oval.

"See? No moat."

Shannon slugged her husband on the shoulder.

They rolled down the drive, missing nothing, and pulled into a large, open valet area. Five other cars sat, all idle and empty. Handsome young men in blue blazers with spiffy gold shields on the breast pockets bustled about. A young man in curly red hair opened Shannon's door. "Afternoon, mam, welcome to Castle Cormack," he said in a reedy voice.

Paul barely got his own door open before another lending hand appeared. "Afternoon, sir. Welcome to Castle Cormack."

"Thank you," he checked the boy's name tag. "Tom."

A third boy pulled their bags out of the trunk and lumbered toward the grand entrance: sets of carved wooden doors that Paul guessed were twenty feet high. Tom shouted to the boy to stop.

"That's Feehan," he said softly. "He's my brother, has a bit of the…" pointing to his head.

Feehan had stopped and waited for Paul and Shannon with a toothy grin that told them he was the happiest man alive.

"Hi there, Feehan," Paul said. The bags hung from Feehan's shoulders like they were rocks. "Sure I can't help you?"

Feehan giggled. "No, suh! I'm doin' my job, and doin' it well, suh!" His teeth broke out again as he turned to chug up a great stone staircase and through the huge wooden doors.

When Paul and Shannon caught up to him in the cavernous lobby, Feehan was panting happily.

"Thank you for your help, Feehan. I can't say that I've ever

Full Irish | 53

had a better valet in my whole life." Paul pulled a €5 note from a wad and handed it to Feehan, who took the note, ogled it and flashed his teeth again.

"Thank *you*, suh!"

"See ya around, Feehan," Shannon said, grinning as Feehan hustled back through the doorway.

"Now," Paul said, looking around for something resembling a front desk. Then it hit him. "The Duggans," he said.

"The what?"

"The Duggans. My client's cousins. They were the two brothers staring at you at *An Croi Dubh*."

Shannon frowned. "Didn't get a good vibe from those gents. Not at all."

* * *

Through experience, Finola had come to split American tourists into two categories—coach and business class. The coach-tourists were usually overweight, wore tracksuits and runners and were constantly looking for directions to either the toilets or the nearest McDonald's. The business class-tourists, on the other hand, were sleek and slim, the men either in Gant golf attire or cashmere Armani blazers and Italian shoes, the women in slim-cut jeans teamed with silk shirts and expensive handbags dangling from their arms. She could spot them a mile away. That couple she had nearly run into in Killarney were most likely business class Americans. But despite the hint of sleek elegance she discerned in the brief seconds of her encounter, the gentleman didn't know how to drive a car with a stick shift. She laughed to herself as she drove her battered Renault Clio up the avenue to Castle Cormack, remembering how he had wrestled with the stick shift to find reverse, blocking the traffic in the main street. She had to step on the brakes to avoid hitting them and couldn't stop herself screaming at them and giving them the finger. That should shake them up, she thought as she'd glimpsed the shocked face of the woman. Later that evening, she saw them going into the Arbutus Hotel. Of course. Where else would Mr. and Mrs. Business Class spend the night?

Too exhausted to tackle the last bit of the journey down the narrow winding road to Waterville, Finola decided to stay in Killarney. She checked into 'Sheila's Guesthouse', forty euros a night, including breakfast. A rip-off, she thought, as she choked down porridge in the drab breakfast room the following morning, thinking about that smart couple who were probably tucking in to a breakfast of smoked salmon, scrambled eggs and newly baked bread, the posh version of 'the full Irish'. Well, beggars couldn't be choosers and she was on a very small expense account, which had to stretch to a weekend in Castle Cormack, no less.

Finola paid the bill and set off up the mountain road to Kenmare, which would take her west around the Ring of Kerry. Although the low cloud cover and intermittent rain prevented her from seeing the spectacular views on the way, she nevertheless enjoyed the drive that took her through the quaint little village of Sneem with its whitewashed thatched cottages and quaint pubs, and on through Caherdaniel, where she stopped to visit the home of 'The Liberator', Daniel O'Connell. She went into the nearly deserted cafeteria and had a quick cup of tea before she set off again in the wind and rain, through Coomakesta Pass, disappointed that the famous viewpoint of the Atlantic was impossible to enjoy. Coming closer to Waterville, she could see the woods that hid the entrance of Castle Cormack.

Finola had only seen this castle in the distance when she did The Ring of Kerry with her mother ten years earlier. At that time, it had just been acquired by Chiar-Tech, at the height of the Celtic Tiger era, when Ireland's economy exploded. She remembered reading about it in the newspapers and being amazed at how this run-down near ruin had been transformed into a luxury hotel in only a year. She had heard about the refurbishments; the pool, gym, en suite bathrooms and luxury suites and hoped the period features hadn't been ripped out and replaced with plastic. Whatever use Chiar-Tech made of it, the Irish government seemed to use it regularly for entertaining visiting royalty and Eurocrats. The gala dinners were a dirty little secret to the Dublin crowd and a source of gossip to the locals.

Things had become more discreet after the bank failures and resulting recession. The dinners and weekends were talked about, but the talk was littered with profanities. Even though Chiar-Tech claimed to be footing all the bills for the entertaining, cynics were not convinced, and there was still plenty of muttering about 'fat cats' living it up while the government announced one austerity budget after the other – all necessary to pay the debts of the banks that fueled the rise of companies like Chiar-Tech. Finola had heard rumors of wild parties behind closed doors. One TD had even hinted at things going on in 'the dungeon' that most had dismissed as fabrication and rumor-mongering, but Finola wasn't so sure.

Everything was still in perfect nick, Finola noted as she pulled up in front of the grand granite steps in a shower of gravel. The immaculate lawns, the tubs of roses and geraniums on the terrace and the newly raked gravel all bore the signs of great care and attention. The castle towered above her, a huge granite pile in a mixture of different styles of architecture. The main part was the original seventeenth century demesne and then two wings had been attached during various periods of history.

Finola got out of the car and opened the boot to get her bag. But before she had a chance to take it out, a hand reached out and grabbed the handle. "I'll take that," a voice said in her ear. Finola turned and discovered not one, but two porters in hotel livery with 'Castle Cormack' embroidered in gold on the breast pocket of their navy jackets.

The other porter held out his hand. "If you give me your key, mam, I'll park your car."

"Um, okay," Finola said, kicking herself for not cleaning the inside of her car before she left. She cringed at the thought of the empty crisp bags, banana peels, old coffee mugs, crumpled tissues and parking slips that littered the floor of her old banger. "I can park it myself. Please don't trouble yourself."

"No trouble at all," the porter said as he won the tug-of-war of the keys. He got into the car, brushing sandwich crumbs off the seat. Finola watched him drive off, the car making the usual spluttering noise from the holes in the muffler. She saw the second porter carry her battered hold-all up the steps, as if it was something he'd rather not touch with his bare hands, and put it beside a stack of designer luggage just inside the door. Finola followed him, running up the steps, pushing the heavy door open and nearly falling into the big lobby, muttering "fuck it."

A couple, standing by the reception desk, turned around. Holy shit, it was *them*. Mr. and Mrs. Business Class. No mistaking that slim woman with the beautiful face or the tall, handsome man beside her. Must be some of the American guests here for the golf and major sucking-up by Irish TDs.

Equally taken aback, the couple stared at her for a moment. Then the wife broke out a smile. "You're the woman who gave us the finger in Killarney yesterday."

Finola beamed her a cheery smile. "The finger? Oh, that. It's an Irish blessing. Means 'may the road rise up to meet you'."

The woman laughed, then put a hand to her head. "Paul, I'm *dyin'*. I'm gonna sit on the couch over there while you and Miss Congeniality take care of business." She directed a weak smile at Finola. "I'm sorry. I'm Shannon McGonigle and this is my husband, Paul Forté. We had a bit too much fun with the locals last night, so I'm not really up to chatting."

Deflated, Finola tried to look sympathetic. She had just delivered an insult that would have flattened most people and here was this woman with her effortless beauty, cool confidence and gorgeous husband being *nice*. Feeling more foolish than triumphant, Finola held out her hand. "Um, hello. I'm Finola. Finola McGee.

Shannon's smile broadened as she grasped the outstretched hand. "Hi, Finola Finola."

Paul Forté followed suit and, in turn, took Finola's hand. "Hi, Finola Finola. I'm Paul."

Finola pulled away her hand. Was he laughing at her? Or just mocking his wife? Or did they both find her ridiculous? "One will do," she snapped. "Hello, Paul."

"Please excuse me," Shannon said. "I'll see you at cocktails, Finola. Right now, I just need to flop somewhere." Without waiting for a reply, she shuffled over to one of the plush sofas and sank down with a groan.

Paul shrugged and smiled. "We're a little—"

"Hung over?" Finola quipped. "Either that or you're coming down with something. You both look very pale around the gills. What was it? Bushmills? Or twenty pints of Guinness?"

"All of the above," Paul sighed. "Those Killarney people sure know how to drink. Quite a coincidence, seeing you!"

Finola laughed, suddenly warming to this man "Well, that's Ireland for ya'. It's a small place. We're always bumping into each other here."

"Did you stay over in Killarney too?" he enquired.

"Yup. Lovely little B and B," Finola lied. "Much nicer than a big hotel." She wasn't going to let this swanky couple know what a dump she had stayed in.

"Too bad you didn't find us at Buckley's. We had a fine time."

"Too fine, by the looks of it," Finola couldn't help remarking. "But now you can have a rest in this fabulous place. Never been here myself." She looked around the lobby, curious to see what had been done to the castle to turn it into a luxury hotel. A lot, apparently. The flagstones, oak paneling and double curved staircase were the same as it would have been three centuries earlier, but the floors were now adorned with Aubusson rugs, and the paneled walls covered with tapestries and hunting prints. A huge mahogany reception desk had been fitted into the recess between the double staircases that rose in two graceful arcs to the first floor. There were a number of doors behind the desk, possibly leading to the office and staff quarters. Sofas and armchairs with bright yellow upholstery were scattered in groups here and there, lit by lamps with silk shades. Enormous urns with lavish flower arrangements stood on marble pillars. The whole effect was, although luxurious, ridiculously over the top.

Finola couldn't help letting out a raucous laugh. "Jesus, this place has been tarted up like a whore's boudoir. I bet the Connolly-Smith ancestors are spinning in their graves."

As if conjured up by her comment, a tall, thin man with receding blond hair appeared at the reception desk. "Good afternoon," he said in a cut-glass British accent. "I'm Alistair Connolly-Smith, the manager." His hooded pale blue eyes aimed a cool glare at Finola. "Sorry to keep you waiting. We have more than forty guests this weekend. Far more than we're used to," he added with a touch of regret. He consulted a list. "You must be Mr. and Mrs. Forté."

Finola giggled.

"Half right," Paul said. "I'm Paul Forté and my wife is over there, sacked out on one of your couches. We're guests of Mr. Fahey."

"Aidan Fahey?" Finola snorted. "Are you a Boston politician?"

Paul laughed. "I'm afraid not. Just touring with my wife, happen to know the Ambassador."

"I see," Finola stepped closer to the desk and Connolly-Smith. "Howerya, Alistair, if you don't mind me calling you that."

"Not at all," Alistair replied, unconvincingly.

"Grand. I'm Finola McGee of *The Irish Telegraph*. My newspaper made the arrangements."

Alistair cleared his throat and consulted his list again. "Yes,

Miss McGee. Mr. Forté, you and your wife are in two-oh-six." He pointed upwards as he handed Paul a key. "Top of the stairs, down the west corridor." He handed another key to Finola. "And Miss McGee—"

"Finola," she interrupted.

Alistair nodded. "Finola, you're in two-oh-eight, next door. I'll have your bags delivered immediately."

"Amazing," Finola chortled. "We're next door. Another coincidence."

"How fun. Well, I'm going to get Shannon upstairs," Paul said. "We'll see you later." He wandered over to his wife.

No sooner had they disappeared up the stairs than Aidan Fahey, resplendent in top-to-toe Ralph Lauren, swaggered into the lobby followed by Feehan, who struggled with a suitcase and a golf bag.

"And here's the reason why we're still in recession," Finola muttered under her breath as her stomach tightened.

"Leave them there, boy," Fahey barked at Feehan and slipped him a few coins.

"Well, if isn't Aidan Fahey," Finola quipped.

Fahey looked startled and for a split second, Finola saw something odd in his eyes. Surprise? Or was it fear? But his expression changed so quickly she realized she had been mistaken as Fahey grabbed her and planted a hot, wet kiss on her cheek.

"Finola! What a wonderful surprise. What is my favorite political correspondent doing here?"

Finola suppressed a shudder at the physical contact and managed a polite smile. "Keeping an eye on you, Minister," she said.

Chapter Five

A power nap, dinner banter, and the art of manipulation

What a miracle time can be. Just a few hours ago, Paul wasn't confident he could get his wife into the room, much less to rally for a cocktail party of 50 and dinner with complete strangers.

But as Paul had learned many years before when he first fell in love with her, Shannon was a resourceful woman. A two hour power nap, and she bounced into the shower, slipped on some skimpy underthings and a chic black wool number that put an exclamation point on her derrière, drew a few lines on her eyes and lips and slipped into a short-cut, white linen jacket. He sat naked in a lounge chair, watching his wife get ready. He loved watching his wife get ready. It was a free floor show.

"How about Finola Finola, huh?" she said.

"Reporter from Dublin. *Irish Telegraph.*"

"She reminds me of Southie so much. Her first thought was a finger in the air. She reminds me of *me*."

"I like her for that reason. And if she's good, we can help each other out, maybe." He was thinking of Corey Fitzpatrick, the kid from the Boston Phoenix, who'd helped Paul expose a federal prosecutor and keep himself out of prison for a crime he didn't commit. The pernicious federal felony that masqueraded as a round of golf.

She padded over to a wet bar in the corner and poured some ice water. "I'll be nice to Finola. You can be nice to Finola, too. Be as nice as you want."

"Let's be nice to everyone. We'll be the two who, at the end of the weekend, everyone will ask, 'who were those annoyingly nice people'?"

"Let's make a scene," Shannon said, stifling a giggle.

Paul picked up a box of matches sitting in a silver ashtray. Gunmetal gray background, with a white swoosh symbol, sort of like the combination of a boomerang and a yin-yang. "Woah."

"Woah what?"

"These Chiar-Tech folks. They don't mind advertising their presence here." He tossed her the box.

"It's on all of the toiletry samples, too."

"It's odd, how closely tied this company is to the government. I wonder how they can get away with it, ethically."

"Well I would think that Aidan Fahey fellow would have all the answers."

"You remember how he was drooling on you in Dublin?"

"He wasn't drooling on me. That's a gross exaggeration."

"He was slavering."

"Was not."

"I want more of him drooling on you. Pump him for information. Promise him you'll sleep with him if he confesses."

"What does he have to confess?"

"I have no idea. It's your job to find out."

"Stand up and let me look at you," she said.

"I don't have any clothes on."

"I know." She waggled her eyebrows.

"My, you *have* recovered well."

* * *

Sometimes Paul could not hide the grin that followed Shannon's spontaneous adventures.

But there was business to do, and as they strolled down the castle corridor toward the cocktail reception, arm in arm, they went over the mission. Find something on Chiar-Tech. Anything that might disqualify them from bidding on the Massachusetts contract. Preferably headline grabbing.

"What about Finola?" she asked.

"Let's play it by ear. If you see an opportunity, take it, but don't be pushy. I'll do the same. Same with Fahey, although," he glanced sideways, "he'd much prefer to talk with you."

Shannon elbowed his nearest kidney.

"Subtlety's the key," he gasped.

They followed the corridor toward the din of voices at the far end of the hotel lobby, a room large enough for a full-on rugby match. With grandstands. Their valet, Tom, spotted them approaching, and hustled up to deliver name tags: gunmetal gray with the Chiar-Tech logo, and a silver pin.

"Thank you, Tom." Paul slid him a couple more euros.

"My pleasure, sir. Mr. Fahey is at the head of the receiving line. He asked me to tell you and Mrs. Forté he is looking forward to saying hello."

"Of course, thanks. Say Tom, do you know Mr. Fahey? Is he a frequent visitor?"

Tom didn't answer right away. "We're familiar with him, sir."

Shannon chuckled. "You fellas keep your cards close to the vest, don't you?"

"Loose lips, mam. But to be frank, Mr. Fahey uses the place like a weekend cottage. He's quite the entertainer."

Paul patted Tom's shoulder. "That's very forthcoming, Tom."

"Sir, your tip to Feehan was more than all of Fahey's combined. Consider it a payback."

"And appreciated just as much." Paul took a step to move ahead, then paused. "Say Tom, what do you know about a basement here? We've been advised to avoid a basement. Do you know anything about that?"

Tom's freckled face turned white. "Uh…We're not permitted to go below ground, sir, not even to the wine cellar. And we're strictly instructed not to discuss anything. We've been told the penalty for breach of the rule is severe and irrevocable."

"Thanks, Tom." Paul slipped him another few euros. "Appreciate your candor."

Paul took Shannon's hand and they moved toward the noise.

"So, they've got the place buttoned up tight," Paul whispered.

"Just makes the challenge more fun."

Down another half football field, Aidan Fahey and several others, all in emerald green blazers and bow ties, stood at the entrance to a gaudy drawing room, greeting guests as they approached. From a distance, Fahey's wavy brown hair and full lips gave him the appearance of a wigged mannequin, but for the smarmy grin glued on his face.

"I think you should have worn your American flag tie," Shannon whispered.

"I'm more subtle, darling."

Fahey's face lit up when he saw Paul and Shannon approach, his eyes lingering on Shannon, assaying her from head to toe.

"Mr. and Mrs. Forté! How delighted I am that you could join us." He shook Paul's hand, grasped Shannon's, raised it to his lips, and kissed it, eyes lingering on her longer than necessary.

"Thrilled to be here, Mr. Fahey," Paul said. "We are in love with Ireland."

"May I present Seamus Nolan, Deputy Secretary of my department."

Nolan had a boyish look. Fair hair, bright blue eyes, smile with a little gap in the middle teeth. "Honored to have you with us," Nolan said. He didn't kiss Shannon's hand, but Paul was quite sure he would have, if he had a little more courage.

"We've enjoyed the trip down," Paul said. "We had a lovely

stay at The Arbutus in Killarney."

"Yes," Shannon said. "And we met that lovely reporter by chance on the street. She couldn't have been friendlier!"

Fahey's face look mildly pained. "Miss McGee? Oh, she can be a bit of a pain. A real thorn in my side sometimes, but a charming lady, for a reporter."

"I hope I'm not out of line asking, but Shannon and I noticed the handsome logo on all of the toiletries and match boxes. Is it something proprietary?"

Fahey kept his mouth shut, and looked to Nolan.

"That," Nolan said, "is the corporate logo for Chiar-Tech, one of our many successful high-tech companies. I happen to be the CEO, and Mr. Fahey here sits on the board."

"I confess I know very little about your high-tech boom, except that is has been a boom and…" Paul searched for the appropriate noun.

"Contraction," Fahey said.

"Yes! Contraction, exactly," Paul said. He reached out and gave Fahey's arm a light squeeze. "Thank you for rescuing me from international embarrassment."

"Yes, well," Nolan jumped in, "we had growing pains similar to those your own tech sector suffered in the nineties, and the global recession has been an incredible challenge."

"Paul, we're holding up the line, honey."

"Yes, of course," Paul said. "I hope we can chat more about it later?"

Fahey and Nolan assured Paul they would, and the American couple moved forward into the room. Paul surveyed the crowd. Equal mix of men and women, slightly more men.

"I was this close to a confession," Paul said, holding two fingers together.

"You softened him up for me."

"Feel like a drink?"

"I'll stick with water."

"Well I think I'll have a bit of the hair of the dog." They moved toward the bar, an impressive polished grey marble behemoth occupying half of the back wall.

"Paul! Paul *Faw*-tay!"

Paul hadn't heard the voice in more than a decade, and didn't miss it. "It's Boyle," he said in Shannon's ear. Boyle in his off-the-truck five thousand dollar suit, holding a double whiskey in a rocks glass. Paul slapped on the automatic smile as he turned to greet his old lobbyist *pal*. He didn't know Boyle for shit, but that didn't matter. To a lobbyist, every rep is a pal. Even ex-reps. Boyle did two terms in the House, then switched to lobbying when his *real* pal, Charlie Sligo, won his senate seat. In Boston, if you're a Boston College guy, you got pals. If you're a "triple eagle," your classmates are blood pals for life. Boyle and Sligo were both triple eagles, classmates, at B.C. High, B.C. College, and B.C. Law.

"Denny Boyle! How the hell are ya?" Paul bellowed. He went in big with the shoulder clap and the man hug. A big fuckin' surprise, this was! "Denny, you know my wife, Shannon? You guys met?"

Denny checked out Paul's wife, like he didn't remember her face, but maybe he remembered her chest. "Nah, I don't think so, Paul. I'd remember. I'd remember," the last bit said with a badly masked leer.

Shannon did not speak or extend her hand. Paul knew that posture. He so admired his wife's people instincts. Boyle didn't even offer her his hand. Maybe he got the message. She could say an awful lot with her eyes.

Paul put his arm around her shoulder. She leaned into him with her arms crossed, and watched Boyle with a poker face.

Boyle swigged his whiskey. "What brings you to Castle Cormack, if I may ask?"

"Shannon and I came to visit the spot where my parents passed away," Paul said. He felt Shannon stir for an instant, knowing she loved his lie.

Boyle's face went slack. "Aw, Paul, I'm sorry."

"No worries, Denny. It was a long time ago. Anyway, we visited the Dáil when we were in Dublin, we were introduced to Aidan Fahey, and he invited us down. Actually, he asked if I knew you. I think that's why he invited us."

"Fahey's my cli- my client's TD. You know what the Irish legis-"

"Yes, of course."

"Yah, so the company that owns this place, Chiar-Tech, they're my client. I've been over twice before, stayin' here." He waved his arms at the surroundings. "Not bad for a parochial school kid from Quincy."

"You have much to be proud of. You bring anybody over with you?"

"Yah, yah, Charlie Sligo's over at the bar. Come on over, you guys look like you could use a drink."

Paul and Shannon followed Boyle as he weaved through the crowd, nodding left and right, saying, "hihowaya" and "howyadoin."

The back of Sligo's cheap suit seemed to take up half the bar as he leaned on his elbows. Paul hadn't seen the guy since he'd left the House ten years ago. Sligo'd put on at least fifty pounds since. His old days as a B.C. football player were way behind him. Like many of his ilk, he'd passed from ex-athlete to fat slob.

"*Chah*-lie, look who I found!"

Sligo rotated 180° without moving his torso off the bar, full rocks glass in hand. From the look of his face, it wasn't his first, and if Paul's memory were correct, it wouldn't be his last.

"Well waddaya know," he said. "Fuckin' Forté! The *giant slayah*. What brings you to the Emerald Isle?"

"'Lo, Senator. Long time no see." Paul shook the man's beefy hand. Sligo squeezed harder than necessary.

"No kiddin'."

"Say hello to my wife, Shannon."

Full Irish | **67**

Sligo surveyed Shannon in the same fashion Boyle did. "Hello, wife Shannon." He stuck out his hand, staring at her chest.

"Senator," she said, giving the hand a curt shake. Senator Charles Sligo did not know her, but somehow she knew him. "Paul, maybe I will have that drink. Scotch for me."

"We're in Ireland, darling. We drink Irish." Paul caught the bartender's eye and ordered two Jameson's on the rocks.

"How'd you weasel your way into this shindig?" Sligo asked again. He held his glass at an angle, the whiskey nearly spilling over an edge.

Paul chuckled. "I'm not a legislator any more, Senator. I don't have to weasel. We were invited by Aidan Fahey. He liked Shannon, I think. But the better question is why *you're* here. Denny tells me Chiar-Tech is his client, but what about you?"

Denny rescued his buddy. "My wife couldn't come. She said, 'take whoever you want.' Senate's in recess till next week, so I invited *Chah*-lie."

"Good thing Bernie Kilroy's not the U.S. Attorney any more, eh, Paul?"

"Ancient history, Charlie."

"Nah, it's not. Your case set a precedent, Paul. No U.S. Attorney's gonna waste his time chasing us for golf dates. You know what happens these days when we play golf with our lobbyist pals? We make a toast to Paul Forté."

"That's an honor I wasn't aware of, Charlie."

"Besides, Denny and I been friends since high school. Our friendship pre-dates my service. His generosity is on account of pre-existing friendship. I'm bullet proof."

That's what Paul thought before his own indictment.

"You bring your clubs?" Boyle asked. Boyle wasn't a bad stick himself, for a once-a-week player. But he had the same hole in his game that most politicians had. He made up his own rules.

"I did, although with weather like this, who's gonna play?"

"You don't wait for the sunshine in Ireland, Paul," Boyle said.

"You dress for the elements and you grind it out. You in? We're playin' in the morning, rain or shine."

Paul hesitated, glanced at Shannon.

"I'm staying right here, honey. You can get drenched to your heart's content. I'll spend the morning trading barbs with Finola. I'm sure we can find some trouble to get in."

"Let's see how it goes," Paul said.

The sound of a clinking glass brought the group to silence. At the head of the room, Fahey addressed the guests.

"Ladies and gentlemen, we'll be moving to the dining room for a buffet dinner in one moment. Seating is identified with place cards On behalf of our Irish friends and guests, we want to extend a warm welcome to our American visitors, and thank them for all they do to advance our common economic interests."

The crowd responded with polite applause, the Americans nodded.

"For our American guests, we've split you up so we can all get a chance to know you. If you could all follow Tom here, he will lead you."

Shannon leaned in close to Paul. "If I'm sitting next to either of these lunks, I'm switching with you - or somebody."

Paul whispered back. "Channel your revulsion. With your charm, you'll have a full confession by dessert."

* * *

When Fahey finished and the crowd began moving toward the dining room, Finola stuffed her notepad into her handbag and joined the scrum. She chatted up a pair of American visitors who offered some colorful comments about how tax advantages given to new business ventures by the Irish government were too generous to ignore. All done to death before, but she might find a fresh angle if she kept asking questions. She hadn't managed to yet meet the American called Dennis Boyle, Chiar-Tech's lawyer in Boston, but she had seen on the seating plan that he was sitting beside her at dinner, so she would be ready to have a go at him. She'd hoped she might catch the Minister of Jobs, Enterprise and Employment, but he had rushed out to greet the Taoiseach, Brian O'Halloran, who had just arrived by helicopter. Schmoozing of the first order, Finola thought, and here she was, stuck in the midst of it.

The guests descended upon the huge mahogany table, where candles flickered in tall silver candelabras. Finola made note of the gleaming parquet, oak paneling and sash windows swathed in red velvet curtains, the way she envisioned it would have looked a hundred or so years ago. High on the walls, the Connolly-Smith ancestors looked haughtily down upon the room from huge portraits with elaborate gilded frames. At least here, the interior decorators had held back on the bling.

In the dim light, Finola spied Shannon at the far end, already sitting beside Fahey. She smiled at Finola and rolled her eyes. Finola giggled. Shannon seemed to have Fahey's number already. Judging from her reaction to Finola's one-finger salute, she could probably cope very well with his clever innuendoes and bawdy flirtations. Let Fahey try to chip away, see where it gets him. Finola delighted in the prospect that Shannon would cut him down to size, but then, she didn't wish him on any woman. To an attractive woman, he was dog poo on the bottom of a sneaker.

Finola found her seat. Neither of her two table companions had arrived, so she remained standing, scanning the room. By the window, Seamus Nolan talked *sotto voce* with a tall, trim man in an expensive looking suit. Was that Boyle? He looked Irish, with his dark hair and fair complexion, but as he wore a gold bracelet and a huge gold watch, he had to be American. Must be Boyle, she decided and looked away as their eyes met. Strange man.

She had observed Paul and Shannon react somewhat coolly to this guy during pre-dinner cocktails, and wondered if they might have clashed in the past. But then Paul gave him the man hug, and she wondered if she had imagined the flash of enmity. But good acting skills were in the bag of any successful lawyer, whether in Boston or Dublin.

She picked up the menu card by her plate and studied it from the bottom up. Catered by '*An Croi Dubh*', Cahersiveen. It rang a bell. They catered for a lot of the big power parties in the area. Castle Cormack's usual staff wouldn't be large enough for something like this, so they would outsource for big events. Her eyes rose to the menu. Typically Irish, with smoked salmon, leek and potato soup, roast leg of Kerry lamb, a selection of local cheeses, and apple pie with vanilla custard for dessert. Not bad. Finola felt stuffed just reading about it.

"*An Croi Dubh.* The Black Heart," a voice said beside her.

Finola jumped. "God, Seamus, you scared me. I was looking at the menu and wondering how I'd be able to eat all that."

Nolan pulled out Finola's chair for her, and Finola once seated, took the next chair. "I know," he said. "But I'm sure they'll present it in fairly small portions. And have you looked at the list of wines? All vintages, even the champagne. Good catering firm, I'm told, despite the strange name."

"Yes. Didn't think of what it actually meant. Funny how we never think in Irish anymore. But that *is* a strange name for a catering firm. Or even a pub, when you think about it. Even in Kerry."

"Not if you know where it comes from," Nolan remarked. "Did you ever hear of Ciaran Ó Dubhagáinn? 'Black Kieran', he was called by the British landowners."

"Of course. A notorious highwayman in these parts in the eighteenth century. But I don't see the connection with the pub. It's owned by the Duggan family, isn't it?"

"Yes." Nolan smirked at her. "Think about it, Finola. What does Ó Dubhagáinn mean?"

Finola slapped her forehead. "Of course! That's Duggan in

Irish. Oh, duh, how stupid of me. Typical Kerry name too. But things are always kind of weird and mysterious here."

Seamus nodded. "Yes. That's the charm of Kerry. It's kind of other-worldly." He leaned across Finola. "Would you agree, Dennis?" he said to the man who had just sat down on her other side.

Finola turned to the man and was hit with a blast of aftershave. She held out her hand. "Hello, I'm Finola McGee."

"The best political reporter in Ireland," Seamus added. "Finola, This is Dennis Boyle, Boston lawyer for Chiar-Tech."

Boyle grasped her hand and squeezed. "A pleasure to meet you, Finola."

"Hello, Dennis," Finola said, trying not to wince as his rings dug into her hand. "Welcome to Kerry."

"Thank you very much." He let go of her hand but rested his arm on the back of her chair. "So you're a political reporter, eh? What do you write about?"

"I cover Leinster House for *The Irish Telegraph*," Finola replied.

He lifted one of his black eyebrows. "Is that so? I thought this event was more about business than politics."

"But they're so very closely related." She sat back a little to avoid his hot breath on her face. "I mean, this party is hosted by a company whose board includes a member of the Dáil, and the Taoiseach is the Honored Guest."

Boyle shrugged. "Well, we would never do that in the States, with the conflict of interest laws."

Finola's hand lurched at a glass of Montrachêt that had just been poured. "You're more subtle about it, then?"

Boyle took his arm away from the back of her chair. "I'm not sure I understand your meaning."

Finola looked him straight in the eyes. "Oh come now, Dennis, don't be a...what's the expression you gents use, 'pussy'? We love our politics here, mostly because we love a dirty business. I'm fascinated by the art of political manipulation!" She glanced at

Fahey down the table and took a long sip of wine. "So, Dennis, are you good at manipulation?"

Seamus slipped his arm around the back of Finola's chair and leaned in front of her toward Boyle, smiling fiercely. "Don't let this woman corner you, Dennis. She's a lovely lady, but she's an ink-stained hack!"

Boyle picked up the origami-like linen napkin by his plate and flicked it into his lap. "Lobbying is an honorable profession where I come from. Every situation in government requires advocates who understand the process and work within it."

Finola glanced again at Seamus, catching a glimmer of expression that suggested even he thought Boyle's reply was absurd. "Of course. I'm sorry, Dennis, I didn't mean to insult your integrity. Maybe I've been around too long to believe there is anything honorable about politics."

Boyle's eyes drifted to the other end of the table, where Paul was talking to a fat man with black curly hair, who had been introduced to Finola as Charles Sligo. "No offense taken, Finola. We have reporters like you in Boston, and we all understand our roles in this process."

Finola glanced at Nolan. "We don't really use lobbyists here to the same extent as the Yanks, do we Seamus?"

"No, that's true," Nolan replied. "We tend to rely on those inside the system."

"Otherwise known as pulling strings," Finola suggested. "Here it's all about who you know, isn't it?"

Nolan squirmed. "I wouldn't say that's unusual, Finola. Remember, the root word of politics means 'people'."

Finola snorted, "Go away out of that, Seamus. You know very well the manipulation going on behind the scenes in Irish politics, and business too, has little to do with the people."

Seamus puffed indignation. "Now don't go indicting us all without trial."

Finola rolled her eyes. "Oh, please. You're the Deputy Secretary of Finance? Nothing going on in your Department that you'd not want me reporting about, eh?" She turned to Boyle. "Do you have corrupt politicians in Boston, like here?"

Boyle cleared his throat. "Of course we do. Boston is famous for its rogues. Mayor James Michael Curley was re-elected from his jail cell."

Finola smiled. "Haven't your last three House Speakers been convicted of felonies?"

Boyle's eyes flashed, and he glanced at Nolan across the back of Finola's chair. "Jesus, Seamus is right about you."

"I suppose he is. So how do they do it over there? Pay for golf? Or offer other kinds of perks? Or do they dispense with subtleties and go for the straight-out bribe?" She glanced at Nolan.

Boyle laughed, showing an impressive row of white teeth. "I'm sure there are many ways of going about it. But I don't get involved in that sort of thing. Not designed for long-term success."

Nolan put his hand on Finola's arm. "I should say not, Dennis. Finola, could you send the shark back to deep water and show us your kind and gentle side?

Finola ignored Nolan. "But what about Chiar-Tech? How do you go about assisting them in their Boston interests?"

Boyle adopted a lawyer face. "Chiar-Tech is an excellent company with an excellent product. They'll perform well under any circumstances. My only job is to help steer them through the labyrinth of the government contracting process."

"Really?" Finola gave him the wide-eyed look of a slightly dim-witted female. "But wouldn't an Irish company have an uphill fight against local firms? How do you overcome the bias in favor of the hometown boys?"

He twirled his wine glass. "That's the other side of the manipulation coin, Finola. Some people hire lobbyists to influence, some hire lobbyists to combat influence, keep the government honest. If there's any bias in favor of local firms, it's my job to make sure it isn't exercised."

Slippery eel. She'd never get a straight answer from him. She turned to Nolan as the first course was put in front of her. She was about to dig into the smoked salmon on a paper-thin slice of brown bread, but Seamus put his hand on her arm. "You can't eat yet. The Taoiseach hasn't sat down."

Finola looked around the room. "But where is he? His helicopter came in twenty minutes ago. Why can't he travel by car like normal people?"

"He's not normal. He's the *Taoiseach*," Seamus said, as if she had just committed some kind of *lèse majesté*.

Finola studied him for a moment. "Jesus, Seamus, he's a head of state, not the Pope." His obsequious devotion was almost embarrassing. He had sold his soul to politics a long time ago. He'd had a choice to back her up against Fahey or not. He had chickened out and stayed quiet. They were on friendly enough terms, but she'd never forgive him for that act of cowardice. She looked longingly at her plate. "I wish he'd hurry up. I didn't have a chance to get an hors d'oeuvre and I've had two glasses of wine. Too busy running around trying to talk to people. That's the problem with this job. You never get to eat when you need to."

"You poor girl." He looked at her with a sympathetic expression in his light blue eyes. "How are you coping, Finola? I know Eoin's death was very hard for many, but you were especially close to him."

Finola sighed. She might have been mollified by Nolan's concern if she wasn't convinced he was just steering her away from further inquiry about Chiar-Tech. Then the image of that screenshot on the flash drive suddenly popped into her mind. Five million euros. But to whom? And for what? "I'm better," she said. "But I'd sure like to know who killed him."

"Wouldn't we all."

Finola made a snap judgment and tossed out a little bait. "Eoin was working on something. I'm going to find out if it had anything to do with his death."

Nolan swallowed. "Was he really? What was it? Do you know?"

As she weighed a response, the crowd stirred. Everyone rose to their feet and began clapping, as the Taoiseach and his entourage entered the dining room. "Let's have some coffee in the conservatory after dinner," she whispered.

Throughout dinner, she struggled to maintain a conversation, fretting over just what she would tell Seamus Nolan, and what she would ask him.

Chapter Six

A stemwinder, biding time, and a right hook

Paul knew exactly what his wife was thinking. *We came all the way to Ireland, drove across their blessed country to the farthest reach of County Kerry, to have a political speech delay dinner.*

She sat across the table from him as *Taoiseach* O'Halloran droned on about the global economy and the rising tide lifting all boats. *Especially stinkpots like this shindig*, Paul could hear her thinking. When O'Halloran finally concluded his remarks ("I'll be brief," he'd lied), the woman to Paul's right, who reminded him of his mother, lowered her head as she stage whispered to him, "that one's got no gift of gab at all."

Shannon heard her and guffawed. Fahey, next to Shannon, turned. "What a delightful laugh, what did I miss?"

Paul rescued her. "Just my irreverent sense of humor, Aidan. My wife loves irreverence. Don't you, darling?"

"I revere irreverence." She sipped her drink. "And Irish whiskey, too."

"Tell me, Aidan," Paul said. "How does the business community regard Mr. O'Halloran?"

Fahey smoothed his hair, weighing his words. "Difficult to find support these days with the drastic measure needed to right the ship. Some are supportive, some are not. Largely depending on the health of their balance sheets. If only the banks would lend again, seems to be the common theme."

"How does Chiar-Tech view him?" Shannon asked. "How healthy is its balance sheet?" She smiled demurely as her eyes surveyed the sumptuous room. Paul made a note to scold her later.

A nervous titter escaped Fahey's lips. "The days of the Celtic Tiger are behind us, I'm afraid. Austerity is the mandate now, for all of us."

As if to mock his words, a flock of black-tailed waiters began delivering the appetizer. A white-gloved hand placed a plate in front of Shannon. Smoked salmon, brown bread, capers, chopped onion.

"Hard to imagine austerity in this environment," Paul said, another glove-with-plate appearing in front of him.

Fahey's face pinched. He smoothed his hair again. "This property is a tax shelter, Paul. The company did the country a favor, buying such an underutilized asset. We were able to preserve hundreds of acres of open space and restore a national treasure. Governments are not very good property managers, as you might know."

"Can't argue with you there. It must cost a small fortune to maintain it, though."

Fahey put his hands on the table, palms down, moved the salad fork an inch. "It has significant intrinsic benefits that do not show up on a balance sheet. I think you call it 'Good Will' in the States."

"Well, Aidan, as Oliver Wendell Holmes once stated, 'it is every man's duty to pay the government what he owes, and not a penny more'."

To Paul's left, Sligo broke in. "I agree with Justice Holmes, Paul, governments could be a lot more efficient with their money."

"The taxpayers' money, Charlie," Paul said. "We must never

forget that governments are custodians, not owners."

"Absolutely," Charlie said. "And they'll be better custodians when they have the right tools. Right Aidan?"

Fahey twirled his white wine glass. "That's right, Mr. Sligo. We're pleased to have your support."

"One thing I'm very impressed with," Paul said, "are the conflict of interest laws over here. An elected member of the Lower House can also serve in a Cabinet level position in the Executive, and *also* hold outside private business interests." Paul sensed his wife's level of glee rising.

"Yes, we've heard this from the Americans before," Fahey said. "We have ethics laws, and we have an entity that is in charge of enforcing them. On some occasions, people think they're too aggressive, other times not aggressive enough."

"Kind of depends whose ox is being gored," Paul said. "As long as there are ethics laws, someone will claim they're being violated."

"That's exactly right," Fahey said.

A pair of penguins swooped in to clear the salad plates.

"Tell me, Aidan, one of the barkeepers on the way down suggested that after Chiar-Tech had purchased this property, it had leased it back to the government for public use. Is that true?"

Fahey froze a moment, patted his lips with a linen napkin and smoothed his hair. "You've been chatting up the locals, have you?"

"Well, Aidan, you know what happens in your pubs. All sorts of 'facts' floating around in the Guinness."

Fahey smiled curtly. "I'm afraid that's just a nasty rumor." He paused, staring over Paul's head for a moment. "You didn't happen to come through Killarney on the way down?"

"We sure did," chimed Shannon.

"Enemy territory?" Paul asked.

Fahey nodded with a thin smile. "You know how it is, Paul, having been an elected representative yourself. There are always…pockets of enmity, rivalry…*skulduggery*," the last bit with emphasis. "I'm afraid it's all a nasty rumor, perpetrated by political opponents."

"You're a courageous man to take it on," Paul said, tipping his glass to Fahey, who nodded in reply. "No wonder they chose you Minister of Finance."

"Thank you," Fahey said, looking around to wave down the penguin with the wine bottles.

"Enough of this politics," Paul said. "Tell me about your government accounting software. You've had a good record of sales in Europe. Did you have to tweak it much to apply to the American system of public spending?"

"Oh, the subject matter is much too dry for such a festive occasion," Fahey said.

The woman next to Paul broke in. "Oh, to the contrary, Minister, I'd be very intrigued to hear more about your methods of bringing more accountability to how bureaucrats spend our money."

Fahey winced. "Yes, well…"

The penguins returned, laying large plates before them.

"Ah, lamb!" Fahey sighed. "I've not had good, fresh Kerry lamb for weeks. Do you know the difference between Irish lamb and American lamb?"

The woman glared at Fahey. "No, Mr. Fahey. What is it? The amount of shite they're fed by the likes of your bunch?"

Fahey blanched and Shannon stifled a guffaw (poorly so). Fahey avoided the woman but glared at Shannon.

"Madam, you're obviously a member of the Labour Party," Paul joked.

"Perish the idea," she proclaimed. "I am an accounting software expert with Muirfield Consultants. Mr. Fahey's product is barely utile and their servicing is almost non-existent."

"Now that will be enough Mrs. Favesham. We were courteous enough to invite you - against my better judgment. I suggest you avoid the ignominy of being the turd in the punch bowl."

Shannon and Mrs. Favesham gasped.

"Paul," Fahey continued, "Mrs. Favesham here is one of those consultants whose opinion depends on who is paying her fee. In this case, she is speaking on behalf of a competitor in Brussels. I think she is just a poor sport. Will you excuse me for a few minutes? I have some hosting duties." He didn't wait for permission, but rose languidly and slid off.

Mrs. Favesham leaned in to Paul. "A crook, that one is," she whispered.

Paul reached into his suit pocket for a business card. "Mrs. Favesham," he whispered.

"Phyllis, please."

"Phyllis…" He handed her his card. "If you have information relevant to Chiar-Tech's performance, I'd be most interested to see it."

She palmed the card. "I'll see what I can do." She lowered her eyes like a conspirator and turned back to her other table mates.

Sligo'd been quiet, a fish out of water, Paul thought. He whispered to Shannon. "Got a zinger for Charlie?"

Shannon smirked, her eyes waiting for Sligo to look at her again. "Excuse me, Senator," Shannon said. "Paul and I were talking on the ride down. There's a Sligo County in Ireland, up north. Is your family from there?" Paul then recalled why his wife knew Sligo. She'd donated one of her paintings to a Croatian Relief Fund auction in Boston. Sligo had received a humanitarian award as Croatian-American of the Year. He'd also been high-bidder on her painting, at $3,500. He never paid up.

"I've never researched it," Sligo said, "but I'm as Irish as the day is long."

* * *

The glass dome of the conservatory reached twenty feet, but Finola barely noticed. She paced around, oblivious of the tall palm trees, the huge ferns and bamboo thickets, the trickle of water from a fountain and the distant hush of rain whispering against the glass panels. She strode past a stand of azaleas and a big planter full of orchids, the pastel hues of their blossoms perfect against the backdrop of dark green foliage backlit by ground lights.

In the far corner, she found a wrought-iron table and chairs with striped silk cushions. She sat down, relieved for a moment of calm after the din of the dining room and the many speeches. She might have drunk a tad too much wine but she needed a little Dutch courage before she confronted—or warned—Seamus. The slight throbbing in her head told her that last glass of Château d'Yquem had been unwise. She pulled herself up and tried to concentrate. She had no idea what to expect, but she was going to get some answers, and in her inebriated state she was ready for anything short of hand-to-hand combat. The clicking of footsteps on tiles made her stomach churn as Seamus Nolan approached, Alistair in his wake, carrying a tray.

"Hello, Finola," Nolan said. "I asked Alistair for some coffee and cognac. You can put the tray on the table, Alistair."

"Very well, Mr. Nolan," Alistair mumbled, and glided off again.

"I don't know how he does that," Finola said looking at his departing figure.

Nolan settled on the chair opposite Finola. "Does what?"

"Walk like that. As if he were on wheels. And so silent. He pops up everywhere and scares the shit out of you."

Nolan shrugged. "Don't know. Must be something Anglo-Irish. Always around when we don't want them." He handed Finola a tiny cup. "Here, have some coffee. Comes in these thimble-sized cups. Don't know what's wrong with a mug."

Finola took the cup. "It's called elegance, Seamus." She lifted the cup and peered underneath it. "These are Royal Doulton antiques. I bet it's from the original Connolly-Smith service."

"How impressive." He downed his coffee in one go. "So what's the big secret?"

Finola looked longingly at the cognac snifter on the tray. Maybe just a sip or two? She shook her hair out of her eyes and opened her bag. "Seamus, ever since the old days at party headquarters, we've always had respect for each other, and I believe that you're basically a very honest person."

Seamus stared at her. "What are you going on about? Come on, out with it, pet. I haven't got time to fool around. I have guests to take care of." He took one of the cognac snifters and raised it to his lips.

Finola bristled. "Very well then." She pulled out the sheet of paper and held it out for Nolan to see. "This was on a flash drive Eoin intended to deliver to me the morning he was killed."

Nolan's hand with the cognac froze halfway to his mouth, his eyes glued to the page. Then he seemed to recover. "So? Why would Eoin want you to have that? It tells me nothing. You think it's some kind of smoking gun?"

Finola met Nolan's eyes, trying to gauge his mood. He didn't flinch or avert his gaze. "Can you show me where the money for the Liffey Project went?" she asked. "Or do I have to start a public enquiry?"

"I have no idea what you're going on about, you daft woman. And neither do you. That's one page of a budget record. What kind of conclusion have you come to, Miss Marple?"

The coldness in his eyes made Finola wilt. Was this the kind man she had always liked? Her fondness for him suddenly vanished. "Five million euros of taxpayers' money was taken out of the account of a very important water project," she said. "And then it went somewhere else. Some unnamed fund. But for what?"

Nolan clenched and unclenched his fists. "Finola, I think this is all over your head, and you're grasping at straws. I see that you think you are onto a big story, but you'd better be very careful before you start slinging accusations around in the press. I'm warning you, as a friend."

Finola stood up. "A little while ago, I decided to show you this, because I cared about you. I thought you weren't aware of it, that you might even have been set up by your boss. I thought I might help you sort it out in my professional capacity. But now I have to wonder if you aren't directly mixed up in it."

Nolan didn't reply.

"You can either cooperate or I will pursue this on my own," Finola continued, her anger giving her courage. "Ever since we worked together at the party, you've hitched your star to Fahey. And it's brought you a long way indeed. But as God is my witness, your loyalty to that man will be your downfall. Get out in front of this while you can, Seamus."

Nolan stood up but remained silent. His face red, the muscles of his jaw seemed to be working on a huge wad of chewing gum.

Finola began to enjoy the feeling of power as Seamus Nolan stood there, speechless. She half expected him to throw up. "But perhaps you'd like to explain how five million euros goes missing on *Prime Time* instead?" She enquired sweetly. "I know Paula very well. She has often asked me to join in some of the debates, but the right issue hasn't come up. Perhaps now it has. We're all living on austerity budgets and the Ministry of Finance is losing money? I don't think you want that."

Nolan said something under his breath.

"What was that? I wouldn't dare?" She took a step closer. "Listen, Seamus, why don't you make it easier for yourself? Just give me an explanation."

"I…I will not."

Alistair appeared out of the shadows, carrying a silver coffee pot. "More coffee?" he asked.

Nolan muttered something, turned away and rushed out of

the conservatory, knocking over a flowering *Duranta Repens* as he went.

* * *

By the time the apple pie and vanilla custard had been cleared, and the last of the Château d'Yquem was wrung from the bottles, Shannon was at the end of her rope, and made no bones expressing it to Paul.

"I'm so tired, I'd turn down an invitation to strangle that Sligo creep. I couldn't get my hands around his fat neck anyway. Did you see that guy eat? Jesus!"

"I averted my eyes," Paul said. "Boy, did he have a keen interest in your form, though."

He escorted Shannon to their room, tucked her in, and returned to the main lobby, where Alistair Connolly-Smith stood sentry at the front desk, alone, an ornate silver coffee pot at his elbow.

"Thank you for the elegant dinner, Mr. Connolly-Smith. The local lamb was exquisite, and your staff is superb."

"You are most welcome, Mr. Forté. As you can see, there is no expense spared here at Castle Cormack for our *important guests*."

Paul did not miss Alistair's dry sarcasm. "Do you have the expression, 'spending money like a drunken sailor' here in Ireland?"

"Regrettably, we do. It seems to be what politicians are good at, especially during an election year. Even when they haven't the money." Alistair's droll delivery did not mask the pain underneath.

"But I understood that this establishment was owned by Chiar-Tech."

"It is, sir." Alistair seemed to consider something before he spoke. "There was the helicopter ride from Dublin for Mr.

O'Halloran. Mr. Fahey and Mr. Nolan each brought their own drivers as well."

"I see what you mean." Paul felt Alistair had more on his mind but was exercising butler's discretion. "May I ask you a personal question, Alistair?"

"You may," he said. "And I reserve the right not to answer." A smile cracked his inscrutable face, something Paul had yet to see.

"Shannon and I read about the history of the castle and the Connolly-Smith heritage. I'm no European history buff, but your roots are British. I mean, losing one's castle tends to leave a lasting scar."

"You want to know how I do it?"

"I can guess how you do it, Alistair. You're a master of holding your tongue. I'm curious about *why*."

"Mr. Forté, I've been doing this for twenty-seven years, and you are the first American ever to ask me that question. To date, your countrymen have lacked your curiousness."

"I make no excuses for them. They look past you because they think they deserve this, and you're 'the help'."

"You are observant of human nature."

"It's a curse."

"Then I will reward your curiosity, on the condition that you honor its confidentiality." His eyes flicked left and right for eavesdroppers. Paul stepped up to the edge of the front desk as Alistair leaned forward. "I'm biding my time."

Biding his time, Paul thought. "The vanquished returns to recover his rightful place. Sir Winston Churchill."

His eyes closed and his face relaxed as though he were savoring an elegant dessert. Then, he flicked a sly smile, one eyebrow up. "If I may be recklessly candid with you, Mr. Forté, which I feel curiously confident I may. Since this land was taken from my family, I have never considered the ownership of it legitimate."

"It was my understanding that you sold the property."

Alistair studied the back of his hand. "A *sale* requires two willing parties. I sold the property, but I didn't do it willingly. And I'm going to get it back."

Paul leaned his elbows on the tall desk and lowered his voice.

"Alistair, if you need a devious legal mind to assist you in that mission, you need only call me. I will help you for the joy of retribution." Paul's mind flashed back to his trial, when an FBI agent who happened to be Shannon's sister arrested U.S. Attorney Bernard Kilroy, in the courtroom, as Kilroy was trying his damnedest to send Paul to prison. He felt the deep satisfaction, schadenfreude, really.

Alistair let Paul's offer hang. "I will remember that." He took two steps back from the desk. "Now then, I should direct you to the billiard room, where most of the American men have gathered to drink more of our whiskey and wine." He extended his arm, a thin, elegant finger pointing. "Past the dining room at the end, follow the corridor until you think you're lost, the billiard room will be the next doorway on your left."

"Thank you so much, Alistair. I'm very glad we could chat."

"The pleasure is all mine, sir." Alistair bowed slightly, turned on a dime and floated through the doorway behind him.

* * *

Shaken from her confrontation with Seamus Nolan, and a little too tipsy, Finola walked unsteadily up the stairs. The image of those cold eyes, normally twinkling with charm and laughter, was still fresh in her mind. A hard, ruthless side of him she had never seen. Of course he knew where that money had gone, it was written all over his face. She had suspected it even before she showed him the document. And the threat, *I'm warning you.* As a friend indeed. The bloody brass neck!

That money had to have gone to Chiar-Tech. But how to prove it was the problem. Once she found out more, this would, apart from providing a strong clue in the murder case, be one hell of a story. It could even influence the outcome of the election. She'd blow the whistle for Eoin and for the values and principles that had been so important to him. It would be a great tribute. She would mention him when she made her acceptance speech for the Journalist of the Year award.

She unlocked the door and stepped into her room, where the soft lamplight shone on the already turned-down bed and the little box of chocolates on the pillow. She put her handbag on the Louis XV chair by the window and closed the brocade curtains against the wind and rain outside. Horrible night, promising an even more horrible day tomorrow. She half remembered her earlier plan to get to MacGillycuddy's Reeks, and do the trail up to Carrauntoohil the next day. But she couldn't contemplate any kind of leisure activity now. All she could think of was how she might find out more about what was going on in Castle Cormack. She could make an attempt at grilling Alistair, who probably knew a lot about the shenanigans that went on behind the elegant scenery. Probably an impossible task, as getting anything out of him would be like trying to prise open a clam. Maybe he could be tricked into talking? Or bribed?

Finola undressed, throwing her clothes in a pile on the chair where she had just put her handbag. After slipping on the fluffy bathrobe that hung on the back of the door, she went into the bathroom to give her face a quick wash and brush her teeth. When she was finally ready to sink into that soft bed, she turned off the taps, switched off the lights and opened the door. About to walk into the bedroom, she saw something by the window, outlined in the dim light of the bedside lamp. A shadow. She froze. The notion that the castle was haunted flashed briefly through her mind and she peered at the shape beside the chair. No. That was no ghost. She reached out her hand and switched on the light in the ceiling. The room was instantly flooded with light and she saw who was there.

Aidan Fahey stood frozen in the middle of the room, holding Finola's laptop.

"Aidan, what the hell are you doing in my room?" Finola snapped.

He didn't move. "Had a little chat with Seamus. What the hell do you think I'm doing?"

She strode toward him, grabbing for her laptop. "Give me that."

Fahey held off the laptop with one hand and seized her arm with the other. "I want to know exactly what you got from Eoin Ryan," he snarled. "And then—" his fingers dug into her flesh—"we're going to destroy this computer and you're never going to inquire about your little discovery again."

"No!" Finola shouted and tried to pull her arm out of his grip. "You must be insane. I'm a fucking reporter for the second biggest newspaper in Ireland. You can't confiscate my property. Who the hell do you think you are, Cromwell? Give me my computer and get out of here or I'll—"

"You'll what?" he jeered. "Scream? Who's gonna hear you? The walls are a foot thick and everyone's downstairs anyway, most of them drunk."

His alcohol-laden breath was hot on her face, sweat beading on his upper lip. She tried to get nearer so she could slam her knee into his groin, but he dropped the laptop on the bed and held her away with both hands. "I spent twenty years to get where I am, darlin'. If you think I'm going to let you ruin it all, you're dumber than you look. "

"You bastard," Finola seethed, tears of rage stinging her eyes. "You miserable little prick. Graduated from sexual harassment to larceny now, have you? I'll ruin you."

They continued to struggle. Finola, knowing she was no match for him, tried desperately to get at him. She pulled her leg back to aim a kick at his shins but before she had a chance to swing, Fahey's torso twisted away from her, and, out of a flurry of white silk, a small but well-aimed fist punched Fahey in the face with a sickening crunch. A fist belonging to Shannon Forté.

Fahey screamed, stumbled back, holding his nose as the blood began to flow. "Ya broke my fuckin' nose, ya bitch," he growled. "I'll get you. I'll get you both." He pointed a bloody finger at Finola. "If I see anything in the papers, it'll be the last story you ever write in this country. Mark my word, McGee." Blood streaming over his mouth and chin, he stumbled out of the room.

Chapter Seven

A grudge match, comparing notes, playing in a dungeon

Paul followed the corridor as instructed, and kept walking until he told himself he *must* have taken a wrong turn. As he swivelled to reverse direction, he heard the unmistakable *click* of marble-on-marble, and followed it to the next door on the left. He smiled to himself. Good ol' Alistair.

The billiard room could have been mistaken for a commercial enterprise, six full-sized billiard tables in rows of three, filling half of a cavernous room full of mahogany woodwork, red leather chairs and couches, and an "honor bar" that took up fifteen feet of one corner. Above each table, Victorian light fixtures floated on almost invisible wires. The air was gray and stunk. Cigar smoking appeared to be mandatory. A dozen men stood about, puffing through a low hum of conversation. Two men wearing designer cowboy boots were engrossed in a billiard game. Sligo and Boyle were not present.

Paul went to the honor bar, poured himself three fingers of Taylor Fladgate 1985. Several bottles of port, scotch, cognac and other apéritifs littered the bar. A pad of "chits" and a cup of pencils loitered next to a slot in the top of the bar. Paul filled out a chit with his name, room number and drink. He tore the sheet off the pad and slipped it through a slot in the top of the bar. He recalled the sage advice of Irish immigrant bartender, Mr. Dooley: trust everyone, but cut the cards.

Paul moved to the billiard table where the two pairs of boots waged their silent battle. The bigger of them, name tag "Clem Winter," surveyed the table with a mixture of concentration and befuddlement.

"Winners?"

Clem's opponent laughed. "Comin' right up," he said. *Raht* up. Name tag, "Will Moore."

Clem shot and missed, leaving Will with a lay-up for the victory. He reached his stick up to the counting beads on the wire above, slid one across. "That's seven points. You're down seven grand."

"A thousand a point?" Paul gasped. "Too rich for me." He turned away.

"Nah, gambling is forbidden," Clem said.

They introduced themselves, both from Dallas, Texas. Clem was the lobbyist, Will the politician.

"So you represent Chiar-Tech in Texas?" Paul asked Clem.

"Yes *ah* do. Been an executive lobbyist for seventeen years. Used to be President of the state senate."

Will was cagier. Just an old colleague of Clem's, along for the free ride.

"Chiar-Tech seems to be making a pretty big push for the U.S. Market, huh?"

Clem nodded toward a group of four standing by a flatscreen television, where a vigorous game of hurling was underway. "Those fellas there, they're from California. Them fella's over there, from New York. Boys playin' cribbage over there, from Florida."

"Mind if I ask what your monthly retainer is?"

"No secret," Clem said, "we're all gettin' the same. Ten grand a month and warrants."

"Warrants?"

"Yeah, piece of the company. You deliver the contract, you get warrants in the new American company. A success fee."

"A bonus, for a job well done." Paul had heard it all before. He also knew that success fees were illegal - in Massachusetts, at least. Even without the success fee, Chiar-Tech was probably bleeding a hundred thousand dollars a month on the polished stone floor of the Castle Cormack billiard room.

Boyle and Sligo entered the room. Sligo went directly to the bar. Boyle stopped at Paul.

"Hey Paul, we got a match tomorrow." A statement of fact.

"We do, huh? You against me? Like the old days?" That was sliding the knife in, just a little.

"Nah, I told Fahey you were a scratch. He wants twenty strokes and a hundred euro Nassau."

If Fahey wanted to play golf against Paul in a pouring rain, and he wanted twenty strokes, it didn't matter whether Paul was a zero or a ten handicap. Twenty was too many on a sunny day. Paul had to hedge the bet somehow.

"C'mon Paul, waddaya say?" A tad too plaintive. "He's my client. I told him I'd fix it up."

He'd fix it up, alright. "On one condition, Denny."

"Name it," he said, almost giddy that he'd set Paul up.

"You and me, we have a side match."

"Okay no problem, what do you say, hundred dollar nassau?"

"No. Five hundred a hole on the front nine, a thousand a hole on the back."

Paul watched the color drain from Boyle's face, but he answered fast.

"Okay, hot shot, you're on."

Paul had no doubt that Boyle had figured Chiar-Tech would cover his bet, but he still stood there, shifting back and forth on his feet, not done with his business.

"So Paul, why are you here?"

"What do you mean, why am I here?"

"I know what you told me. I think it's bullshit. I don't believe in coincidence. What's your game, rep?"

"Denny, you still can't hold your liquor. Or are you asking for Fahey?"

"You workin' for Duggan?"

The word stopped Paul's heart for a beat. "What? Who's Duggan?" He was a little rusty at the rank deception game, but it was like riding a bike.

Alistair Connolly-Smith appeared at the doorway. "Mr. Forté?"

"Yes, Alistair?"

"I believe your presence is urgently needed."

Paul excused himself.

"Don't forget," Boyle said, "in the lobby at 9:00 am sharp. You pull out, you lose the bet."

Paul paused and looked back at Boyle. "Fuck you, Dennis. Don't stay up too late."

He followed Alistair into the hallway. "Everything okay?" he asked as they hurried along.

"The ladies are fine. But there's been an incident," he said.

"An incident involving my wife? Couldn't be."

"Your wife and the reporter, Miss McGee, seem to make quite a team."

"It would appear to be fate," Paul said.

"An awful thing, that."

"Say, Alistair. Apparently, I've got a golf match tomorrow against Mr. Fahey, and another against Boyle. You know if Waterville has any good caddies?"

Alistair smiled as he glided along beside Paul. "As luck would have it, I do. I will make a call in the morning and make sure you get Gavin Corkery. He was runner up in the Irish national amateur. Impressive young man."

"That would be wonderful. I don't like to gamble at golf, but

I am forced into this, and I'd like to hedge my bets."

"You may have to hedge them a little further, Mr. Forté."

"Why is that, Alistair?"

"Mr. Fahey cheats."

* * *

Still trembling with pent-up anger, Finola sank down on the edge of the bed and glared at Shannon. "Fuck you."

Shannon gaped. "*What?*"

"Did I look as if I needed help? Jesus, what do you take me for? I could manage very well by myself, thank you."

Shannon crossed her arms. "Oh yeah? He had you pinned to the wall."

"I was about to get him right in the balls. Fuck it, I wanted to give it to the bastard big time, right where it'd hurt him the most. But you had to come and bloody rescue me."

"Oh, I'm sooo sorry," Shannon mocked, as she slunk into an overstuffed chaise next to the minibar. "You're right, I should have waited by the door until you were about to be raped."

"He wasn't trying to rape me, you eejit." Finola picked her laptop from the bed and waved it in the air. "This is what he wanted—or something in it."

The door opened. Paul stepped into the room, surveyed the scene, put his hands on his hips.

"Ladies, do you have anything to do with the bleeding politician in the hallway?"

Shannon raised her hand and lowered her head. "Guilty, your Honor."

"You make a fine diplomat, darling. Finola, you look terrible. Are you okay?"

Finola slowly straightened up. "I'm fine. I'd have managed all by myself though, but Superwoman here thought I needed help.

Nice right hook, I have to say."

Paul strolled over to Finola's minibar. "Why don't you tell me the story while we unwind a bit. Cognac?" He didn't wait for orders, just cracked the nips and began to pour.

"Yes, please," his contrite wife said.

"Me, too." Finola suddenly burst out laughing. "This is ridiculous. I'm sorry for overreacting. Now that I think about it, it wouldn't have been so good for my career if I had managed to crush his nuts. So, after mature reflection, as they say in Irish politics, I suppose I should thank you."

"Apology accepted," Shannon said. "Let's toast. Where's the bartender?"

Paul handed her a glass and noticed her red knuckles. "Your hand okay?"

"Maybe ice isn't a bad idea."

"Okay, Finola, tell me what happened, if you would." He returned to the minibar and set about filling a washcloth with green ice cubes shaped like shamrocks. "Here, some Irish good luck for you." He sat beside his wife.

"Vulgarity rules. Even in the fridge." Finola threw back her brandy in one go and coughed. "Ugh, oh, yeah. Better." Her eyes focused on Paul. "What happened? Well, I was in the bathroom brushing my teeth and all the rest and when I came out, I found that creep Fahey with my laptop in his hands. He was after—certain information. I tried to take it back and he was wrestling with me, and then Shannon just flew in and—wham!"

"You beast," Paul whispered, looking at Shannon. "Remind me never to pick a fight with you."

Shannon sighed and put her head on his shoulder. "I'd never, ever punch you. Pinch you perhaps, and slap you around a little bit but never punch you."

Paul sighed and put his arm around her. "I feel so much safer." He turned to Finola. "We're all exhausted and I have a death match with Fahey on the golf course tomorrow, so let's make this brief. You said Fahey was after *certain* information. Did this certain information have to do with Chiar-Tech?"

Finola stared at Paul. Who was this man? What was he doing here? "What do you know about Chiar-Tech?" she asked.

Paul looked at Shannon who nodded as if to say 'go ahead'. He cleared his throat. "Well… It's a little complicated but…"

"But what?"

Paul sighed and drained his glass. "I'll cut a long story short so we can all go to bed. I'm here to gather information on Chiar-Tech. It has to do with some business in Boston I am considering taking on. I came here partly by accident, but as luck would have it, the place is crawling with people connected to Chiar-Tech. So then I thought I'd keep my eyes and ears open and see if…"

"If you could find something that would damage their reputation?" Finola asked softly. "You're working for a competitor. Just a wild guess, of course."

"Not exactly, but awful close," Paul said, looking at her with admiration.

Finola put her glass on the night table. "Well, if it wasn't obvious before, it is now. I want to screw the bastards. But it's time you left. Your wife is falling asleep and so am I. We'll talk some more in the morning."

"Shall we plan to meet after I finish my grudge match?"

Finola nodded. "You bet."

* * *

Paul's eyes snapped open bright and early. Rain assaulted the windows. A relentless gurgling droned from the downspout. He looked at Shannon, face planted into a down pillow, like she was trying to asphyxiate herself. He picked up her right hand and kissed the red knuckles.

"Hey, bruiser."

No movement. Then a low, muffed few words. *I am so ashamed*, it sounded like.

"You gonna be okay on your own all day?"

"Ah be fuh." Sounded like *I'll be fine.*

"Don't beat yourself up. Not many women can say they punched an Irish politician in the nose."

The hand he'd just kissed moved. It made a fist, save for the middle finger.

"Well, I'm sure you'll have fun bonding with your new friend. Don't get into any more trouble."

The head swivelled, Shannon propped herself on an elbow. "Did I hurt your mission, Paul? I feel like I've stepped in shit."

His insides smiled. "Nah, you didn't hurt a thing. Might have helped, in fact."

"Why?"

He patted her hip and kissed her. "I'll tell you when I get back from golf with Fahey's money in my pocket."

* * *

When Finola came downstairs in the morning, she thought she had missed Paul but spotted him sitting on the window seat in the lobby, dressed for a deluge and looking none too happy about it. He was glancing at a newspaper and sipping coffee, now and then looking out the window, as if the weather would, by some miracle, improve.

He looked up when Finola approached. "Good morning. Sleep well?"

Finola stifled a yawn. "Like the dead. I think I slipped into a coma after you left. How about you?"

He put down the newspaper. "Same here. Shannon's still out. I let her sleep. I think bed is the best place in this weather. But sit down. I want a quick word before I head out."

Finola sat down beside him. "I see the Boston Globe gets around. Didn't know you could get it here."

"You can get anything here, it seems. No expense spared in Castle Cormack."

"Ain't that the truth."

"Coffee?"

Finola jumped and discovered Alistair behind her, holding a tray with coffee cups and a silver coffee pot. "Oh, God, Alistair, you scared me. No thanks, I'm grand. I might have something later in the library. I'm going to do some work there."

"I'll bring you some then," Alistair said and faded into the shadows.

"Where did he go?" Finola asked. "One minute he was here and then—poof—gone. He's like a spirit you can conjure up by just thinking about him. He must have extra-sensory perception."

"You okay? You look a little pale."

Finola rubbed her face. "A bit tired despite the deep sleep."

"Not surprising." Paul leaned closer. "Listen, I won't be able to hit a golf ball if I'm wondering what you've got. Can you help a guy out?"

Finola nodded. She told Paul about Eoin Ryan and the contents of the flash drive.

He pulled back and looked at her. "Those documents mention Chiar-Tech specifically?"

"No. But why would Fahey assault a reporter and steal her computer to get it back?"

"It's a long way from admissible evidence, but we're not in a court of law, are we now?" Paul got up. "I have to go. We'll talk more later."

"Okay. Good luck." Finola winked and pushed her fist into his shoulder. "Give 'em hell."

Paul grinned. "It'll be my pleasure."

* * *

Following a light breakfast, Finola carried her handbag and laptop down another endless corridor in search of the library. The smell of stale tobacco smoke wafted from an open door and she looked in to discover the billiards room where Feehan was pushing a vacuum cleaner across the tartan carpet with great gusto. He grinned at her and waved.

"Library?" she mouthed. He pointed to the right and she continued until she arrived at a set of double doors with brass handles. She pushed them open and entered a huge dark room lined with bookcases that climbed two stories to the ceiling. A spiral staircase rose to a catwalk along the upper racks. A musty smell of old books mingled with wood smoke from logs blazing in the fireplace. The room had been spared the tsunami of modern design that had flooded other parts of the castle and there was an eerie sense of stepping back in time. Lamps with green glass shades cast their soft light on oak floorboards covered in faded oriental carpets. The Adam fireplace, flanked by leather armchairs, sported the head of a stag above it. Finola looked up at the stag and met its glassy stare. "You poor thing," she muttered.

"I agree," said a voice from the depth of one of the chairs. "He hasn't been dusted in ages."

Finola jumped. "God, woman, don't frighten me like that. I thought you were in bed."

Shannon sat up. "Sorry. So tired I couldn't sleep. I've decided to visit every room in the castle before I leave, but this one was so comfy."

Finola sat down on a chair opposite Shannon and found herself disappearing into leather cushions. "These chairs sure are squishy," she said, trying to pull herself up.

Shannon laughed. "Don't fight it. Just let yourself go. They're very comfortable once you settle in. Like the inside of a very expensive purse."

Finola relaxed against the back of the chair. "Very comfy. I love the smell of old leather."

Shannon smirked. "You don't look like the type who goes for leather."

Finola couldn't help laughing. "God no. Only when it comes to furniture."

"I had a pair of leather pants once. I wore them three times."

"Three times? You're a brave woman. Was it the chafing or the sweating?"

"Both."

Finola noticed the big leather-bound book in Shannon's lap. "What's that you're reading?"

Shannon opened the book. "It's a history of the castle from the mid-nineteenth century filled with beautiful illustrations and etchings. Very interesting. It says there was a moat around the castle in the early days, and a drawbridge. All that was demolished during the Victorian era, when they modernized the castle and built the entrance that's there now, and laid out the gardens. Nothing's left of the mediaeval porch with the portcullis and that hole above where they poured boiling oil on their invaders."

Finola winced. "Charming practice."

Shannon flicked a page. "Hey, there's supposed to be a dungeon here. Look." She turned the book toward Finola.

Finola craned to see the picture. "Oh, yes. I wonder where it is." Was Shannon thinking the same thing? "I've heard rumors and jokes about it, but thought it was all a load of *piseog*."

Shannon's eyes narrowed "A load of pish what?"

"*Piseog*. Irish for superstition."

"Oh." Shannon giggled. "Sounds kinda dirty. But the dungeon… I've heard about it."

"Like what?"

There was sudden gleam in Shannon's eyes. "From the bartenders in Killarney. They said 'stay out of the basement.' Sounds intriguing."

Full Irish | 101

"Intriguing? That's putting it mildly. I would call it an invitation to explore."

Shannon waggled her eyebrows. "Shall we?"

Finola considered it for a second. "Hell, yes. And we should do it right now. There's nobody around. Most of the guests boarded a bus for Muckross House and Gardens in Killarney about half an hour ago. They won't be back for hours. Perfect opportunity to snoop."

"And Fahey's out dragging my husband around in the rain. He's the only one I'd be concerned about." Shannon got up. "I'm dying to see what's down there. Come on, maybe we'll meet Quasimodo," she added with fake doom in her voice.

Finola extracted herself from her chair. "Okay, then. Let's go hunting for the spirits of tortured souls."

Shannon opened the door and peered down the corridor. "The coast is clear."

Finola joined her. "Feehan was cleaning the billiards room a while ago."

"There's not a sound from there. Probably gone on his coffee break."

Finola looked down the deserted corridor. "What about Alistair?"

"Who knows? He could be anywhere. Never knew anyone who can appear and disappear like him." Shannon started to saunter out of the library like she owned the place. "Come on," she said. "Let's go play in the dungeon."

Chapter Eight

Playing for pride, an invitation to leave, a collaboration

The low-slung clubhouse of Waterville Golf Links hunkered into a bluff overlooking the North Atlantic Ocean and Ballinskelligs on the Iveragh Peninsula. It was one hell of a lonely outpost at 9:30 that morning. Paul had played his share of golf in lousy weather. As a veteran of many Seagulls tournaments at Hyannisport in April (snow or shine, the invitation said), he knew how to prepare for rain and wind. He also knew when *not* to play golf, and this would have been one of those times.

But this was work, he kept telling himself.

Fahey looked like he'd been in a car accident, but the black eyes and bandaged nose didn't begin to describe the man's condition. Try as he might, he couldn't hide the raging indignation. Paul had gone to sleep thinking the man would beg off, get the hell out of Dodge and go home.

But no. There he was, zipped into his tidy rain gear, face sticking into a steady gale, pellets of rain bouncing off his cheeks. He reminded Paul of Ahab. Grim.

Boyle, naturally, had adopted his client's silent aggression as well.

The conversation was stiff, awkward. The terms of the bet

settled. They might as well have gone to the dueling station, Paul thought. Fahey was playing to restore his honor. Paul was playing for his wife's right hook. It wasn't a fair fight.

With his trusty caddie, Gavin, at his side, Paul plodded down one side of a fairway, Fahey and Boyle the other. The wind-whipped tide barreled up the mouth of the River Inny. The fescue on the mounds of the dunes whipped and swished. Not even the seagulls were out. The only words exchanged were to declare the score at the end of each hole.

Each endless, excruciating, unplayable hole.

Paul had hoped that after the front nine, his opponents would find reason and sanity, but no. Fahey walked off the ninth green (three down) and marched directly toward the tenth tee.

Paul looked longingly at the clubhouse.

"Don't you guys wanna get some hot chocolate, something stronger maybe?"

"No, thank you. You're up."

* * *

Finola and Shannon skulked through the corridor that led back towards the billiards room and turned sharp left through another, narrower corridor with rough stone walls and worn uneven floor tiles. Shannon ran her hand over the wall. "Amazing. Still like it was originally. I wonder why they didn't do this part up like the rest?"

"Maybe they ran out of money," Finola suggested. "Or wanted to make it less attractive to snoops."

They came to a door at the dead end of the corridor. Shannon tried the handle. Above the knob, a brass key lock glinted against the black metal. "It's locked."

"Or just stuck?" Finola pushed past Shannon and put her shoulder to the door and gave it a good thump.

"Stop, you'll wrench your shoulder. The door opens out, not in, you nitwit."

Finola smirked. "I'm sure you've already got a surefire way to get in then."

"There has to be another way than this one door. Let's go through the kitchen, there's bound to be a back entrance for the service."

"Good thinking."

They worked their way back to the dining room, to the swinging doors where all of the black-tailed waiters had emerged. The doors were shut, and a single deadbolt in their center attached them. Finola pushed on the two together. They gave several inches before the deadbolt caught on the opposing socket, and resisted.

"There's no floor anchor on either door. Nobody threw the floor locks," Shannon said.

"Hope it wasn't poor Feehan." Finola reared back, and thrust her upper body into the doors. The deadbolt caught again, but when Finola gave a second thrust, the deadbolt popped out of the socket, the door flew open and she stumbled onto the tile floor of a large industrial-sized kitchen.

Shannon helped Finola to her feet. "You survive that one okay?"

Finola scoffed as she dusted her knees. "I'm a tough ol' broad." She straightened up and looked around. "Where to now?"

"I used to work in the kitchen of a place that served on more than one floor. Let's look for a dumbwaiter."

"A what?"

"A dumbwaiter. An elevator for food."

"What the hell good is that going to do us?" Finola wandered across the kitchen floor, past polished steel tables and sinks big enough to bathe a car. "What's this then?"

Shannon hurried to her. "I believe that is called an elevator for people."

"Okay, I'll take this one. You can take the dumbwaiter." She pushed the call button, and the white metal door slid away to reveal the empty inside of an elevator car.

"I might as well join you in this one, in case you get claustrophobic."

They crept into the car, and Finola hit the button with the "B" on it. The doors slid closed with excruciating slowness, and the car began to sink.

"I hope these fucking doors open," Shannon said.

"Don't worry, if we get stuck, I can entertain you until they discover us."

The car groaned downward and slowly came to a halt. The doors didn't move. Shannon punched on the "open" button a few times, and the door opened with equivalent lassitude.

They looked down a long, dark corridor, stone walls on the sides, a polished concrete ceiling busy with pipes and ducts. At the end of that corridor, another door, this one freely swinging.

Finola led them through the door, into another room. They looked around. "Strange. Just a few bits of furniture." She walked to the window and looked out. "The herb garden. We're at the back of the castle, opposite the kitchen courtyard. And here's another entrance to this room, just beside the window. I wonder what this room was for?"

"Maybe some kind of parlor?" Shannon walked around, looking at chairs and sofas, stacked together in a corner. "Old stuff. Some of it antique. Must have been what they didn't need for the hotel. Wonder what's behind those doors?" She walked to a set of doors opposite the window and opened one of them. "Cleaning equipment. Buckets and brushes and stuff."

"And the other one?" Finola went to open it but Shannon beat her to it. The door opened easily, as if the hinges were oiled regularly.

"Brilliant." Finola peered in through the door. "Black as coal. Where's the light switch?"

"Let's go inside and see if we can find it."

They sidled in through the door. It closed behind them with an ominous 'clunk'. They suddenly found themselves in complete darkness.

"Shit," Shannon gasped. "I can't see a thing."

"Oops," Finola whispered, a cold finger of fear creeping up her spine. "We'll never get out of here now. Gee, it's dark. And hey, there's a funny smell in here."

Shannon sniffed. "It smells a lot like grass."

"That's what I thought. I wonder what goes on here." Finola tried hard not to panic. "God, I hate this darkness. I have to have some light. The switch must be here somewhere…" She ran her hand all over the wall until her fingers met a series of buttons. She pressed one of them and gasped as the room was suddenly illuminated in a reddish light. Dazzled and speechless, they stared at the big vaulted room. It was like an Aladdin's cave with dark red walls and low sofas along the walls. At the far end was a low bar counter with easy chairs surrounding a brass pole. The back wall was lined with a half-dozen booths, each with just a bench against the wall, no table, a curtain hanging from the ceiling for privacy. A half wall held an assortment of kinky looking things. A feather. A whip. A ball gag. Handcuffs. Shelves behind a wet bar beside it were crammed with bottles.

"Whoa," Shannon whispered. "It's a sex club."

Finola jumped when the room was suddenly coursing with loud, raunchy music. "Where the hell did that come from?" she half-shouted.

"Sorry, I just pressed a button here." Shannon hit the button and the music stopped.

"What's the pole for?" Finola stepped up on the stage to examine it.

"Pole dancing," Shannon laughed. She hit the button again, joined Finola on stage, and pushed her aside. "Observe." She grabbed the pole and started to gyrate to the music, swiveling her hips, her eyes half closed. "Maybe I'll put one in my penthouse."

Finola kicked off her shoes and pushed Shannon away from the pole. "My turn." She started to sway and grind as the cheap porn movie music moaned and groaned. She reached up the pole with one hand and undid the buttons of her blouse with the other, eyelids at half-mast, lips pursed, as Shannon doubled over at the hilarity and silenced the music. "I'm stopping you now, you crazy woman."

Finola guffawed as she buttoned back up and stepped off the stage. "I bet they have strippers perform here."

Shannon nodded toward the row of booths along the wall. "I have a feeling they're doing more than stripping," She added.

"Sex, drugs and rock n' roll. Jesus, this sure is a den of iniquity. Wonder what else is around here."

"Video cameras," a voice came from the shadows.

They spun toward the door. "A…Alistair," Finola stammered.

"Busted," Shannon said.

Alistair strode into the room. "I'm afraid that's the case. Must say that you ladies are adventurous. I've been searching for you for twenty minutes. I have to confess that I'm a little disappointed to find you here."

"Aw, come on, Alistair, this isn't such a big deal," Shannon protested.

"If it were this alone, I would agree. And I would be happy to keep our little secret, but I don't control the surveillance equipment. I'm afraid it's only a matter time before your trespass is discovered."

Finola propped her fists on her hips. "Discovered by whom?"

Alistair smiled politely. "You reporters are always so *inquisitive*. I should perhaps also tell you why I was looking for you."

Finola and Shannon looked at each other. "Why?" they said in unison.

"It is my unpleasant duty to inform you that you are no longer welcome at Castle Cormack."

Two open mouths gaped back at him.

"He's *kicking us out?*" Shannon gasped.

Finola glared at Alistair. "By what right? The British rule is *over*, even if it doesn't seem to have sunk in with some people."

Alistair, his mouth in a thin line, raised one eyebrow. "This is not about history, it's about the wishes of the owner, who has every right to invite *any* undesirable guest to leave, for whatever reason."

"So we're undesirable now?" Finola enquired.

Alistair's eyes drifted to Shannon and his expression softened. "Well, perhaps that's putting it a little too strongly. But since your adventures were caught on video, it would be prudent for you to leave."

"What the hell am I gonna tell my editor," Finola protested. "I have a story to write." She looked Alistair straight in the eye. "What's on the videos?"

He looked as if he wasn't going to answer. Then he cleared his throat. "I have nothing to do with the video apparatus. I loathe the idea. It is so…tawdry." He shivered. "I rather suspect that the visitors on them are, like you, unaware."

"Blackmail!" Shannon barked, her face twisted in disgust.

"I have no idea what purpose they serve."

"Feck," Finola muttered. "I have the biggest story in Irish political history in front of me, and no way to prove it."

"Yes…well, Miss McGee, as your own inspired performance has been memorialized, I think you would be wise to keep this particular episode confidential."

Finola's eyebrows rose. "Oooer…Well, I hadn't thought of that. I'm supposed to report the news, not make it."

"The danger of spontaneous action is that it lacks circumspection. Do not be alarmed on my account. I have no intention of bringing this to anyone's attention."

"Gee, Alistair, your loyalty appears rather fickle," Finola said

Alistair Connolly-Smith stared coolly at Finola. "Loyalty is sometimes a fickle virtue, Miss McGee. Now if you'll both follow me, I will escort you out through the more conventional exit."

* * *

In the midst of the rain, wind, engaging conversation and hard-fought sportsmanship, Aidan Fahey did on the tenth tee what anyone in his position would do. He pressed.

Not one to follow, Boyle reneged on the back nine bet and promised to pay Paul the three grand when they "got home."

Down three on the back with four to play, Fahey doubled his bet. And he also got into Paul's face. As they marched briskly side-by-side along a path on the edge of a cliff that fell to the Atlantic, venom spewed from Fahey's lips.

"I looked into your past, Forté. You're a shady one, you are. You know how to travel on someone else's dime. Everyone's favorite guest, eh? Why are you here, Forté? What's your business? What kind of scam are you and your pal Barkley trying to pull?"

Paul didn't answer, just finished the march up the trail to the green. If that's what Fahey wanted to think, no reason to stop him. "You're away."

Fahey managed to cut into Paul's lead. He was one down when they arrived at the final hole, a mammoth par five that ran along the beach, facing the full onslaught of a furious onshore Atlantic gale. On the line Gavin instructed, Paul's ball rode a long, high flight out over the beach, headed so far out of bounds it would have been laughable. Then the gale turned it over, and swept it fifty yards back, to the center of the fairway.

Fahey continued his nattering until he got to his ball, which lay a few inches into a wispy fescue. He examined the lie and scowled. "This is ground under repair," he said.

"Play it as it lies, Fahey."

"I'm entitled to relief, ya fuck."

"You're entitled to nothing."

"You're a hustler."

"You're a cheater, but I'm not complaining. Hit the ball where it lies."

Fahey appealed to Gavin with a look that might suggest his employment hung in the balance.

"Um sorry, sir, but the ground's not marked. The ball is in play."

Fahey chopped it out, advancing it down the fairway.

"I have no business in this, Mr. TD, but I tell you, I'm awful curious why a man in your position would attack a well-known Dublin reporter over material given to her by a murder victim."

"You're right, it's none of yer fuckin' business."

"Yeah," said Boyle, the first word he'd spoken since the twelfth tee. "It's none of ya fuckin' business."

"Yah, well maybe I'll make it my business, Denny. You guys sure know how to make enemies." Paul followed Gavin to his ball. Gavin handed him his three wood, pointed out over the beach.

"Why not just hit a five iron down the middle, wedge it up, two putt for par? He's in meltdown."

Gavin leaned close. "Put the dagger in, man. Finish this fucker off or I'll kill him in the fuckin' parking lot."

Heh, good boy.

Paul striped the three wood out over the beach and watched the wind carry it over the last beachside bunker, bound off the fairway beyond and roll to the back of the green.

Fahey shanked his ball out of bounds. He dropped a new ball and hooked it into waist high gorse. He threw his club after the ball, stormed up to Paul, and stuck his thin finger in Paul's face. "I want you out of that castle by sunset. You're not welcome any longer. You're not welcome in this country. Get out. Go home. Ya fuck."

He turned his back and strode off toward the clubhouse,

abandoning the match. Boyle scurried after him.

Paul and Gavin watched them disappear over the dune.

"What do you think?" Paul asked.

Gavin looked up at the sky. "Rain's let up. Might as well putt out."

They ambled up to the green.

"Lovely golf course, Gavin. I'd be pleased to play it with you another time."

"I'd be pleased to oblige, sir."

"Say Gavin."

"Yes, sir?"

"You think Mr. Fahey will send me a check?"

* * *

At the clubhouse bar, Paul bought Gavin a second pint of Guinness while the club manager arranged a ride back to Castle Cormack.

"Awful rude of the man, ditching you like that," Gavin said.

"Can't blame him too much. After such a dramatic exit, he couldn't very well stick around."

"Now that we're drinkin', you mind me asking how he got the nose?"

"My wife," Paul said.

Gavin laughed. "That explains a lot."

A scruffy young man in a scally cap stuck his head in the door to the bar. "Someone lookin' for a ride to Castle Cormack?"

Paul and Gavin exchanged cards and mutual promises to play golf in the indefinite future. Gavin offered to get Paul's bag, but Paul refused, got it himself, and threw it into the back of the cab. On the ride to the castle, the cabby gave a few one-word answers to Paul's attempts at conversation, so Paul stopped trying. He paid the man while Feehan wrestled the wet golf bag out of the car trunk and lugged it inside.

Paul found Feehan in the hotel lobby and gave him a €5 note, and saw Shannon and Finola standing together, bags at their feet, arms crossed.

"What's going on?"

"Time to leave," Shannon said. "I packed your bag."

"We've been ejected," Finola said. "I've been thrown out of better dumps."

"He told me to leave, too. Walked off the golf course. Stranded me there."

"We saw him come into the lobby," Shannon said. "He looked quite grim."

"You can't imagine the day. Did he say anything to you?"

"No," Shannon said. "He walked right past us, went behind the front desk and into the back offices."

"Then Alistair came out," Finola added, "and with Fahey watching from the door, Alistair made a great drama of asking us to leave."

"Which was funny," Shannon remarked, "because he'd already told us earlier, so he was just doing it for show."

Paul smiled and shook his head. "You guys got in more trouble while I was gone, I guess."

"We found the dungeon," Finola said.

Paul rolled his eyes. "Why am I not surprised?"

"Wasn't hard," Finola bragged. "Practically stumbled into the place by chance."

Shannon smirked. "Alistair caught us down there. Guess what?"

"What?"

"It's wired for video."

"It is, eh?"

"Yup," Shannon said. "And there was some kind of wild party going on down there last night. I'm crushed we weren't invited."

"Find anything interesting?"

"Place reeked of dope," Shannon said, her eyebrows dancing.

"It's a *sex club*," Finola whispered.

Alistair appeared at the half-open door to the back office, caught Paul's eye, motioned with his hand. Paul approached and Alistair backed into the office to give them privacy. The space was tight, a dead space that had been converted during renovation.

"Exciting times, eh Alistair? Those girls are born troublemakers."

"Your presence has provided me with a welcome respite from the usual drudgery, but regrettably, we must say goodbye."

"No problem at all. I understand completely. Nobody likes to be the skunk at the garden party."

"Quite." Alistair pushed the door until the latch clicked. "I thought I ought to warn you, sir. The ladies were up to some… mischief…that might be discovered on a video surveillance. There was…immodesty on display. I wouldn't like to see you embarrassed by it."

"Me? Embarrassed by my wife's immodesty? You don't know us well enough, I'm afraid."

"I just thought I'd mention it, sir."

"I appreciate your candor, Alistair. If I might impose on it further, may I ask if you are aware of the nature of the information Mr. Fahey was attempting to steal?"

"Not specifically, no."

"Alistair, I know that you are employed by Chiar-Tech, so I ask this at some risk that my confidentiality is misplaced, but is the Irish government paying for the maintenance of this monstrosity?"

"I'm not aware of such a thing."

"Miss McGee is in possession of documents showing that five million euros was siphoned from an important public works project to pay your bills."

"I understand Miss McGee's suspicion, Mr. Forté. She is a tenacious woman, and Mr. Ryan's shocking death has made it quite personal for her."

"You're a well-informed butler, Alistair."

"Mr. Forté, I am not in a position to divulge more details in this matter."

"I understand that."

"I don't think you do, quite yet. Were Miss McGee to be premature in publishing her suspicions, I'm afraid it might impact on certain… arrangements that have been carefully planned."

"I assume you mean the company's business development efforts in the U.S.?"

Alistair hesitated. "Somewhat," he said.

Paul handed Alistair a business card. "Let's just agree to keep in touch. My only interest in this is personal. Mr. Fahey is not the kind of man I want to see doing business with the Commonwealth of Massachusetts. If only on general principle."

Alistair's face relaxed. "That is understandable, in the present climate. Frankly, I'd prefer to deal with you, and not Miss McGee. I have nothing against her personally, but I don't trust the press."

"I can't imagine why not," Paul said.

Alistair cracked the door open, peered out, and they both slipped back into the lobby, where Finola and Shannon waited.

* * *

Finola looked at Alistair's inscrutable face as he followed Paul out the door of the office. She wasn't going to get anything from him now. He would be a hard nut to crack under the best of circumstances. As their eyes met, she saw something in his expression she couldn't quite decipher. Was he trying to tell her something? Or was he just willing her to leave? "I'm ready to go," she said. "Is there is anything extra on my bill that I should pay straight away?"

"No," Alistair said and handed her an invoice. "It's all paid for."

"Thank you." Finola picked up her bag. "I'll get going, then. Don't worry about the valet parking rubbish, Alistair, I can find my car myself."

Alistair nodded. "As you wish."

When Paul had settled his bill, he exchanged a look with Shannon. "I think we'll do the same."

"Absolutely," Shannon said and picked up one of the bags from the pile beside the desk. "And we'll carry our own luggage."

As she said it, Feehan scurried across the lobby to her side and took hold of the strap around her shoulder. "If you please, mam." Shannon would not deny him his final tip. He hefted her bag and Paul's golf clubs and wobbled toward the door.

Paul took the other two bags and they all proceeded out the entrance doors, down the steps and around the corner to the parking lot behind the rose garden.

Shannon sighed and squinted up at the sky that had miraculously turned blue. "Look, the sun! I had forgotten what it felt like to be warm."

"Just my luck," Paul remarked. "I could have done with some of that earlier."

"Irish weather," Finola said, walking ahead. "Drives you bonkers."

Finola found her battered Renault against the far wall. She stopped with Paul and Shannon by the rear of his rented Skoda, wedged between a Mercedes and an Audi. She waited as Feehan hefted the bags off his shoulders with a grunt.

"Thank you so much for your excellent service, Feehan," Paul said, handing the boy a €10 note.

Feehan looked at it like it was a winning lottery ticket. "Aw, suh! This is too much money."

"It is commensurate with the quality of your work, young man. You are dismissed."

Feehan displayed his crooked teeth one final time and trotted off like a peacock.

"What did Alistair say in the office?" Finola asked when he was gone.

Paul put down the bags. "Not much. How could he, with Fahey hovering around? Let's get out of here and find a place where we can talk."

Finola picked up her bag. "Yes, of course. There is a lookout point out on the main road, about a kilometer north. A good place to talk, and lovely views, now that the weather has improved."

"Sounds good," Paul said.

Less than five minutes later, they had pulled their cars off the main road into a car park area perched at a bend in the road, above a valley that framed the deep blue Atlantic glimmering in the brilliant sunshine. They parked behind two overgrown gorse bushes and walked to a low stone wall below, out of sight of the roadway above.

"Wonderful view," he said. "You would never have guessed this was here earlier."

"No. The clouds were too thick." Finola sat down on the wall. "As you're involved in all of this, I thought I'd tell you-confidentially-what the hell is going on over here. And maybe you can tell me what the hell is going on at your end?"

Paul nodded. "Agreed. Everything said remains confidential, without exception."

"Okay then. Did you see the news regarding a member of the Irish Parliament murdered?"

Paul glanced at Shannon for recognition, and she nodded. "Yes," she said, "it was on the telly in our hotel room."

"Murdered on his way to see me," Finola told him. "Pushed under a train. There were witnesses. The police launched a murder inquiry. But they found nothing, of course."

Paul and Shannon both gawked at Finola. "And?" Paul prodded.

Finola looked at Paul, cleared her throat and started to talk very fast. "A large sum of money was shifted from a water project budget into an unnamed account. I think it was done by Fahey, and I think the recipient was Chiar-Tech."

"You have evidence of this?"

Finola sighed and shrugged. "All I have are pictures of the transfers, but the receiving account has no identification."

"That's not much to go on," Paul said.

"It wouldn't be," Finola said, "except for Fahey breaking into my room and trying to steal my laptop. And you should have seen Seamus Nolan's face when I showed him a printout of the screen shot. He nearly had a heart attack."

Paul blinked. "Huh. Where did you get the pictures?"

"They were on a flash drive that was in his possession when he died. His widow gave it to me."

"Do the police know about the flash drive?"

"No. Orla—my friend's widow wanted me to have it first."

"What do your editors plan to do with the information?" Paul asked. "It seems you would have to turn it over to the authorities. And now that Fahey has physically attacked you, I would think that's enough to run with a story and suggest a tie between the two events."

"I plan to write it when I get back to Dublin," Finola agreed. "Should cause quite a stir, if my editor will run it."

"Yes, and I think that story will help me in Boston. Here," Paul gave Finola a business card. "I need you to email me a link to any news stories that mention Fahey in connection with the murder, the money, or his attack on you. I will send you back any information out of Boston that feeds into your own investigation. We've got an investigator looking into the people behind Chiar-Tech. I'll share that with you when I can."

Finola took the card and stuffed it into her pocket. "Will do. Bye for now. Got to go. We can always talk via Skype, if there's a need. Bye Shannon. Great to meet ya."

They returned to their cars and headed north, Finola in the lead, her old Renault belching black smoke as it sputtered to gain speed. Paul overtook her at speed down a hill. She glanced sideways as he passed, and spied Shannon pinching her nose.

Chapter Nine

Unauthorized pursuit, a turf war, and fighting dirty

Paul sat at an outdoor table at Miel Brasserie Provençal, one of the chi-chi restaurants at the Intercontinental Hotel. He pulled his blazer together and buttoned it against the gusts coming off Boston Harbor. It was still cool in May, but just warm enough to be comfortable, if his client wasn't a half-hour late for a meeting *he'd* arranged. Paul was comfortable, but a little peeved.

But Duggan was the client, after all. One must never forget that. So Paul sat under the shade of a raspberry-sherbet colored umbrella, swirling a glass of Pinot Noir, admiring its tint against the blue sky and waited.

Duggan rushed across the patio and, amid a flurry of apologies, pulled out the chair next to Paul and sat. He extended his hand to Paul and when Paul took it, he clasped the back of Paul's hand. You couldn't get any more effusive than that, Paul thought.

"Sorry I'm late."

"No problem at all, Francis. I'm just enjoying the view and the unseasonably warm weather. After the drenching I took on the Waterville Golf Links while engaged in a grudge match with the Kerry TD, I'm just tickled to be warm and dry."

Their waitress arrived with a bottle of Cortôn-Charlemagne

in an ice bucket, two fresh glasses, and a platter with a dozen oysters.

"I called this in on my way here. I hope you don't mind," he said.

"What's to complain about?" *He could have called me, too,* Paul grumbled silently.

Francis poured wine for both of them as Paul finished his red. "What is this about a grudge match with the Kerry TD? You don't mean *Fahey?*" He kept a neat poker face.

"I do indeed."

He swirled the glass, sniffed, and sipped. "Tell me more," he said, eyes glued to Paul's.

Paul told him about the dinner and the after-event in the reporter's room.

"Your wife socked Aidan Fahey in the nose?"

"She did."

He shook his head in amazement, brought an oyster shell to his mouth, slid the oyster between his lips, rolled it around in his mouth, and swallowed. "Magnificent."

"The story?"

"The oyster," he said. "The story is *fuckin'* spectacular."

Paul had never heard the man curse before, so his particular choice of words was laden with ambiguity. Nevertheless, Paul did not see the necessity in apologizing for his wife's chivalry. The waitress took their orders and retreated.

"What was the grudge match? Your wife punched him, so he made you play golf in the rain?"

Paul choked on the white burgundy, coughed into his napkin. "Sorry," he wheezed as his windpipe clenched. "That's about it, yes. Thank God there wasn't a dueling range. He tried to cheat on the last hole, I called him on it, he told me to leave Ireland and stormed off the course, left me with my caddie. Boyle was with us, he followed Fahey."

Duggan's poker face couldn't hide the gleam in his eye. "Why did your wife deck Fahey?"

Paul explained about the reporter, Finola Finola.

"Finola Finola?"

"Sorry, the wine," Paul said. "Finola McGee, political reporter for *The Irish Telegraph*. She was in the room next to us." Paul repeated his understanding of his wife's assault.

"Fahey attacked a political reporter? Because she had some information?"

"Information supplied to her by the murdered TD, Eoin Ryan."

"Murdered TD?" Duggan's interest had lost its casual quality.

Paul explained what he knew about the flash drive and McGee's suspicion about its contents. In the back of his mind, he wondered how his client could be oblivious to news of the suspicious death of an Irish member of parliament.

"But this reporter," Duggan said, frowning. "What's she got to connect this to Chiar-Tech?"

"Nothing concrete. Money disappeared from a budgeted program account. It was transferred elsewhere, no explanation or detail."

Duggan twirled his glass and stared at the wine. "Nothing, in other words. She has nothing."

"Nothing except a company director, who happens to be the Minister of Finance, trying to steal her computer. I think the reporter had a special relationship with the TD. She really has it in for Fahey, she's taking it personally. And then there's the butler."

"The butler? Don't tell me the butler did it." Duggan slid the last oyster into his mouth.

"Not exactly a butler. More like a concierge. Former owner of the castle who now runs the place," Paul said. Alistair Connolly-Smith had been an inscrutable concierge, as tight-lipped as the Irish bartenders who were unwilling to discuss "the dungeon," yet he'd confided his selfish interests to Paul with unusual candor for a man of his position. "The man wants his castle back."

"He wants his castle back," Duggan repeated. "He told you that?"

"Not in so many words. He said he was 'biding his time,' as the saying goes. I offered to help him."

Duggan did a double-take as a piece of pan-seared Idaho rainbow trout was placed in front of him. "What the hell could *you* do for him?"

A hand slid a plate of soft-shelled crabs in front of Paul. "Probably nothing, but how many chances do you get to help an old Englishman reclaim his ancestors' property from a bunch of Irish Catholics? I'm sure his rights have been trammeled."

Duggan ate as Paul goofed around. "What is this Finola McGee going to do?"

"She is going to write a story about Fahey's attack on her, and suggest a link to the documents in Ryan's possession."

"When?"

"She's fighting it out with her editors right now. The story is written."

"Really?" Duggan's eyes flicked to his phone and back to the fish.

"Sure, and then she'll file a public records request, looking for information about the recipient of the transferred funds."

Duggan scoffed. "That's a waste of time."

"Maybe," Paul said, "but it does bring the matter into the news."

Duggan didn't react. "What else?"

"I have Rex Barkley looking into the corporate ownership of Chiar-Tech."

"That's a hard nut to crack. Non-public, Irish registration. Nothing will be found in any legally accessible filings."

"Rex doesn't rely on public filings."

"What's private is private," Duggan said, "and what's private isn't necessarily true."

"What Rex finds is indelibly true."

"What kind of research?" Duggan focused on his trout, the grilled potatoes, the *haricots verts avec amandes*.

"It's best that we not discuss that," Paul said. "Let's put it in the 'attorney work product' category." He'd had the argument with Rex a dozen times, when he'd insisted on knowing specifically what methods were used to obtain company financial data. Marital records, criminal history, real estate, licensed vehicles, tax liens, law suits, political contributions, parking fines, even neighbor complaints about loud music were public information, available to anyone to review on public archives, and online for a small fee. But private business records - what hedge fund might be invested in a particular company, for instance - was none of the world's business. Absent a lawful judicial order compelling its disclosure, a private business record is safe from discovery.

Which has nothing to do with hacking. When the ever-patient Rex first explained the practice of computer hacking for the enemy's private company data, Paul was horrified. Then he learned about the rules of legal "ethics," and was astonished to learn just how far "attorney work product" travels.

"I don't want you to do anything further on that."

"You want me to stop investigating your competition?" Paul crunched into a soft shell crab and maneuvered it toward his mouth.

"I don't want to risk any-*any*-possible allegation of corporate espionage. Under *any* circumstances. I know what information is legally available. I have it. You are not authorized to pursue other means. Do you understand?" Duggan was done with his trout. He patted his mouth with a white linen napkin.

"I understand." Paul made a few mental notes, one of which was to contact Rex later.

They discussed the engagement letter and retainer, and talked about Ireland while Paul's crabs and the wine were finished off.

"Say," Paul said as they were wrapping it up. "On the way

to Waterville, we went through Cahersiveen. We passed a pub called *An Croi Dubh*. Two gents standing in front, reminded me a lot of you."

"That would be the cousins. *An Croi Dubh*. The Black Heart."

"Odd name for a public accommodation," Paul said.

"It's a part of Irish history we're not particularly proud of - story for a different day," Duggan said, rising.

"They catered the dinner at the castle."

"They do a lot of that, I guess. Good business for them. Can't rely completely on selling booze - no matter what you hear about the Irish."

Paul did not describe his wife's reaction to Francis Duggan's kin.

* * *

As Dublin basked in unusual heat, Finola trudged to the office, wiping sweat from her forehead intermittently. Her mind on the events at Castle Cormack, she hardly noticed the office workers on unofficial coffee breaks, flaked out on the grass of St Stephen's Green in various stages of undress. Averting her eyes from bright pink flesh, she pondered the questions stuck in her mind: who knew that Eoin had the flash drive? And did they know he was bringing it to *her*?

She arrived at the Telegraph to find Maureen and Liam Quinn, the crime reporter, in Maureen's cramped office, waiting to speak with her about the Eoin Ryan case, as well as Finola's report of Fahey's bizarre attack that she'd relayed to Maureen via email on her travel back to Dublin.

"Do we know where Eoin Ryan got the information?" Maureen asked.

Finola shrugged. "Does it matter? He's a member of the Dáil, and very involved in environmental projects. He must have been briefed on the Liffey Water Project by any number of people."

"Have you asked Orla?" Liam inquired, peering at Finola over eyeglasses that always seemed to be in danger of plummeting from his long, pointy nose. Finola once wondered if he viewed himself as the unlikely cartoon superhero, wrists sticking out of shirtsleeves that came halfway down his arms, skinny white ankles unmolested by trouser legs; thin, sandy hair plastered across his skull as if he had just had a shower. His appearance might not have suggested a man of superhuman feats, but it did hide a sharp brain, and a great talent for writing brilliantly crafted crime stories.

"No," Finola said, "her husband just died. But now that the funeral is over, I will pursue this lead."

"I could ask her," Liam suggested, too quickly for Finola's comfort. "This is a homicide case. Should be my assignment, don't you think?"

"No, Liam, I don't." Finola tried to keep her voice level. "This is a political story. *TD murdered in the act of whistleblowing on a colleague.* I have the right contacts, the widow is a close personal friend of mine, a fragile source of information, and I might add, the highest human interest angle." She crossed her arms and hugged against the revulsion.

"You're not reporting the story, Finola, you're making it," Liam said.

Maureen broke in. "And that's great. A TD attacked you for your computer, and it may be connected to this murder. It's a great story, and you can tell it from your point of view, at the right time. But you're now personally involved, and so you shouldn't be *reporting* on the unrelated events about Ryan's murder."

"What do you mean, *at the right time?*"

"I haven't gotten approval to run your story yet. The lawyers are discussing it with the publisher."

Finola fumed deep inside, barely maintaining her temper. "Un-feckin'-believable."

"Now Finola," Maureen started.

"Bah, '*now Finola*' nothin'! I'm bloody certain that gobshite Fahey is responsible for my friend's murder. I'm certain he's responsible for the diversion of five million euros from the Liffey Water Project to pay the expenses of Castle Cormack. I'll wait on that until we have more proof, but why wait to report on that bastard's assault on me?"

"I'm sorry, Finola, but that's the deal."

"And another thing," Finola said, jabbing her finger toward her colleagues. "If Liam Quinn wants the by-line on my story, he can have it, but this is *my* story. It's *my* story." She turned and glared at Maureen, a mere arm's length away in the cramped office. "I expect this fecking newspaper to back me to the hilt, I don't care against whom. If I can't get that when the goin' gets rough, I might have to look elsewhere."

Maureen and Liam gaped at Finola.

Finola used the lull to her advantage. "In the course of my… research into Ryan's evidence, I came upon an American couple at Castle Cormack. The wife, Shannon McGonigle, was the individual who thwarted Mr. Fahey's attempted assault."

"She was an eye witness?" Liam pressed.

"As my report to Maureen states, she interrupted Aidan Fahey's attempt to steal a computer belonging to this newspaper. And she stopped Fahey's physical assault on me."

Maureen asked, "The woman who punched Fahey in the nose witnessed him assaulting you?"

Finola grinned. "Yes. And she's very attractive too. Makes a lovely witness. Name's McGonigle. Shannon McGonigle Forté. Husband's a lawyer from Boston."

Liam interrupted. "Let's get back to the murder, if we could." He turned to Maureen. "Who are you giving the murder story to? Me or Finola?"

Sitting behind her desk littered with coffee mugs, newspapers and computer printouts, Maureen tapped her teeth with a pencil. "You're going to work together on this one. I'm surprised either of you could possibly consider anything else. So, if we could dispense with the childish arguing, we could discuss whether the flash drive and the information on it should be turned over to the police."

"It's criminal evidence," Liam said.

"Is it? I mean technically, it's just—" Finola started.

Maureen picked up the front page of the Saturday edition of The Irish Telegraph and handed it to Finola. "I don't think you've read this. It's Liam's report about the murder case. The Guards are investigating. They know that Eoin may have been working on some sort of new exposé."

Finola looked from the article to Liam. "Have they any idea? If it was on his person when he was…recovered, you'd think they would have inventoried his belongings."

"Apparently they missed it," Liam folded his arms and swung back on his chair in a way that grated on Finola's nerves. "But if they found out about it from someone else, I'm sure they'd get tough with Orla, and then she'd spill the beans on you."

"Oh, shut the fuck up!"

"Stop it!" Maureen shouted.

"What an awful thing for her," Finola said. "The police grilling her and possibly searching the house, right now, when she's coping with her grief and looking after those children."

"That's true," Maureen said. "I'm thinking it would be good for you to visit her, Finola. Make sure she's…okay. See what The Guards were after." She turned to Liam. "Why don't we stall for a bit and see what Finola can come up with? After all, what's on the flash drive reveals only that some money went astray. I don't think The Guards will have better luck than Finola."

"Exactly," Finola cut in. "And in any case we don't know whose pocket The Guards are in, do we?" She shot a glare at Liam.

"What are you insinuating?" he demanded.

"Stop squabbling, children," Maureen said. "Could we not hang onto it for a while? Do we really have a legal obligation to turn it over?"

"That's debatable, of course," Liam said. "I mean, it was in Eoin's possession when he was killed, but it was handed over to Orla *before* his death became a suspected homicide. Then, it was just a tragic accident and anything found on him was the widow's property."

Finola nodded. "Exactly."

"But now," Liam cut in, "when we know it had something to do with the murder…"

"I suggest we don't rush into anything," Maureen interrupted. "Journalists don't have to reveal their sources."

"It's evidence in a criminal case," Liam remarked.

Finola glared at Liam. "You're just trying to cover your ass, you big chicken. Even when we don't have to."

"You want to end up in jail?"

"I'll bring you some chicken soup. You have a very short memory, Liam. What about the *Keena and Kennedy* case of 2009? The Supreme Court of Ireland ruled that they were not obliged to reveal their sources in that one. I remember that case so well. I wrote a great piece about it at the time. The ruling went something like this…" She closed her eyes and held up a finger. "The Supreme Court cited Article 40, section 6,1 of the Irish Constitution, which guarantees freedom of expression, as well as an earlier journalist's privilege case, *Goodwin v. United Kingdom*, European Court of Human Rights 1996, in which the court recognized a 'vital public interest in the protection of the journalist's source,' to support its ruling, that the High Court failed to strike a proper balance between the public interest derived from compelling Keena and Kennedy to testify and the public interest in the journalists protecting their source." She opened her eyes. "I'll never forget it. It's burned into my soul."

"That was different," Liam remarked with fake conviction. "Nobody was murdered."

"You're nit-picking," Finola said.

"Stop arguing," Maureen ordered. "It's not up to us. It's in the hands of the paper's lawyers. We can't publish anything about Fahey, his attack on you or your suspicions until I've checked the legal position with them and cleared it with the publisher. And I'll have to see what they say about the flash drive. So we'll have to wait for the go-ahead. In the meantime, we hold on for a while and try to do our own investigation."

"But I have nearly finished the article," Finola protested. "It's going to set Dublin on fire. I sent you a draft early this morning, Maureen."

"I know. I read it. It's good but we simply can't publish it yet. I'm sorry, Finola," Maureen said. "My hands are tied until I get the go-ahead. But why don't you go and have a chat with Orla? She might have something that will make your case even stronger. Liam, you keep leaning on your contacts at The Guards to follow up on these witnesses and the identity of the suspect."

"Okay, then." Liam's chair swung forward and landed with a bang. "We'll stall for a bit. But I just want to point out that there is one important question we need to focus on."

"—who knew Eoin Ryan had that information?" Finola said.

Maureen nodded. "And was it worth murdering for?"

* * *

Rex called Paul from the comfort of the Oahu office lanai. Paul answered his cell phone from a stool at the distressed wooden bar under the tent top of The Barking Crab, where he and Shannon were sharing a quart of overpriced fried clams and a few pints of Harpoon.

Paul excused himself and walked out to the street. "Waddaya got, tough guy?"

"Very little, like I told you."

"Well give it to me."

"I'm not telling you where I got it."

"I don't want to know *where* you got it. I want to know what *it* is."

"You already know about Nolan and Fahey, right?"

"Right. Financial disclosure forms from the Dáil."

"Right. But they don't show either as owners of Chiar-Tech equity or as employees or directors."

"They don't?"

"No, their financial disclosures show they are equity owners, officers and directors of a different company, Falan Ltd."

"Falan, eh? A melding of Fahey and Nolan. And what is Falan Ltd.? What do they do?"

"They do nothing. It's a shell company. They file a tax return with zeros."

"So how do they represent themselves as officials of Chiar-Tech?"

"One way they could do that legitimately would be if their services were contracted through Falan."

"Chiar-Tech purchases the services of its CEO and director through a separate company? Why?"

"One supposes to create an extra layer of separation between Fahey and Nolan, and Chiar-Tech. Might have something to do with the Irish ethics laws."

"Okay, so what about Chiar-Tech? What'd you get on them?"

"Not much. In their bid to the government of France, they disclosed cash on hand of $3 million and that 35% of the company was owned by a hedge fund called The Talon Group."

"Who's The Talon Group?"

"We're working on that."

"Who owns the other 65%?"

"We're working on that."

"I don't trust a man who uses the word 'working' while lying in a hammock on Oahu."

"I said 'we.' I have agents in the field."

"Still, appearances are important. I think you may be needed in the field."

"Are you suggesting I leave this paradise to fly halfway around the world to Ireland?"

"Well, you could do the first leg to Boston and we could see if that's absolutely necessary."

"I don't see the utility."

"Shannon misses you."

"Don't fight dirty."

"I miss you."

"You slut."

"Promise me you'll ask your wife if she'd like to visit Shannon and me on the Cape? There are other aspects of this case that I would love to have your help with."

"I'll ask. Don't get your hopes up." Click.

Good ol' Rex.

Chapter Ten

An exhortation, a heads up, and a sucker punch

Finola made her way through the front garden of Orla's house, where the grass was ankle-high and the flowerbeds dappled with newly sprouted weeds. Gardening had been Eoin's favorite way of relaxing at the weekend, she remembered. He spent hours digging and planting in the springtime. Then they'd have a barbeque at the end of May to celebrate his efforts. No more. Finola rang the doorbell and tried to shake off the gloomy thoughts. Stay cheerful, she told herself. Positive and supportive.

There was a long wait before the door opened a crack and Orla peered out. She swung it open when she saw Finola. "It's you."

"Of course it's me. Who else would it be?"

Orla looked past Finola down the garden path. "Anyone. I've had lots of callers recently since the story broke. But come in. I've made coffee. We can have it on the deck out the back. It's such a lovely day."

Orla led the way through the hall crammed with coats, jackets, wellies, football boots, tennis rackets and hurling sticks, into the living room and through patio doors to the deck.

Finola sat down on one of the deck chairs. "It's such a lovely view," she said, looking at the hills behind the overgrown garden.

"I always find this spot so peaceful."

"Yes. We bought the house partly because of that."

"It's very quiet. Where are the children?"

"My sister took them all swimming. Just a minute, Finola, I'll get the coffee. I made a lemon sponge too."

"Oh, lovely. How thoughtful."

"I needed something to do. Besides, I know how much you like it."

Finola tittered awkwardly. "I suppose."

When Orla came back carrying a tray with coffee and cake, Finola got up to help her. "Here, I'll take that."

"I've got it, thanks." Orla put the tray on the table and sank down on the chair opposite Finola. "I'm still a little weak, but getting stronger."

Finola sat down again. "Of course you are. You've been through so much." She looked at Orla's pale face and bleak eyes and wondered if it had been wise to come here to ask questions.

Orla poured coffee into a mug and handed it to Finola. "Help yourself to some cake." She sat back and folded her hands in her lap, looking at Finola. "So, anything new to tell me? You know, the one thing that would give me the closure I need is to get the bastard who wrecked my family and ruined my life. Grief is awful. I can't sleep, thinking about it, wondering who hated Eoin so much they took his life. I want to see him hang, Finola!" Orla nearly shouted.

Finola put down her mug, feeling guilty that she didn't have some good news to report. "You will, Orla, I swear." She took a deep breath.

"The Guards have been here several times, of course. Asking me the same question over and over, interviewing the neighbors, even grilling the kids. I'm so sick of them. Do you know what kind of mess they make when they search a house? Worse than any burglar."

"They searched your house?"

Orla nodded. "Yes, they did. Made me feel like some kind of criminal."

"What did they ask you?"

Orla shrugged. "What you'd expect. Did Eoin have any enemies, blah, blah." She rolled her eyes. "Wouldn't it be obvious that he had enemies? He was a champion whistle blower. Everyone knew that."

Finola nodded. "Of course they did. He was always getting up the nose of one politician or another, wasn't he? And he felt so strongly about all the corruption and cheating."

"That's for sure," Orla said with feeling. "Jesus, he got so upset sometimes, he shouted so loud he scared the kids. The last time, I thought he'd explode." She paused for breath. "That was a week or so before the… it all happened," she ended.

Finola nodded and leaned forward. "Who was he upset with, Orla? Was it Aidan Fahey?"

Orla considered the question. "I suppose he was the most recent I can remember."

"Did you tell The Guards?"

"I did mention that he'd been angry with Fahey about something, but they didn't seem to be interested in that."

"As though it was out of the question that Fahey could be involved. He's fooled everyone with that fake smile and all the promises." Finola thought for a moment. "Did he ever mention a company called Chiar-Tech?"

"Not specifically. Of course, it's quite well known and on the news now and then. But not in any other way."

"You didn't…" Finola paused. "You didn't say anything about the flash drive you gave me?"

"No, of course not. I don't trust them. Eoin has…had no love for the police." She stopped and blinked. "Anyway, go ahead. What else did you want to know?"

"Just one more question: "Did Eoin always take the 9:00 am train to work?"

"No. He usually took the ten past eight. He liked getting into the office early. But that morning, he took the later train because he was meeting someone in town and there wasn't any point in going into the office first." Orla sighed. "Of course it was you he was meeting."

Finola nodded, her mind on what had happened the night before that fateful morning. "Someone knew that he was going to meet me," she muttered. "Or that he was meeting *someone,* in any case. But who knew that? And how?"

"Could anyone have overheard him at the book launch?" Orla asked.

Finola pondered the question for a moment. Eoin had pulled her into a corner, his face determined. He had been looking around and then whispered in her ear that he wanted to meet her the next day. "I don't think that was possible," she said. "They could have seen us during the brief time we talked, but there was nobody near enough to hear. Did he speak to anyone the night before or that morning?"

"I only heard him on the phone with his secretary, telling her he'd be in the office a bit later."

"I'll have a word with her. So, if nobody overheard him arrange to meet me, the logical thing is that someone was spying on him. They could simply have waited for him to leave, followed him to the train, or eavesdropped on his phone call."

"Oh, I don't know." Orla sighed and rubbed her eyes. "All this cloak and dagger stuff is over my head. Just keep digging, Finola. Just keep digging!"

"I will, Orla. I'll do everything I can." Finola took Orla's cue that she was tired of discussing it, sighed and cut a slice of cake. "Pity to let this go to waste."

When they had finished cake and coffee, Finola got up to leave.

Orla accompanied her to the front door. "I'm sorry I wasn't much help."

Finola kissed her on the cheek. "Yes you were. You might not realize it, but you were a huge help."

* * *

Early in his partnership with Mickey Ford, Mickey had observed that Paul didn't have the shark instinct: attack first, and make your opponent fight with one leg.

Ford's remark had rumbled around in Paul's mind ever since, as he recalled the story about his father telling the head of the SEC's enforcement division to go fuck himself, threatening to sue the U.S. government for civil rights violations.

He thought of that story again on the morning he walked from Melcher Street up to the State House, for a personal meeting with the State Treasurer. It was a privilege he had earned years before, when Arthur Logan was a wide-eyed rookie sitting next to Paul in the House chamber. Arthur was a rabid Bruins fan, and Paul had an excellent source for red line seats. In the Great and General Court, that's all it takes to buy a man's loyalty.

Although that was ancient history, Paul was kept waiting for less than three minutes (in an ante-room crammed with too much furniture) before Arthur Logan burst through the doors of his office.

"Heya, rep! Howaya!" Logan was a boyish thirty-five, lanky with a long face and dimpled chin. He wore a good suit well and liked British shoes. And he knew how to pump a hand like he'd won the lottery. He looked Paul up and down. "Jesus Christ, you look great."

"How are you Arthur? It's great to see you."

"C'mon, c'mon, check this place out." As he ushered Paul into his office, he asked his receptionist to hold his calls.

Paul had seen the Treasurer's office a few times in the past, and Arthur hadn't done anything to make it more or less opulent than it always had been. Big oriental rugs (commercial grade), chest high walnut paneling, carved sconces and crown moldings, a lot of dark red leather and thick wooden furniture.

Arthur directed him to the biggest high-back armchair, then sat at the end of a leather couch abutting it. "Tell me what'cha been up to since you left town to a hero's goodbye."

Paul gave him the three-minute executive summary.

"Everyone tells me you found quite a lady." Big smile.

"Dumb luck, Arthur. One in a million, you find someone who's so true a fit."

Arthur's faces sagged for a moment. "Yah, well Paul, I remember what you went through, what with the ex-wife dyin' like that, right in the middle of your trial. It broke our hearts."

"None more than Shannon's," Paul said. He fought not to choke up at the memory, he and Shannon holding Kate's weakening hands as she uttered her final words: "Joyful, joyful." The song the three had sung together on Trinity Place, so close to the end.

"So," Arthur mercifully cut in. "What is the nature of your business?"

Paul chuckled. "Well Arthur, I'm going pretty far over someone's head, but you're my favorite Treasurer ever, and I'd hate to see you end up holding this bag of shit." If Paul was still Catholic, he'd have put that one on the List for his next confession.

"I'm listening, Paul. You remember, we used to talk about the strengths and weaknesses of the politician?"

"Of course I do." Another to add to the List.

"You told me the thing that brought down good politicians more than any other was placing too much trust in the wrong people."

"Especially when you don't know them."

"When they're someone else's hire," Arthur said.

"Right."

"So who's the hire, and what's the problem?"

Paul identified the project, the agency, and the bid committee chairman, Teddy Price.

"Don't know the name," Arthur said. He picked up the telephone on the side table. "Bernice, get ahold of a fella named Edward Price in the Comptroller's Office, ask him to come down here—"

Paul reached over and disconnected the call. "Please don't do that."

"Why not?"

"Ted Price is the head of the procurement committee conducting the process. Under no circumstances should he be meeting privately with counsel for one of the bidders."

Arthur wrinkled his face. "What do you want me to do?"

"Arthur, I'd never ask you to interfere with a procurement process. I just wanted you to know what's going on under your nose. If you look into it and determine that it's something that requires your input, you do whatever you think is prudent. If you decide it's not worth getting involved, that's your call."

Arthur stared at him with his mouth shut. "So what's going on?"

Paul told him about the software bidders, Dennis Boyle and his role.

"I hate that fuckin' guy," Arthur said.

Paul told him about Boyle bringing Sligo to Ireland.

Arthur put his face in his hand. "Paul, that kinda shit disappeared the year after your acquittal. What the fuck are they thinking?"

"They have a 'prior personal relationship,' apparently."

"What? B.C. High? If Triple Eagle relationships were exempt from the ethics law, they might as well just repeal the ethics law."

"Arthur, I'm gonna ask a question. You can find out the answer for yourself. This contract is $75 million. Where's the funding for it? How'd it come about? Usually this kind of stuff percolates from the bottom up. Where'd the impetus for this come from?"

"I'm kind of embarrassed I'm not aware of it myself."

Paul was ready to close. "Arthur, I really can't think of a legitimate reason to put the local guy at a disadvantage, and I don't like the idea that Mr. Price or anyone in the Comptroller's Office is being influence or controlled. This process is being steered to this Irish company, and it's wrong."

"Seventy-five million, huh?"

"For the first five years."

Arthur's baby face wowed. "I'll look into it, Paul. I'll fuckin' look into it. You sure you don't want me to get this Price guy down here now? I'll do it."

"No, Arthur, not while I'm here, and you probably want to keep some distance from it - inquire down the line, but not directly. But I need you to understand. Regardless of what you do or don't do, if my client loses this bid, I will make a big deal out of it. I'm just giving you a heads up. My guy's qualified, and he's got a superior product. If he loses, it won't be on the merits. We'll litter the building with so many subpoenas, it'll look like a parade came through. "

Logan frowned and nodded. "I appreciate the heads-up. I'll look into it."

They spent another ten minutes shooting the shit, catching up, swapping stories, and then Paul watched as Arthur got up from his seat, walked behind his desk and pointed to a framed pair of tickets to the fifth game of the Stanley Cup Finals, procured by Paul, used by the two of them.

"Ya remember that? Huh? Huh?"

* * *

Liam reached the murder scene exactly an hour after the body had been found. His contact at Guarda headquarters had called him at six in the morning, pulling him out of a deep, dreamless sleep. He dressed quickly without showering or shaving, grabbed a coffee and donut at an all-night café on the way to the scene: an alley in Temple Bar in the city center. He made his way to the police barrier just as the forensic experts came out of the tent erected over the body, followed by State Pathologist Geraldine O'Meara in her white overall.

"Hi, Geraldine," Liam called. "What have we got?"

Geraldine pulled off her cap and shook out her blond hair. "I'll give you the basics only, Liam. I haven't even spoken to the Superintendent yet." She nodded at a man in uniform sitting in one of the squad cars nearby.

"Okay." Liam pushed his glasses further up his nose. "What can you tell me?"

Geraldine sighed. Small and frail-looking, she looked more like a primary school teacher than the most famous forensic expert in the country. "The victim was male, about thirty-five years of age, medium height and weight. Shot in the chest at point-blank range."

"That's it? No ID?"

"None. No wallet, cash, phone. Nothing."

"How long has he been dead?"

"Don't know officially but between you and me, I'd say about four hours or so."

"Is this related to the drugs ring, do you think?"

Geraldine backed away. "How the hell would I know? I'm a pathologist, not a detective."

"Aw, come on, Ger, we're friends, aren't we?"

Geraldine pursed her lips. "I don't know if I'd call it a friendship. More like a professional hazard."

Liam winced. "Ouch, that hurt, Ger. C'mon pet, just a little something?"

She cracked a wry smile and turned to leave. "Autopsy report will be done by tomorrow noon."

* * *

Paul occupied a stool at Temperance, nursing a Sapphire as he awaited the arrival of Rex Barkley. His cajoling had worked; Rex was due into Logan at 2:30, which put him in a bar stool by 4:00.

It was a Thursday afternoon, and the House had just adjourned for another of its many four-day weekends, while the House-Senate Conference Committee ironed out their differences in the budget. True to prediction, Sligo had slipped an amendment into the Senate's budget, funding the first year of the anticipated contract with the winning software vendor - whomever that might be, *wink wink*.

Paul took a copy of the amendment from the breast pocket of his blazer, and was looking at it again, when the paper was slapped from his hands. He looked up at the grimacing face of Dennis Boyle, body tense like he was restraining himself from battery.

"You sneaky fuck," he sneered, jabbing his finger into Paul's chest. "I'm reporting you to the Board of Bar Overseers. You fuck!"

"Dennis! How's it goin'? Have a drink? It's on me."

"Fuck you, you slimy prick. You spy on my clients, you don't disclose your relationship, then you come back here and go crying to Logan?"

Paul waved at the bartender. "Chip, can I get a Bud Lite bottle? You don't use a glass do you, Dennis?"

"I'm not drinking with you."

"Oh, calm down. I was not retained by BosTech until after I returned. When you and that asshole Fahey both welshed on your bets, I decided to look into your big project when I got back here. Mr. Duggan was happy to meet with me. I found out what's going on, and I'm going to stick this process up your ass sideways."

"You accusing me of bid rigging to Arthur Logan? It's fuckin' slander, is what it is. I ought to sue your ass."

"This isn't Junior Golden Gloves at the Y, Dennis. You're in a legal process. You fight dirty, you better know how to take a punch."

Boyle leaned in close to Paul's ear. "Back off. I'll show you how to fight."

"You owe me five hundred bucks, ya cheap prick."

Boyle straightened, and moved to pass by Paul, then threw an elbow as he passed, catching Paul flush on the cheekbone, rocking him back against the bar.

Lights flashed behind Paul's eyes, the pain of the blow radiating through his skull. In a gauzy haze, he saw flashes of movement, heard bursts of loud voices. Through blurry eyes, he made out the spinning image of Rex Barkley, standing next to his stool, looking down to the floor.

And Dennis Boyle, prostrate thereon, unconscious.

"You okay?" Rex asked him.

Rex's face came into full focus. His big, gruff, hard face. "You're late," Paul said.

Chapter Eleven

An identification, an accusation, and a phone that doesn't ring

While the damn lawyers and suits sat on her story and wrung their hands about political scandal and libel suits, Finola researched every news article and photo of Aidan Fahey, Seamus Nolan and Chiar-Tech available within the international press library. They'd finally come around, and when they did, she'd be ready with the next volley. She was the political editor of the biggest paper in Dublin, and Fahey had tried to rob her of her computer! Why had the paper even asked her to not make a police report?

Her story had plenty of evidence to point the finger at Fahey in a subtle way that would result in questions asked in the Dáil. Liam was off her back for the moment, busy with the latest murder case and that body found in Temple Bar.

Neither Finola nor Liam, nor any other reporter in Ireland, could dig up any new information on the identity of the unknown murder victim. The following day, a photo of his face along with a detailed physical description was on every front page in the country with the caption: "Who is this man?" Links were posted, reposted, shared and retweeted on Facebook and Twitter thousands of times across Ireland. As Finola looked at the photo of the dead man, she couldn't imagine it would take long before he was recognized. Such a distinctive, rather ugly face, with rough features, a broken nose and that birthmark on the cheek. There was a threatening, evil feeling to him, despite the still expression. She shivered and turned back to her research.

But other thoughts distracted. Her exposé would make big headlines and cause a scandal even greater than the corruption cases a few years earlier. Her follow-up articles would then further expose Fahey and Nolan until they had not a shred of honor left.

The story would drive other sources to her door. The drip-drip-drip of negative press drove men like him insane. A slow chipping away at the image would be the way to go.

She could supplement the main story with a sidebar about how a TD's salary could possibly stretch to the lavish lifestyle some in the Dáil flaunted. Of course it couldn't!

She flicked through the Internet and the archives of gossip magazines until she found what she was looking for: a picture of Fahey on holiday in Marbella in *VIP* magazine. There was more: Fahey drinking champagne with the Taoiseach in the VIP tent at the Galway Races and another shot of him on the deck of his sailing boat at the Dingle Regatta. Finally, to cap it all off, the bold Minister coming out of the Carlton Hotel in Cannes with a blonde hanging on his arm. Yes, Finola nodded to herself. This would work. Photographs…yes, these days, photographs are everywhere.

The door of her office flew open, and Maureen stood in the void, gripping the jambs. "Have you heard the latest?"

Finola looked up from her laptop. "What's happened?"

"The dead body has been identified."

Finola stared at her. "And—? Who is he?"

"Could be the man who murdered Eoin Ryan."

"What?"

"Oooer…" Maureen stammered. "Liam was tipped earlier… One of the witnesses in Eoin's case has identified him as the man she saw push Eoin under the train." Maureen caught her breath.

Full Irish | 145

"That's the big news."

"Christ," Finola muttered. "Okay. Big news I suppose. It would be even bigger if we knew who he was, though."

"I'm sure they'll find that out fairly quickly. A funny detail," Maureen added. "The witness noticed this face staring at her from the wrapping of her fish and chips she was just about to eat. I bet she choked on it, coming face to face with the dead guy. And Liam's Garda contact has just told him they're going to contact the second witness to see if he agrees."

"So, then…" Finola started. She tried to focus on what Maureen had just told her. "That won't tell us much until the man is identified, though, will it?"

They both jumped as Liam stuck his head through the door. "More news. Second witness agrees with the first and they have an ID. The stiff was known to the police. His name was Rodolfo Eduardo Silva, a Brazilian national who came here as an asylum seeker ten years ago. Such an ugly dude. Easy to identify. He did time for burglary and assault and came out of prison only two months ago. My guess is that he was hired by someone to bump Ryan off. We have a good story now."

"Yes, Liam," Finola said. "You have a story about a murdered immigrant criminal. It's very intriguing, but I'd rather connect the man to the murder of Eoin Ryan, and both of them to Aidan Fahey."

"And I bet you think you're going to do it before me," Liam said.

Eat my dust, Finola thought, as she glanced at a stern editor and replied to Liam, "No Liam, we are working this story as a team, you and me."

She turned back to her research.

* * *

DEAD MAN IDENTIFIED AS EOIN RYAN'S KILLER

The news shouted from the front pages of every newspaper in Ireland. Finola smiled to herself as she read the first paragraph of Liam's report while walking to her car. It was the best piece of them all, she had to admit. The revelation was big news, but her own article about Fahey's attack and the contents of the flash drive would be even bigger. Although the lawyers still objected, this latest blockbuster story had convinced the publisher that her story was worth the risk. His business was selling newspapers, after all.

Maureen had scheduled it for the following day. All Finola had to do now was add a few sentences tying her story in to the latest discovery. Anticipating it would probably be one of the biggest political stories in Ireland since the Mahon Tribunal, Finola felt butterflies as she drove to work, hoping the traffic wouldn't be too bad. Living in Rathgar, she always took a shortcut from the bridge at Portobello, down South William Street towards St Patrick's Cathedral and the bridge across the river. This was the best route during the rush hour- or any hour, really.

When she got to the office, she discovered a missed called from Orla on her phone. Finola rang her back immediately.

"Finola!" Orla said, breathing hard. "They found Eoin's murderer."

"Yes, they did."

"It gave me such a jolt to see that face. How horrible. Do you think it's true, what Liam says in his report, that he was a hired killer?"

"That's what The Guards suspect."

"Someone put a contract on Eoin. This is more horrible than I thought. These people, whoever they are, must be desperate. And very dangerous."

"Probably."

"What happens next? How will they find who hired the killer?"

"Difficult to say. I'm concentrating on another angle right now. I think you'll like it. First page tomorrow."

"Should make quite a stir. But I suppose you won't be popular with some people when it's published."

"Who cares? They hate me already," Finola laughed.

Just as Orla rang off, Maureen stuck her head through the door. "Deadline at noon for your final final. Sorry to rush you, but I need to take one last look before we put the paper to bed tonight. That okay with you?"

Finola glanced at her watch. "That's fine. I'm just adding some material to tie in the latest development."

"Terrific," Maureen said and closed the door.

Images crowded into Finola's mind. Orla's pale face. The neglected garden. The children left without a father. Fahey's face, distorted with rage. The water scheme, so important to the Dublin area. Money stolen from a government account. Greed, avarice, vain men drunk with power. Aidan Fahey.

Aidan fecking Fahey, his filthy, lecherous mind and disgusting sense of entitlement. She couldn't do anything about it then, when she was young and vulnerable.

But she sure could now.

* * *

Rex Barkley's international team of former spooks, detectives and "computer technicians" did not contain slackers, fakes or amateurs. When his clients asked him to obtain information, he called upon only those who possessed the skills suited to the task.

Brooks Kelly was such a man. In his early sixties, Kelly had conducted financial sleuthing as a consultant to Scotland Yard, Mossad, the CIA, and an uncountable number of private firms able to pay for his talent. Since the failures of Anglo Irish Bank, the Bank of Ireland and Allied Irish Banks, he'd become a busy man indeed.

He knew as well as the man who'd commissioned him, however, that uncovering the identities behind the investors in private hedge funds was not easily done. This assignment required shoe leather, visits to contacts he'd accumulated over the years in bank offices throughout County Kerry. Many of those contacts were no longer in the banking business, several thrilled to be invited anywhere and not pay for a meal, to say nothing of the chance to screw their former employers. Kelly bought more pints of Guinness than he needed to, and one day on a golf course in Limerick, his guest (who could not have afforded the golf otherwise) gave him the information he sought.

Brooks Kelly took that information and bounced it off a few more confidential sources, and got confirmation. Sitting at the desk of his home office in Clondalkin, south of Dublin, he punched up Skype, dialed Barkely's number, waited for the *whoosh* sound and the appearance of Barkley's stern mug.

"Mr. Kelly."

"Mr. Barkley." Kelly couldn't tell where Barkley was, exactly, but he was outside, possibly at a restaurant, and in the foreground of the camera sat a short glass filled with an amber-colored liquid. "Am I interrupting important business?"

Rex moved the glass out of view. "Have we found something?"

"You bet yer arse we have. I recommend you to have a good slurp of that soup before I talk."

"If you insist." Barkley brought the glass to his lips and kept it there for more than a sip.

"The Talon Group, I am informed, is a holding company for

the assets of a particular Kerry clan."

Outside of Kelly's view, Paul Forté smiled and shook his head.

"How fascinating," Barkley said. "Do we know who this clan is?"

"We do. Brothers, they are. Rather a colorful history in the family. They are descendants of Ciaran Ó Dubhagáinn, a notorious criminal from the seventeenth century, famous for robbing castles of their lucre. Their business is—"

"Pubs," said a voice off-stage.

"That's the client, I assume," Kelly said.

"Affirmative." Rex turned his iPhone. "Meet Paul Forté."

"Good ta meetcha, Paul."

"The brothers are twins named Duggan, I bet," Paul said.

Kelly beamed at the screen. "I'm impressed. How'd you know?"

Paul looked at Rex. "Their cousin is my client."

"There's more," Kelly said, just as his doorbell rang. He glanced at his watch.

"Sorry mates, this is probably my daughter and her son. They're always early. I'll have to ring off. Emailing you what I have right now. Call you tomorrow."

"Stay in touch, Mr. Kelly."

Kelly rung off, hit "send" on his email, closed his laptop, went to the door and opened it without hesitation.

The beaming smile on Kelly's face faded as a single 22 caliber bullet from a silenced handgun entered his forehead, slightly to the right of center.

* * *

Finola's article appeared on the front page of the Irish Telegraph above the fold:

WAS EOIN RYAN'S MURDER LINKED TO A NEW CORRUPTION SCANDAL?

By Finola McGee

Dublin, May 2014

This article is a tribute to Eoin Ryan: a friend, but above all, the bravest, most decent man I have ever known.

Earlier this month, as I was working on an article about Ireland's poor ranking in the global corruption index, I wondered how they had arrived at such a figure. How can Ireland still be so corrupt? After the long and costly years of the Mahon Tribunal and the shocking revelations of the behavior of the then Taoiseach and his closest allies, one would have hoped that such things were now in the past. The assurances of our present government that they would introduce new laws and increase vigilance lulled us all into a sense of security. So where is this corruption that has us at the bottom of the list? Sadly, it's still everywhere, and Eoin Ryan dedicated his public life to fighting it.

The day before Eoin was murdered, he asked me to meet him at a local café, so that he could provide me with some important information. He was on his way to meet me when he was pushed in front of a train. The information I believe he intended to share with me was contained on a flash drive that came into my possession before the death was found to be suspicious.

The flash drive contains pictures of government budget accounting, in which a large sum of money (over 5M euros) was transferred out of an account for the Liffey Water Project, into an unnamed account.

Last weekend, I attended an event at Castle Cormack, jointly hosted by our government and Chiar-Tech, on whose board we find certain members of the Oireachtas, including the Kerry TD, Aidan Fahey. I took the opportunity to show the documents I'd been given to an official of The Department of Finance. He refused to answer my questions and left my presence, but not before warning me that things would get "sticky" if I were to reveal what I'd been given. Later, Minister of Finance and TD Aidan Fahey broke into my room, demanded to know who had given me these documents, accosted me, and attempted to take my laptop by force. After a brief physical altercation that he lost, Fahey left. In the photo accompanying this article, Mr. Fahey is sporting a bandage across his nose, covering a wound he later said had been cause by a golf ball. Not so.

These events raise a lot of questions. Why would the Minister of Finance and his Deputy be so concerned that a member of the press was in possession of official government budget records? What did Aidan Fahey find so important about this reporter's possession of government documents that he would commit a criminal assault?

Why was $5M euros transferred from the Liffey Water Project account? And where was that money transferred to?

Most importantly, why was Eoin Ryan murdered, and did it have anything to do with the flash drive he intended to give me?

All of these questions require a serious inquiry by powers greater than me. For the memory of Eoin Ryan, I shall make it my mission to insure that they are answered and that the people responsible for his death are held to account.

By noon, the article had been linked over a hundred times, tweeted and retweeted nearly a thousand times, and the Irish Telegraph Facebook post of the article had been shared in seventeen countries.

And Aidan Fahey had spent the morning repeating the two-word reply of the guilty: "No comment."

* * *

The phones were hopping the next morning and the girls at the switchboard of the *Telegraph* could hardly keep up. The three biggest radio stations vied for first crack at telephone interviews with Finola, which she crammed in between two live-shot TV appearances. She had the feeling that this scandal was cheering everyone up after the long dreary months of the austerity budget. At last there was an opportunity to attack a government who had promised so much and delivered so little. Looking supremely indignant, members of the opposition made grave statements on the morning news, all the while trying to keep the glee out of their voices. There was an echoing silence from government representatives.

Finola had just come off the phone after an interview with the morning show on RTÉ, when she saw Liam through the glass partition. She knocked on the glass to attract his attention. "Liam, did you hand over the flash drive to your friend at The Guards?" she called.

He nodded, looking flustered. "Yes. Just came back. And now I'm going out again. There's been another shooting."

"Connected with the one in Temple Bar?" Finola asked.

"Don't know. It happened out at Clondalkin. Guy in his sixties called Brooks Kelly. I'll know more, once I've spoken to the police. They're still out there, so I'm off."

"Very far away from Temple Bar," Finola remarked.

"Yeah, but you never know. I'll call you later when I have some more news." He stopped in his tracks. "Forgot to say that Maureen asked me to tell you that Aiden Fahey will give a statement to the press after lunch."

Finola grinned. "He has to say something other than 'no comment.' That'll be interesting. But I'm going home for lunch. I'll listen to it there. I'll be back."

Liam nodded and rushed out of the office.

Finola sent a text message to Maureen, put her laptop in her bag and left the office through the rear entrance. Her head spinning after the past few hours, she didn't want to talk to anyone. She got into her car and started the engine, looking forward to a quiet lunch. Things were bound to pick up again after Fahey's statement. The slimy bastard would probably try to wiggle out of the mess he was in. She could see the headline of her next article already.

The traffic was light and for once, she enjoyed the views of the ancient towers of St Patrick's Cathedral outlined against the blue sky. It might be a good idea to visit it one day. She stopped at the traffic lights outside Marsh's Library, looking into the park. So peaceful at this time of day. She wound down the window to catch the warm spring breeze and barely noticed a motorcycle pulling up beside her car. Then she saw the pistol. A split second before the shot rang out, Finola threw herself onto the passenger seat, feeling a force hit her shoulder before the searing pain told her she had been shot. Stunned, she watched the rapidly growing dark red stain on her shirt and heard the motorcycle roaring away.

* * *

If he was being honest with himself, Paul *did* expect Arthur Logan to get back to him, even if he told Logan otherwise.

Paul had Logan pegged as a boy scout. A skilled politician, but prone to gullibility. Guileless in a business where guile was a coin of the realm. Paul had been confident that his meeting would compel Arthur to look into things, if only to cover his own ass, and not be pleased with what he found.

Paul's latest discovery put him in a tough spot. How could he be sure the Irish Duggans' involvement in Chiar-Tech was unrelated to his client?

He couldn't. And as long as he didn't know, he had no reason to question his client about it, and thereby create an impossible ethical dilemma. He had been hired to represent BosTech in a procurement process. If that meant taking down Chiar-Tech, the collateral consequences were immaterial, as long as he was acting with the approval of Francis Duggan. Why would Francis Duggan knowingly go to war with his cousins? Well, they were Irish, who never forget a grudge. It was possible he had no idea. After all, he did send Paul over to Ireland to investigate the company. Besides, there was nothing illegal about competing against relatives.

He turned these thoughts around in his mind as he held on the phone, trying for the fourth time to get through to Logan.

"I'm sorry, Mr. Forté, but the Treasurer is in meetings for the rest of the day, and he'll be leaving town tomorrow for a three-day conference in Phoenix."

Paul had an uncanny knack for discerning untruthful underlings. "Can I please leave you my cell phone number, and ask him to call me at his earliest convenience. It's very important."

The reedy Dorchester voice hesitated. "Well, uh…sure. What is it?"

He gave her the number, but it was plain from her demeanor

she was going through the motions. He hung up, resolved that his ploy with the Treasurer hadn't achieved its desired effect.

If only Arthur Logan read the Dublin news.

Chapter Twelve

An insider, pouncing jackals, and a fetching photo

It took Rex a few days to find the guy, check out his routine, find his regular barstool. It would have taken him one day, but the guy called in sick, Friday before a holiday weekend.

Paul and Rex met him, by coincidence, at the Eire Pub, the storied Dorchester neighborhood bar made famous by Ronald Reagan's 1983 visit. The guy sat alone at the bar, 5:15 on a Tuesday. He'd just ordered a Pabst draft when Paul and Rex book-ended him.

Rex started. "Felix Rogal?" A voice from his shoes, matching his bushy eyebrows and thick mustache in intimidation.

Rogal's head snapped right. "Who wants to know?"

"Eventually, the Justice Department," Paul said.

Rogal's head snapped left, then waggled back and forth like he was watching a tennis match.

"Who the fuck are you guys?"

"We're angels of mercy," Rex said. "We're here to offer you a gold star for your honesty."

"And with that star, you will avoid all the evil about to befall your boss, Edward Price," Paul said.

"The fuck you guys talkin' about?" Rogal had a tough exterior, but it was eggshell thin.

"You want to end up defending your involvement in the current FMIS software procurement?" Rex barked.

"When the subpoenas start to fly, you're at the top of our list," Paul said gravely.

Rogal stared at his glass. "You're that Forté asshole, aren't you?"

"Well I would choose a different noun, but yes."

Rogal looked to his right. "Who're you? Lurch?"

Rex bared his teeth.

He considered his position, took a long pull on the Pabst, and sighed. "I told the guy he'd never pull it off."

"Tell us what you know."

"Why should I?"

Rex leaned in. "Because no crime has been committed yet. You sit back and let it happen, you're going to be asked the same question by an FBI agent."

"If we can put a stop to this, it'll just disappear."

"Yah, well, good luck with that. They're voting on the award tomorrow."

"What? They can't do that! My client hasn't been notified of the public meeting."

"It's not a fucking public meeting, counselor." The bartender delivered some salted peanuts. Rogal snagged a handful. "They don't have to post notice."

"Where's the meeting?"

"Twelfth floor, Ashburton, two o'clock. Be there or be square."

"Who's behind this," Rex barked from his shoes.

Rogal flinched a little at the voice. "It's that asshole, Sligo. He's the one twisting arms."

"Why? What's he got in it?"

Rogal waved his arms to ward off the question. "Woah, I got no idea. He and that Boyle guy are old friends, but beyond that, all I know is who wrote the language for the bid specs and the bidder qualifications. And it *wasn't* fuckin' *me*." He tipped the glass to his lips, drained it, tapped the glass on the bar and pled to Paul. "Can I drink while we talk about this?"

* * *

The bullet had grazed her shoulder and caused a deep, painful flesh wound but no major damage. Finola flinched as the junior doctor in the A&E department of St James' Hospital stitched the wound and put on a bandage.

"Does that hurt?" he enquired. "We gave you some pretty powerful pain killers."

"Don't seem to have kicked in yet." Finola grunted through clenched teeth.

"It usually takes half an hour. Sorry about this but I had to stop the blood and clean it up as fast as I could."

"Where's the bullet?" Finola asked. "I'd like to see it."

"They found it embedded in the door of your car," said the young Garda who was hovering just outside the cubicle. "You were shot with a HK VP seventy, is my guess. But we'll see what the forensics say."

"Oh. Okay." Finola settled back against the pillow. She looked at her watch. Half past twelve. Fahey would be on the news in half an hour. She sat up again. "When can I get out of here?"

"As soon as we're finished," the doctor replied. "Shouldn't be long, now that you're all stitched up."

"You can say that again," Finola muttered.

"I'm afraid we'll have to ask you to come to headquarters for a statement," said the young Garda, Sean Murphy according to his name tag. He looked to be about seventeen.

"Hell, no," Finola said. "I have to watch the news. It's of utmost importance. I must go home. Where is my car?"

"I'm afraid we have it," Garda Sean said. "You'll get it back once it's been examined."

Full Irish | 159

"You shouldn't drive for a day or two in any case," the doctor remarked. "Your arm will be stiff and sore, and you'll want to keep on the pain meds."

Finola struggled to get off the trolley she was lying on. "Feck it, I have to get to a TV."

The doctor put his hand on her arm. "Do you need a tranquilizer?"

Finola pulled away. "No. Are you deaf? I need to watch the fucking news!"

The doctor exchanged a glance with Garda Sean. "What should I do?"

"I'd suggest you let her watch the fucking news," Sean said. "It appears that's what she wants to do."

The doctor sighed and snapped off his gloves. "There's a TV set in the waiting room. I'm finished here in any case. You need to come back to take the stitches out in a week." He handed her a piece of paper. "Here is a prescription for Solpadeine. Take two before you go to bed tonight and two three times a day for the next few days."

"Yeah, yeah," Finola said and stuffed the prescription into her pocket. She pulled on her shirt, grimacing as she saw the hard red-brown stain on the shoulder. "Thanks," she said to the doctor.

"I should really put that arm in a sling," the doctor said.

"Stop fussing. I'm fine." She got off the trolley, swaying slightly, but righted herself, ignoring Garda Sean's outstretched hand.

"I'll go with you," he said and they continued down the corridor to the deserted waiting room, where the big wall mounted flat screen TV showed the weather forecast that preceded the lunchtime news.

"Great." Finola sat down on a chair as close to the TV as she could get. "Just in time."

"I'll get you some coffee," Garda Sean offered.

"No. Please stay. I'm sure you'll want to watch this. It'll be fascinating. The beginning of the end of a political career."

"Okay." The young Garda sat down on the chair beside Finola. "Sounds interesting."

"It will be," Finola said with glee. Forgetting the pain in her shoulder, her eyes were glued to the screen as the headlines were read out. Fahey's story was the very first item. As the news reader set the stage, Fahey came into view, standing in front of the Department of Finance behind an array of microphones, a piece of paper in his hand.

He cleared his throat. "In response to recent accusations by political journalist Finola McGee, I have this to say: During the goodwill event at Castle Cormack last weekend, I observed Miss McGee during the welcome dinner on Friday night becoming increasingly inebriated. Not surprising, considering the amount of alcoholic drinks I watched her consume both before and during the dinner…"

Finola sat up. "WHAT?"

Fahey continued: "After dinner, she wobbled into the conservatory and mumbled something incomprehensible to one of my officers and then proceeded to go upstairs to her room. Worried that she would come to some harm, I followed her. I knew she was, as we all are, upset about the death of Eoin Ryan, who was a close friend. Feeling sorry for her and concerned that she might hurt herself, I attempted to help her into bed, when she suddenly panicked and began lashing out. In the course of subduing her violent outburst, I was struck in the nose by accident. I had attempted to pass this off as a golf injury for the sake of Miss McGee's reputation. I can only say how saddened I was to see such a talented journalist in this state and I hope she will feel better very soon. I am going to contact Finola and ask her to retract her accusations. I might also recommend a good therapist." He paused and looked into the camera with a mournful expression. "Finola, if you're watching, I just want to say no hard feelings here at all, I assure you." He stopped reading. There was an avalanche of questions from the assembled journalists, but Fahey waved his hand and, with a "no further comments", disappeared into the building.

Speechless, Finola looked at Garda Sean.

"Holy shit," the officer said. "That is one smooth bastard."

* * *

"Look at this." Liam waved the front page of *The Daily News* at Finola.

She snatched the paper and read the headline: **The Telegraph's Failed Hatchet Job.**

Is anyone surprised at reports that Irish Telegraph Editor Finola McGee was falling down drunk on free booze? Why is the Telegraph sending someone with an obvious drinking problem to an important State event? Is this the best they can do when it comes to reporting?? It's bad enough that she embarrasses her newspaper (a hard thing to do), but now she's accusing a respected member of the Dáil with assault and burglary? One wonders if The Irish Telegraph will soon be sending one of their editors out to pasture – or at least into rehab…

Finola suddenly found herself unable to breathe, gasping and sputtering.

Liam scowled at her. "She's a bloody gossip columnist. Everyone knows it's crap."

Finola gripped the paper with shaking hands. "Yes, well that feels much better, Liam. Thank you for your sympathy." She folded the paper in half and began ripping it into long strips. "This is Fahey's doing, I'm sure of it."

"No shit, Agatha."

Finola threw the newspaper on the desk. "I should sue her for that."

"Time to face the music, girl," Maureen said as she came into Finola's office with a load of papers under her arm. "Here's one from *The Irish Times*, asking the same kind of questions but in a more measured way, of course. An opinion piece." She flung another one down. "Allegations of insensitivity, sloppy research, lazy journalism, begrudgery and mudslinging. And one last paper slapped the others. 'Peddling gossip and innuendo as truth'."

Finola blanched. "Jesus," she whispered. "And from *The Irish Times*. I don't mind pip-squeaks like that reporter of a sleaze tabloid like *The Daily News*, but the Times…"

"I know," Maureen said. "Can't believe they wouldn't support us. Must say that I'm taken aback by the orchestrated hostility."

"Professional jealousy?" Liam suggested.

"Feck no, it's shameless bootlicking," Finola said. She suddenly slapped her desk and laughed. "I never thought it would happen. Me, getting bad press? I usually hand it out, now I'm seeing the other side. Serve me right, eh?"

Liam shrugged. "One thing Irish politicians are good at, payback."

"This is not making me laugh," Maureen growled. "Finola, you're going to get to work on this. I want you to keep digging and find something on this miserable excuse for a politician. I want this smarmy little shit's head on a platter."

Finola snapped to attention. "Yes, mam."

"Feckin' right," Maureen replied. "We have to get the bastard. And when we're done with him, we'll go after those who stood by him, and I mean *all* of them, even the Taoiseach—"

"Yes?" Finola asked. "What about him?"

"He's defended Fahey as an honest and indispensable member of his government."

"The fucker had me shot at!" Finola shouted.

"And we'll never prove it," Liam said.

"We'll get proof. We'll nail him on that too," Maureen said, sticking out her very square jaw.

Finola glanced at the time and turned to her computer. "I'm going log into the Dáil debate."

"Should just be ending," Liam remarked.

"They never start or finish on time." Finola logged into the website of RTÉ, clicked on the Dáil debate and flinched as Fahey's self-righteous voice filled the room.

"In response to all these comments, I have this to say: Miss McGee, in her recent article, asked some strange questions, and revealed she had these…documents. But we've seen no documents, and until she has graced us with a copy of them so they may be verified, the woman's story is just that, a story – and a rather fanciful one at that. In any case, one would wonder, if she was in possession of evidence that might be relevant to the murder of Eoin Ryan, why hasn't she turned it over to The Guards? Is she interfering in the investigation of her friend's murder? Why?" He paused. "Finally," he continued, as though he were on stage, "I'm beginning to believe Miss McGee to be under instruction from *the opposition*," he said, hurling it like an epithet at one side of the room as they jeered his slander. "An underhanded way to fight a general election, I must say. And it has failed spectacularly, as this dupe of theirs, this…*reporter* clearly has displayed her unreliability in a spectacular way. I would strongly advise the chamber to now let this matter rest and that we move onto more important things, such as running this country and working hard for its people." His words were followed by shouts and catcalls before the broadcast ended.

"Holy mother," Liam whispered. "This will be one hell of a fight."

"I'm looking forward to it," Maureen said with a grim smile. "Now the ball is in our court."

"I'd vote for suing his scrawny ass," Liam said. "And that gossip bitch at *The Daily News*. There were a lot of people at that dinner. There must be someone who'd be willing to vouch for you."

"Nah," Finola scoffed. "I only need one of them." She stared off as though she were hatching a diabolical plot.

"What do you mean?" Maureen asked.

Finola held her gaze against the empty wall. "Fahey miscalculated."

"Talk to me," Maureen said.

"He told the country he got his black eye from me, right?"

"Thinking you'd never get a strange woman you'd only just met to come to your defense."

"Exactly. Well, he's wrong. I'm going for the jugular. Please get out of my office. I'm going to be very busy."

"Great stuff." Maureen moved to the door.

"What's she going to do?" Liam asked, looking at Maureen.

Finola scoffed at Liam. "Watch and learn." She clicked away on her keyboard. "Like my dear old dad always said, I'm smarter than a shithouse rat." She scanned *The Daily News* article and emailed it to Paul Forté, with this cryptic message: *"Could Shannon join me in Dublin for some fun and games?"*

* * *

The conference room on the twelfth floor of One Ashburton Place was government dull, matching the wits of too many of the workers in the building. Linoleum floor, drab, off-white walls, fluorescent lighting, metal-framed molded plastic seats (not made for comfort but stackability) in rows, facing a set of tables set end-to-end, where the bid committee members loitered while staff members stood around trying to look important.

For a meeting that was not advertised, it was certainly well-attended. Every seat was filled. In the back left corner, along the wall, Paul Forté and Francis Duggan waited. In the opposite corner, Rex Barkley sat military straight. In the front row, Dennis Boyle waited to claim his prize. Paul couldn't see Boyle's face, but he imagined it to be a mixture of smugness and nerves. Behind Boyle, a man named Cory Fitzpatrick sat with legs crossed, his reporter's pad open, his ballpoint pen uncapped. He looked older than the day he'd met Paul in Clery's Bar and soft-peddled his way into covering Paul's angle during his trial.

The committee took their seats, Teddy Price in the middle of a row of five bureaucrats, all eyes scanning the audience, faces fixed with tension and, Paul thought, a little guilt. Twenty minutes past the scheduled time, Price rapped on the Formica table with a small gavel, and the murmuring came to a halt.

"This is an open meeting of the bid selection committee for Request for Proposals Number one-two-oh-oh-six," he began.

Paul rose to his feet. "I protest the conduct of this meeting," he bellowed. "My client is entitled to notice of the meeting. He was not provided it. We learned of this meeting by rumor. I want to know why an attempt was made to prevent him from being here."

He remained standing as a hundred and twenty pairs of eyes stared at him. The room was as still as a moment of silence for JFK.

The committee members, all but Price, stared at their hands. Price spoke up. "This is not a public hearing. There is no opportunity for public comment at this time."

"I'm making the time," Paul fired back. "This proceeding is a sham. The bidding process has been unfairly slanted to a single competitor."

"That will be all," Price said. "If you attempt to interrupt the conduct of this meeting again, I will call security and have you removed."

"What is this, Nazi Germany?" shouted Rex, now standing. "This is a public meeting. Let the public have their say!"

Price rapped the table hard with his little gavel. The sound was hollow, weak. "We are conducting public business. The time for public comment has passed. We will now proceed to the purpose of this meeting."

Cory Fitzpatrick waved a hand in the air and didn't wait to be recognized. "Is it true that the CEO and a Board member of the Chiar-Tech bidder are being investigated for corruption in Ireland?"

Boyle spun around. "That's a Goddamn lie!"

Cory ignored him. "There is a news report out of Dublin that Mr. Aidan Fahey, Board member of Chiar-Tech, assaulted a reporter and attempted to steal her computer, which had documents showing the disappearance of five million euros in government funds. Does this information bear upon the suitability of Chiar-Tech as a bidder for this contract?"

Boyle's face turned crimson. "Who's feeding you this garbage? Is Forté behind this?" He spun back to face Price. "I object!" His voice echoed feebly.

Paul jumped to his feet again. "I request that this meeting be continued for a period of time that allows for an examination of Chiar-Tech's suitability. New information has come to light that should bear upon this committee's deliberations."

Price couldn't hide his anger, hammering the table. "Clear the room! Clear the room!"

Rex jumped up. "You can't clear the room! It's a public meeting! I'm going to sue!"

Cory stood, stepped into the center aisle, only ten feet from the front of the committee table. "Is it true that Senator Charles Sligo has been involved in the drafting of the bid specifications and bidder qualifications for this procurement?"

"You're out of order!" Price shouted.

"Is Charles Sligo responsible for the $5 million budget line-item that funds this contract?" Cory was on a roll.

"That is irrelevant to this proceeding!"

"Has Senator Sligo pressured you to award this contract to Chiar-Tech?"

The gavel bounced and bounced.

"Have Mr. Sligo and Mr. Boyle ever met with you privately, outside of this building, to discuss this contract?"

Boyle bolted from his seat, trembling with fury, took two

steps toward the reporter, put his finger in the man's face. "I'll sue your fucking paper back to the Stone Age!"

"For asking questions?" Fitzpatrick's pen never stopped moving as he smirked. "Answer my question, did you ever meet with Mr. Price outside of this building to discuss this contract?"

"This is not a press conference," Price hollered. "Sit down and shut up. Everyone shut the hell up." Price laid the gavel down and put his hands flat on the table. The air vents rumbled above. Fitzpatrick's pen continued to move.

"This committee stands in recess," Price said, raising the gavel.

"You can't do that," one of the committee members stage-whispered. Paul heard it in the back row.

Paul looked along the row of staffers behind the committee table. Felix Rogal sat with his knees together, hands in fists atop them. He flicked his eyes at Paul, a squiggle of a smile flashed.

The meek voice belonged to a balding, doughy Irish face. "Adjournment requires a motion and a second."

Price sighed. "May I have a motion to adjourn."

No committee member stirred.

"Okay, then," Price said. "I move that we adjourn."

No committee member seconded.

The meek one continued. "I move that the committee recommend to the awarding authority that a contract be awarded to Chi-ar-Tech upon the terms specified on the bidder's price proposal."

* * *

Finola spent the day digging around in press archives and other sources on the Internet for pictures of Fahey that might give her good material. She found several with good potential and added them to her "research" file. The best defense would be counter attack, not a denial of his accusations. That would only start another flame war in the press, with Fahey's supporters adding fuel to his fire. Other journalists would join in, trying to come up with the best headline and the best angle. She wasn't going to offer up her head on a plate for them.

Liam stuck his head in. "Howerya doin'?"

"Not bad," Finola replied, her eyes on a photo she had just found in an old issue of *The Independent Sunday* magazine. "Look, here he is in bloody Marbella with that floozy from *The Daily News*. Sheila whatshername."

"Killian."

"That's the one. She wrote the piece about the failed hatchet job. What a bitch."

"Sure is. We'll get her too. Hey, listen, there's news about the murder victim in Clondalkin."

Finola looked at Liam, trying to focus. "Which one? I'm getting confused with all these dead bodies. You mean the Brazilian guy?"

"No, the other one. This one's Irish. Guy in his sixties, called Brooks Kelly."

"Oh. That one. What about him?"

"Turns out he was some kind of private investigator, shadowy bloke. My contact says he had a past with all the spooks, Scotland Yard, MI, all of 'em. Also worked for the banks, chasing assets. His place was cleaned up really well. Highly professional job."

"They know what he was after?"

"Nope. They don't see any connection to the Ryan incident. That suburb is rife with gangs. He could have come in the way of something he wasn't even connected to."

"Terrible," Finola muttered. "What's this country coming to? Life seems so cheap these days." She turned back to her computer. "I'm just going to have a quick look at what the tabloids are up to. Today's issues should just be out." She clicked on a link that would take her to the front page of *The Daily News*. The page loaded from the top down as she saw her own face coming into view, then the rest of her. She stared at it for a full minute. Bent backwards, holding onto a pole, her shirt gaping open and a silly smile on her face. "What—" she gasped. "How…"

Liam looked over her shoulder. "Finola McGee reveals more of her talents," he read. "Jesus, girl, you do know how to do a twirl."

Chapter Thirteen

A monkey wrench, a chauffeur unmasked, a command performance

Paul looked down the back wall to Rex, who stared back. *What now, cowboy,* Paul heard him think.

They had done what they could. Price himself had pushed to postpone. All they could hope for, the delay. Now, the committee had arm-locked Price into proceeding against his will. What the hell was going on? At least they'd get a wild story out of Cory that'd shake Sligo to the core of his Croatian soul.

"Very well then," Price said, exhaling the tension bursting inside him. "There is a motion. Is there a second?"

"Second," murmured a rail thin woman with a permanent scowl.

Price seemed surprised that the members who had just denied him a simple procedural vote were now falling in line as he had expected. He only needed three votes. He had a mover, a seconder, and himself.

"The motion has been made and seconded. All those in favor of the motion, say 'aye.' Aye."

Price's voice rang out alone.

Before his word had gotten to the back row, murmuring

rippled through the crowd. Price's wide eyes glared at his two connivers.

"You made the motion," he said to the doughy one.

"I don't have to vote for it," he said flatly.

Price looked to the woman, who stared back with her scowl. He didn't bother to ask.

"Nay," she said.

"Nay," said the man.

"Nay."

"Nay."

Price was paralyzed. Hands back in the desk, palms down, he stared into mid-space, above the clock on the back wall.

"I move that we adjourn," the meek one said.

"Second," said the lady.

"Aye.

"Aye."

"Aye."

"Aye."

The committee members slowly gathered their papers and departed without a word. Price remained in his seat. The staffers hesitated without the direction of their boss. Except Rogal. He was already gone.

* * *

Paul, Rex and Francis Duggan walked across the street to the park behind the State House.

"What the hell just happened in there?" Duggan asked.

Paul was embarrassed that he didn't know, exactly.

"Rex and I had a lengthy heart-to-heart talk with one of the staff members. We thought we had worked out a way to postpone the meeting until we could build a stronger case for debarment."

"Looks like he did you one better. You must have been persuasive."

"This isn't the end of it," Paul said. "The committee's vote is just a recommendation to the awarding authority. It's followed routinely, but no contract arises until the awarding authority signs it."

"So what now?"

"They could have moved that the award be made to you, but they didn't. Maybe they went as far as they could, to cover their own asses, but not so far that they risked their jobs."

"So they just threw us a bone? Give us more time?"

"Or themselves. In the typical instance, they're used to seeing the table tilted toward one candidate, but they tend to get nervous when there is a whiff of scandal in the air. Nobody likes being served with a subpoena, especially if it's from a grand jury."

"What do we do now?"

"We could sue the committee to compel them to finish the process and make an award," Paul said.

"We can do that?" Duggan asked.

"We can. Once the bidders have complied with the submission requirements, they are entitled to have final action without unreasonable delay."

"But we want the delay," Duggan said.

"If we file suit, nothing's going to happen right away, but we'll be in a position to have the Court oversee the process. And we can seek discovery, which will fuck them up good."

"You mean the court could control the process?"

"Not necessarily control it, but they'll be more reluctant to shove this thing through if they know a judge is a phone call away."

Duggan winced. "I'm not sure I want to be that aggressive. If we get this contract, we have to work with these people."

"Then we better hope that Irish reporter has some luck with her investigation of Chiar-Tech," Rex added.

"I don't know if that's likely," Duggan said. "She's getting hammered in the press over there. That Fahey has people coming out of the woodwork to paint her as a reckless drunk."

Paul couldn't help but chuckle. "She's a tough gal, Francis." Paul made a note of his client's close attention to what was going on in Dublin.

"She better be," Duggan said, "Politics in Dublin is a contact sport. Over there, you practically have to kill someone before they turn on you."

* * *

When Finola McGee's image appeared on Paul's Skype screen, Paul glanced at Rex and Shannon. The woman was frazzled, didn't matter how many pixels.

"How's business, Finola Finola?"

Her nervous guffaw said it all. "Great! Great! I'm the fuckin' talk of the town! My mum is so proud!"

Shannon elbowed Paul aside. "Finola! What is this shit about you being a drunk?"

"Awful, innit? There was a roomful of people at that dinner. You'd think my behavior would have been apparent to more than one person."

"None of them prepared to cross Fahey," Paul muttered.

"Well I am," Shannon said. "Fuck him."

"What do you think," Paul asked Rex.

"I think he bet that his assailant would not cross the pond to defend a woman she'd barely met."

"Do you think it'll help?"

Rex thought about it until half his mouth smiled. "I don't see how it could hurt." His eyebrows did a little dance.

"I'm taking Virgin Air, business class," Shannon said.

"They don't fly to Dublin," Finola said. "You'd have to go through Heathrow."

"So I spend a few days in London. What's wrong with that?"

Paul rolled his eyes. "Nothing a few thousand dollars won't fix."

Shannon grinned fiercely. "I got my own money, you misogynist prick."

Finola howled.

"Okay then," Paul said, "I can't bear to be without you any longer than necessary."

Shannon socked Paul's shoulder and hugged him. "Right answer. Okay, I'll fly direct to Dublin. Where do I stay? Can I stay with you, Finola?"

Finola blanched at the thought of Shannon seeing her flat. "Oooer…I'm afraid I'm a little short of room."

"Okay, I'll stay at the Four Seasons then."

Paul groaned. "Sure you wouldn't be comfy in a B&B?"

Shannon glared at him.

"The Four Seasons would be fine," Finola said, "but the Merrion would be better. It's right across the street from the Ministry of Finance and one block from Leinster House. We could schedule a press conference right there, and we're guaranteed to have a full house. Serve some food, you'll have them ink stained wretches by the balls."

Shannon looked at Paul for a response.

He looked back and shrugged. "Finola ought to know. I sure wasn't the best friend of the press."

"You don't have my looks, either."

The three kibitzed for another twenty minutes on specifics, strategy, and above all, what not to say. Shannon was there only to speak to what she saw of Finola McGee during dinner, what she heard to draw her to Finola's room, what she saw and heard, and above all, why she punched a member of the Irish lower house in the nose. If the questioning got aggressive and Shannon was grilled to explain why she'd fly across the Atlantic Ocean to defend Finola, she would describe her initial introduction to the woman, and her visceral hatred of cowardly, conniving men.

What could go wrong?

* * *

While she waited for Shannon to arrive, Finola stayed busy constructing her own missile. The photo of her pole dancing had been spread all over the first page of every newspaper in Ireland and also appeared briefly in the evening news on TV3. But RTÉ remained aloof, stating they would not publish something that could have been photo shopped or simply taken out of context. Finola thanked her friends in the RTÉ news room and promised them first shot at anything new or startling about Fahey before she published it herself.

RTÉ might have remained aloof but the bloggers on the Irish Independent political blog did not.

It's scandalous that Finola McGee is still given a voice in the media, one blogger wrote.

Another chimed in: *That journalist is dragging the Irish Telegraph to an all-time low.*

And it went on and on: *Someone who was so obviously legless should not have been allowed at an official dinner. What kind of impression did that give of Ireland? Don't we have enough trouble to shake off our image as a country full of drunks?*

The woman should be fired and locked up in a rehab center.

Fuming, Finola typed out half a dozen responses she would love to have posted, but deleted each in turn. Commenting on that blog would be both fruitless and stupid. Shannon would be able to prove it was all lies, anyway. Finola turned back to her therapy – an article titled, "The High Life on a Shoestring. *Aidan Fahey's amazing housekeeping talent stretches to the lifestyle of the rich."* She knew it would never run, which allowed her to take some license.

While doing some research to find material for a political analysis before the imminent general election, I was astonished to discover that certain members of our government seem to be enjoying a very lavish lifestyle. This, during a period of recession, seems like a slap in the face to the people of Ireland who are now trying to make ends meet after the recent austerity budget. Apart from that, one would wonder how this is possible, considering the reduction of TD's salaries last year. Could it be that TDs in general and one TD in particular are simply 'very good with the housekeeping money', to use a quote from the first Pink Panther movie? If this is the case, should Mr. Fahey not use these talents to run our country's finances rather than swanning around at the Galway races, to which he travelled in his chauffeur driven Mercedes (see picture below) accompanied by the leggy blonde gossip columnist who, upon closer examination, appears to have lost her knickers?

Finola let out an evil cackle as she added the photo to her draft. "Take this, you floozy," she muttered, reveling in the photo, Sheila Killian baring herself while exiting the Mercedes. The livered chauffeur with the dark shades and black cap would add even more fuel to the firestorm she would like to ignite.

"What's this?" Maureen said when she looked at the photo on her screen. "A remake of Basic Instinct?"

"It's an exposé," Finola chortled. "Or a lesson in how not to dress on a windy day. But read it and tell me what you think."

Maureen read, and guffawed. "Marvelous. I'd love to run it, but no."

"And waste that terrific photo? And the revelation that Sheila Killian is one of Fahey's allies?"

Maureen glanced at the photo again. "I know. It's a pity to—"

Finola clicked on the photo and zoomed in. "Shut up," she suddenly interrupted as she stared at the photo. "Sorry, Maureen, but I've just realized something." Her eyes were glued to the picture, her face suddenly pale. "Jesus, why didn't I see this before?"

"What?"

Finola stabbed her finger at the screen. "Look at the chauffeur, for God's sake!"

Maureen leaned forward and looked where Finola was pointing. "What about him?"

"Hang on." Finola went into her image file, pulled up the photo of Ryan's murderer and moved it next to the blow-up. "Look at that face."

Maureen clapped a hand to her mouth. "Christ, it's *him*!"

"I think we have a new angle to pursue," Finola said.

* * *

Groggy from her seven-hour red-eye flight, Shannon checked into the Merrion Hotel at 9:00am, a mere two hours before the press conference. She found her room (cozy and elegant, if a little dated), showered off the grime of the all-night flight, took a cat nap, donned a demure, charcoal grey pants suit, and returned to the hotel lobby to meet Finola, who she found sitting on a red satin love seat between two giant potted trees, dressed in a blue blazer and beige pants. They greeted with a hug and air kisses.

"Look at us," Finola said, "dressed like a couple of church marms."

"I'll say. I feel like an impostor."

Finola checked her watch. "We have about forty minutes. How about we have a stroll over to St Stephen's Green, try to relax."

"Sounds good. I'm as nervous as a cat on a raft."

They left the elegant, white-tiled front hall onto Upper Merrion Street, Finola leading. "I can't tell you how much this means to me, you coming all the way over here at great expense to do this." She reached into her shoulder bag and handed Shannon a copy of the release announcing the press conference. "This went out yesterday to the entire press corps covering Leinster House. I even left a pile of them in the lobby of the Ministry of Finance, in case any of Fahey's underlings couldn't suppress the urge. There are seventy-five seats in the conference hall. I expect it will be SRO."

Shannon read the release as she walked, and butterflies began their fluttering. The only public speaking she'd ever done was in art galleries during her shows. She hadn't done anything political since the days she used to help her father, an old ward lieutenant for the Mayor.

Around the corner, they reached St Stephen's Green, where they strolled along the wandering paths.

"What does your editor think of all this?" Shannon enquired.

Finola snorted. "Hah! When the broadsides began, I thought she was going to cut me loose. But when the bodies started piling up, she realized that, despite my blundering, I was onto a pretty good story. So she's behind me, but until this morning, I wasn't confident how strongly, or for how long."

"What happened this morning?"

They'd reached the bandstand, where a group of young boys pretended to play music while their mothers stood in a group, cigarettes in one hand, coffee cups in the other.

"I found a photograph of Fahey getting out of a limousine, and the chauffeur holding the door was the man who murdered Eoin Ryan."

Shannon stopped, mouth agape. "What?"

Finola nodded. "Yup. My editor is turning it over to The Guards."

"Aren't you going to do a story on it?"

Finola grinned. "Yes, but not quite yet."

"What do you mean? Why would you sit on a story like that?"

Finola's eyes scanned the innocent children playing their make-believe game. "The way my editor put it was, she wants to kick him in the balls before we shoot him in the head."

Shannon's heart skipped a beat at the metaphor. "So, tomorrow my press conference is reported, then after that you connect him to a murderer?"

"Once he's had a chance to return volley, dig himself deeper with his smug arrogance."

Shannon thought about the picture of Finola on the stripper pole. "Jesus, that man is going to get what's coming to him. I can't wait for this."

Shannon's sanguinity impressed her friend. "You're quite a brassy lady. Did you get that from your ma or your da?"

Shannon didn't reply, her mind traveling back over her younger life, her father's imprisonment, her mother's death, and her rough upbringing on the streets of Savin Hill.

"I'm sorry," Finola said. "I've hit a tender spot."

"If you only knew."

Finola hesitated until the reporter in her won out. "Tell me."

Shannon gave her the executive summary, not wanting to dredge up too many of the details. Her father's role as a political foot soldier, the token-skimming scandal at the MBTA, his frame-up, the political machine throwing him under the bus, her mother's illness. She did not tell Finola what she was doing when her mother had the fall that killed her, or that she had blamed herself. That was too much information. Her crazy brother, her FBI agent sister.

"You have a sister in the FBI?"

"Yes. We were estranged for many years, after my mother died. She didn't think much of my lifestyle. Paul's trial brought us back together."

"Paul's trial?"

Shannon told the story of Paul's indictment, the trial, the corrupt prosecutor and his thirst for revenge, the acquittal.

Finola listened in silence as they moved out of the park, heading back toward the hotel.

"Paul was indicted for playing golf with a lobbyist?"

"That's about it."

"Jesus, if they ever started with that here, we'd have no Dáil."

"The whole case didn't go over very well," Shannon assured her. "And it likely won't be done again. Paul came out of it as kind of a folk hero to his former colleagues, but it didn't sit well with him."

"Why not?"

"I don't think Paul honestly believed he was innocent."

Finola waited for more but didn't get it. "Why not?"

Shannon measured her words. "He played a hell of a lot of golf." Realizing that wasn't much of an explanation, she added, "Paul has a very sharp conscience. He feels things very deeply."

"A lawyer with a conscience, there's something you don't see a lot of."

As they approached the hotel, ten minutes before the scheduled time, Finola nudged Shannon. "Look." She pointed across the street from the hotel, where a steady stream of suited men were exiting the gates leading from the Ministry of Finance, crossing the street and entering the hotel.

"Lunch crowd?"

Finola scoffed. "The Merrion's too expensive for them. They're coming to see *you*, Shannon darlin'!"

"Let's give 'em hell, then."

They followed the crowd flowing into the lobby and up the stairs to the Wellington Room.

* * *

Finola had predicted accurately. Every seat was occupied, and standing bodies lined the side and back walls. Most of them held no spiral-bound pad, marking them as rubberneckers, there for the show, or perhaps the buffet of Schadenfreude.

An intern from the newspaper stood awkwardly at the door, handing out copies of a statement to anyone entering. The moment she saw Finola, she blushed, as though the woman was there to be exorcized. She held out a copy to them.

"Thanks, pet, but I don't use notes," Finola said.

Shannon followed Finola through the space between the line of men along the wall and the end of the seat rows, to the front of the room, where Maureen sat in a chair next to a podium, her legs crossed, looking elegant, utterly confident and calm as the day before a hurricane. They took the two chairs next to Maureen.

Finola introduced Shannon to Maureen, they exchanged pleasantries.

"Shall we begin?" she asked Shannon. "Are you ready to go?"

"Ready as ever," Shannon said, not able to tell whether she felt elation or terror.

Maureen rose and stepped to the lectern. Shannon looked out at the audience. In the first three rows, every occupant held a notepad, pens at the ready. Cameramen from local television stations rolled away. Photographers sat on the floor between the front row and the podium, cameras loaded.

"As all of you know, Aidan Fahey, the Minister of Finance and member of the Dáil for South Kerry, recently leveled scurrilous charges against Finola McGee, a well-respected veteran political reporter for the Irish Telegraph. The next day, a photograph appeared on the front pages of practically every newspaper in Ireland, without attribution or explanation, purporting to show Ms. McGee engaged in inappropriate conduct involving the use of a stripper pole. Not one single member of the Dublin press corps thought to corroborate Mr. Fahey's slanderous claims as to Ms. McGee's sobriety, and none paused to authenticate the photograph that was so prominently displayed on the front pages of your respective publications.

"We have called this press conference today because it was a condition of an agreement I made with Ms. McGee. That agreement was that Ms. McGee would refrain from suing anyone (besides Mr. Fahey himself) who participated in this travesty, and in exchange, the Irish Telegraph would afford her this press conference in which she could speak to you directly.

"I have my own opinions on how my professional colleagues have behaved in this event, but I will hold them to myself, perhaps permanently, perhaps not. For today, the platform belongs to Finola McGee, the Political Editor of our newspaper, and a woman in whom I have the utmost respect and confidence. Finola?"

Finola had sat rigid and stone-faced through Maureen's introduction, fighting not to allow herself to crack. Damn that Maureen, she thought as she blinked away a tear and rose to take the podium.

"Good afternoon, everyone," she said, raising her chin, surveying the audience. "I am so pleased that you all decided to hear the other side of the story, and I hope you will be as diligent about reporting what we have to say as you were to report Mr. Fahey's story. I only wish you might have given your colleague the courtesy of a phone call for comment before running with a story without any confirmation or corroboration.

"In response to my first-hand account of Mr. Fahey's physical assault upon me and his attempt to steal my property, Mr. Fahey claimed that I was intoxicated, that he merely attempted to protect me from myself. He expressed his concern for my welfare after the death of my good friend, and his colleague, Eoin Ryan. Why he chose to pursue this line of counter-offensive, I cannot know. What I do know is that what he has told you, and what you have all reported, is false and malicious. And rather than telling you myself, I will leave it to an eye witness of the events that took place at Castle Cormack, leading up to, and including, Mr. Fahey's attack. Mrs. Shannon McGonigle Forté and her husband, Paul Forté, were guests of Mr. Fahey at Castle Cormack that weekend. Mrs. Forté has traveled from Boston to be here today to tell you what she saw and heard. Mrs. Forté?"

As Finola took her seat and Shannon rose to the podium, cameras clicked like a thousand mechanical crickets, pens moved across pads, video lenses zoomed, all without a murmur of human sound.

Shannon unfolded a single sheet of paper that contained a few notes, just in case.

"Good afternoon," Shannon said in a strong, confident voice. She scanned the faces of the first three rows with the same smile that changed the course of Paul Forté's life. Consequently, she didn't have an enemy in the room.

Chapter Fourteen

A breakfast ultimatum, front page news, and unlikely allies

Paul's iPhone whistled at 6:32 am. He dove for it and almost fell to the floor, certain that it was the wife he desperately missed.

"Baby, I've been tossing and turning all night. Tell me all about it," he warbled.

"This is the office of the Senate President," a male voice said.

"Oh." Paul resumed his balance, checked the time. "Why are you calling me at 6:30 in the morning, and how'd you get my cell phone number?"

"Meet the Senate President at The Hungry Eye at eight o'clock."

Paul had tried to place the voice, but drew a blank. He knew the place, a hole-in-the-wall on the backside of the Boston School Committee building on Court Street. "I can be there. Make sure he's on time."

"Just you, just him," the voice said.

"How did you get this number?" *Click.*

He spent his shower trying to figure what the hell the Senate President wanted with him, besides the outlandish idea that he could be mixed up in Sligo's blundering attempt at influence peddling. Not a chance the man would be that foolish, to get behind a goon like him. Then again, McDonough wasn't a Mensa candidate, either.

When he finished in the bathroom, he checked his phone, added five hours and wondered when Shannon would call. The press conference was at eleven. Even allowing for a late start, it would be over by 11:45, then maybe fifteen minutes of grilling. She'd be calling any minute, but he had to get to The Hungry Eye.

His phone whistled again as he climbed into his Saab at the curb.

"You slut. How could you keep me waiting like this?" He made sure to apply sufficient mockery.

"I'm sorry, Mr. Forté, I didn't know I was expected earlier." A baritone British accent.

"Alistair?"

"Do any other English butlers have your mobile?"

"I'm expecting a call from Shannon any second now, Alistair."

"Excellent, I won't take much of your time then. I would like you to have her meet me for tea at 5:00, the Café en Seine. It's quite close to the hotel."

"But what about the press conference?"

"The press conference was marvelous. Your wife is quite a woman."

"Did you see it? Are you in Dublin?"

"It is due for airing on the one o'clock broadcast. The Internet sites are starting to report. I would like to keep our meeting confidential. Please ask her not to tell Miss McGee."

Paul's phone gonged with an incoming Skype call. He checked the caller ID.

"Alistair, Shannon is calling."

"Five o'clock, Café en Seine. Tell her I have something for her." *Click.*

* * *

Finola and Shannon had bolted from the conference room to the elevator and up to Shannon's room, to escape the ravenous jackals feeding off the red meat Shannon had so elegantly fed them.

Finola could hardly contain her glee. "Jesus, woman! You sure know how to cut a man's balls off! I've never witnessed anything so ruthless. 'Aidan Fahey is a liar and a sissy.' What a closing line!"

Shannon's nervous energy consumed her. She still fought to control her breathing, as she had throughout, but when she heard Finola's reaction, her lungs expelled air that her throat turned into a cackle.

"I was looking at the reporters in the front rows the whole time, like you said, but I never saw any of them. What were they doing?"

"They were scribbling like mad."

"What about when I talked about the location and circumstances of the stripper pole photo?"

"Hahahahahahah! That was the best part. Half of them slung their cell phones to their chests and began tapping away. I have a feeling poor Alistair will be overbooked for the next three weeks. There'll be a road rally to Waterville this afternoon, I'll tell ya."

"Oh my God, I have to call Paul!" Shannon whipped out her cell phone, opened Skype and hit the blue bar. In seconds, her husband's face appeared. "Hi, honey!"

"How'd it go?"

"It was fabulous. Do you want a full report?"

Paul checked the time. "Maybe later, I'm on my way to meet with the Senate President and don't have much time. Can we speak privately? I'm sorry, Finola, this is confidential."

Finola stiffened slightly and began to stand. "Oh, of course, no trouble at all."

"No, you sit tight, Finola, I'll go out on the balcony."

Shannon stepped through the French doors onto a small balcony overlooking the street and the Ministry of Finance. "What's the big secret?"

"I just received a call from Alistair Connolly-Smith."

"You *did*?"

"Yes. He is in Dublin right now. He wants you to meet him for tea."

"What for? Was he at the press conference?"

"I don't know how he learned what you said, but in any event, he wants you to meet him at 5:00, at a place called Café en Seine. It's close to the hotel."

"What for?"

"He says he has something to give you, but he doesn't want Finola to know."

"Why the hell not?"

"I suppose it's because Finola's attracted a lot of attention lately, and he doesn't want to be seen with her."

Shannon frowned. "Well…what the hell's this cloak and dagger stuff?"

"I have no idea, darling, but you remember what he said to me when we were leaving Castle Cormack."

"Okay, then," she said, still doubtful. "High tea at Café en Seine."

"Yes. And contact me after, as soon as you can. I'd like to know what the hell he's up to myself."

Shannon was struck with a bolt of panic. "Paul, do you think I have anything to be worried about?"

Paul pictured the upright old butler. "I can't imagine you're at risk of more than a lengthy discourse on the history of Castle Cormack under the Connolly-Smith rule."

"Okay. What'll I tell Finola?"

"Tell her you've got some McGonigle relatives taking you sightseeing."

"What, like long lost Uncle Dermott up there in Kilcummin?"

"Make some up. From Tipperary. A rich cousin Deegan or something."

"I don't like lying, but I'll come up with something."

"Okay, ring me back when Finola's gone. I want to hear all about it."

"Okay, honey. I miss you."

"I miss you like crazy," Paul said, and disappeared from the screen.

Shannon held the phone, watched the traffic below as she concocted her fib, and moped back inside, where Finola could not contain her curiosity.

"What's the matter? Is anything wrong?"

"No, nothing. Some family misunderstanding." Shannon plopped down on the bed. Her face sagged, not so much with feigned sadness as the discomfort of lying to a friend. "I'm sorry, Finola, but all of a sudden, the excitement has gotten to me. I'm feeling exhausted. I think I need a long nap."

"Yes, that's a grand idea, dear. I've got to get back to the paper anyway. Shall we meet for dinner, say about six? I'll meet you downstairs, and I'll get Maureen to have the paper spring for it. We can celebrate properly."

"Oh…" Shannon could not think. "I suppose. I mean, I don't know. I'd love to, of course, but…"

"Well why don't you have your nap and see how you feel. You can ring me later on and we'll wing it."

"Okay, that sounds good. I'm sorry."

Finola patted Shannon's leg. "Say no more. Ring me later."

Shannon covered Finola's hand with her own. "Thank you, Finola." She smiled weakly. "I had a blast."

Finola chuckled. "Oh, I have quite the feeling we've just begun!"

* * *

Paul parked his Saab in the alley behind his office building and walked at a brisk pace toward Court Street. He had no doubt McDonough would be late – all important people are late – but he was incapable of tardiness.

The beauty of The Hungry Eye was that it had no eyes. It was the "no-tell-motel" of breakfast venues. The windows were opaque, and the owners knew every trick in the book and face in the crowd. No conversation was witnessed, at least by anyone reliable.

Paul was halfway through his hash and eggs before his host showed up twenty minutes late.

"Sorry to keep you waiting," the Senate President said as he slid his large body into the seat across from Paul. He wasn't that big when Paul served with him in the House. He was tall, broad-shouldered, a linebacker at Northeastern. But the years of climbing up the political ladder rung by rung hadn't been enough exercise to keep the fat off him.

"No you're not," Paul said, wiping a corner of wheat toast through a runny yolk.

"I'm sorry?"

"No, you're not. You're late on purpose." Paul popped the yolk-sodden toast into his mouth and talked through it. "You had some guy call me, sounding all mysterious, telling me to meet you at a specific time and place. Like an idiot, I show at the designated time, and you don't have the courtesy to show up at the time you specified. It's a cheap tactic."

Jackie McDonough put his hands on the table. "Well this isn't off to a good start."

"No. It isn't," Paul said. He stabbed a few home fries, wiped them in the remaining yolk and ate them. "What do you want?"

"Why the hostility, Paul? We're old colleagues."

Paul slid the empty plate to the side and looked at McDonough. The man's pockmarks seemed to have gotten deeper. "There's only one thing I'm involved in that's important enough for a man of your stature to call me about."

McDonough played all indignant. "How do you know I wasn't handing you your next meal ticket, wise guy?"

Paul ignored him. "You want me to back off on this Chiar-Tech contract award. I'm not backing off. We can have a conversation about anything else, but if that's your purpose, we have nothing to talk about."

"Think about what you're doing."

"Help me out. Tell me why what I am doing is wrong."

"I'm not saying it's wrong or right," McDonough said. "I'm saying it isn't smart from a career standpoint."

"So, you, the President of the Massachusetts State Senate, are suggesting to me that my continued involvement in this matter will cause harm to my legal practice?"

"I think you know that's a risk. I think maybe you're underestimating that risk."

"And the fact that the Senate President is delivering the message? I should conclude that you'll see to it?"

"I didn't say that."

"Of course you didn't say that. You're too smart to make overt threats. That's not the way you guys work. Don't speak when you can nod, don't nod when you can wink. Are you winking at me, Jackie?"

McDonough leaned back in his chair and studied Paul. "You're quite a cowboy."

"Yippee ta-yay."

McDonough inspected his fingernails and shook his head. "How much is this Duggan guy paying you?"

"Why would you ask me that? You think you can buy me?"

"I'm asking because it can't possibly be enough to make the fallout worth the trouble. You succeeded in getting the committee to vote your way. Once. It won't happen again. Tell Duggan you can't continue."

"Now who's being the cowboy?"

"I'm serious, Paul."

"Do you know that you're committing a crime right now?"

"Your word against mine. And I haven't threatened you. I am merely telling you that you will generate a lot of enemies in the building, and you know how important relationships in the building are. If you fuck them up, your effectiveness will evaporate. You won't be able to get a vote on a street naming." Paul watched McDonough tilt his head down, so his eyes peeked out from under his bushy eyebrows.

"Can I ask you a question?" Paul asked.

"Go ahead."

"Neither Charlie Sligo nor Dennis Boyle could be so important to you. Why get involved yourself? What's in it for you?"

"I help out my guys," McDonough said, shrugging as though he were giving away a few Fenway seats.

"Whatever it is, Jackie, it's not worth it."

McDonough shrugged again and stood slowly. "Okay Paul," he said with resignation, "remember, I tried to help you. There's no going back."

"Well, Mr. President, there's another saying that comes to mind."

"What's that?"

"A fish rots from the head."

"Take care of yourself, Paul," the big man said, and lumbered out the door, leaving Paul to finish his breakfast in peace.

* * *

Despite the sumptuous bed, the pristine cotton sheets, the elegant down comforter, Shannon spun like a top through the afternoon. Every time she felt her eyelids get heavy, they would snap back open, she would roll around to a different position, but it did no good. The impact of her involvement in attacking a sitting member of the Irish Dáil hadn't really occurred to her when she'd so enthusiastically volunteered to come to Finola's defense. The punch in the nose was one thing. Standing in front of the entire Irish press corps to call Fahey a liar and a sissy was another matter, and foolishly, she hadn't properly considered the impact of what might come of it. *To hell with Fahey*, she tried to convince herself. But she knew she would soon find a newspaper and see a picture of herself under a headline.

What would it say?

A hundred versions flitted through her mind as she twisted in the sheets. She finally dropped off as the clock read 4:17.

She was awakened by a knock at her door, and bolted upright, fearful that she'd overslept. The time was 4:45. She scrambled out of bed, ran to the door, and opened it a crack. Sitting on the carpet, face up, the afternoon edition of *The Daily News*. Below the masthead:

Witness: Fahey a liar and a sissy

Below the headline, columns of text bracketing a full color picture of Shannon, in mid-word. She didn't look too bad, she thought, as she let out a *WHOOP!* and dove back into the bed with the paper.

The room telephone warbled.

"Hello?" she said.

"Mrs. Forté, this is the hotel manager, Brian Burns. I'd like to let you know that we are receiving a spate of calls asking for your room, and we are taking the liberty of blocking them for you. I hope this is your wish."

"Oh!" she said, startled. But of course they would hound her. "Yes, yes, of course. I appreciate it greatly."

"And I should add, there are many members of our press outside of the hotel, awaiting you, I am to assume. You have plans to leave the hotel?"

"Yes, I do." Her heart raced. "I have a five o'clock meeting, not too far from here. What should I do?" *Jesus, this would have been page 12 in Boston.* Maybe not. She clutched the phone cord and twirled it around her wrist.

"Here is my cell number," he said, reading out the digits. Shannon lurched for a pen and scribbled. "When you're ready to come down, text me, and I will meet you at the elevator and we will take care of it."

"You can do that?"

Mr. Burns smiled through the phone. "We've done this before, I'm sure you might guess. We are but two blocks from the Dáil."

Shannon exhaled. "Okay, Mr. Burns. I will do that. I can't tell you how much I appreciate—"

"It's our pleasure," Burns said, and rang off.

Shannon jumped out of bed, headed to the bath to freshen up. She applied minuscule make-up, dressed (stylish pants suit with a dashing tweed blazer), and started for the door. She stopped, went back for the newspaper, took a photo of the front page, close-ups of the story, emailed them all to Paul with a big smiley emoticon. The one with the tongue sticking out. After the email whooshed away, she texted Brian Burns, and he replied almost immediately, "Ready."

As the elevator crawled down, Shannon realized that the anxiousness she felt was not anxiety at all, but exhilaration. She loved being a painter, an artist, and a creator. But she was a Savin Hill girl, for crissakes. She'd been in fights growing up, she had thick skin, and she could take a punch, at least figuratively. *Bring it on*, she said to herself. And the door opened.

Burns took her hand swiftly, without introduction. "This way, please."

He led Shannon through a doorway to a corridor, through the back end of the hotel, finally through a door that opened into a stunning courtyard, adorned with hedges and fountains, tables with canvas umbrellas sprinkled throughout. Above the ivy-covered courtyard walls, surrounding buildings were dotted with ornate railed balconies.

"Wow, what is this?"

"This is our garden terrace," he said over his shoulder. He pointed up at the building ahead. "I live in this building. My car is in the private garage below."

They whisked through the garden to a door, he unlocked it, and she followed him into a dark hallway and down a short set of stairs to another door, and then into a cramped garage with a short ceiling. Shannon ducked down.

"No need to duck," Burns said. "It's a natural reaction, but it is plenty tall, I assure you."

"Thank you," Shannon said. "I really can't tell you how much I appreciate this."

Burns reached the car, a sleek, late model Jaguar, black with tinted windows. He blinked the locks and opened the passenger door for Shannon.

"We…are happy to repay you in some way for your service to our…friends." Burns smiled warmly. "What you did was very brave, Mrs. Forté. Brave and noble. We are pleased you chose our hotel to do this."

Shannon had not even considered that the ownership of the hotel might have an interest in what she and Finola had arranged. *Of course* they could never have booked the press conference in a place where Fahey's allies prevailed. She had left those arrangements to Finola and her editor, and only assumed they had chosen The Merrion because it was convenient to her. But no, they had chosen it because it was the turf of Fahey's enemies, whoever they were.

Shannon slid down into a soft leather seat, and the door shut with a muffled thump. Burns got in, and a minute later he maneuvered the Jaguar through a narrow concrete tunnel to a steel door that clanked open, and the Jaguar rolled into a narrow alleyway.

Burns pointed at a storefront across the street. "There's the Trib office right there," he said, and she read the lettering on the blue and white sign, "*The Sunday Tribune*."

"Oh, my." How helpless she would have been, trying to slip out the back herself. "I supposed I should tell you where I am going."

"No need," Burns said, "I know where you're going. Sir Alistair asked me to help."

Shannon's mouth dropped open. "Huh?"

Burns chuckled. "Just a small favor for an old friend."

* * *

After Paul's breakfast with McDonough, he'd grumbled his way back to the office, reflecting on McDonough's veiled threats and mulling precisely when and where the retribution would come from.

If he didn't change his mind.

He'd long ago come to the conclusion that state legislators too often over-estimate the depth and breadth of their power - even a Senate President - and in any event, he wasn't so dependent on work involving political business that he couldn't sustain a few hits. Besides, what better endorsement did one need in his business other than that politicians feared him? With word on the street that McDonough was out to get him, no procurement chief in the state government would screw around with him. He tried to convince himself this was true, but hadn't yet succeeded.

At the office, he reported in to Francis Duggan, then Rex Barkley. Duggan expressed mild concern, but seemed distracted to Paul. Rex suggested that he stick around a few more days and provide Paul with "protection."

"That sounds dramatic."

"It is dramatic, and you know how into drama I am," Rex's voice dripping sarcasm.

"Okay, so meet me for lunch at Les Zygomates, one o'clock. We'll talk about it."

"Take a table in the back, and face the entrance. They always face the entrance." *Click.*

Paul checked his phone. Ten o'clock. Just enough time to drive to a scheduled pre-trial conference in Dedham and make it back. He left the office and strolled to the back alley where he hid the Saab next to a dumpster. He unlocked and opened the door when the first blow landed on the side of his head, just above the occipital bone, sending his equilibrium into a cyclone. His body careened as he tried to grab the door for balance, but he felt himself falling backward. Inside his head, the spinning vision of two men rolled by then away as his head cracked against the brick wall next to the dumpster. The number of blows that followed, or the number of fists and feet delivering them, were unknown to him. The only conscious thoughts he remembered later were that he hurt like hell, he was afraid he was going to die, and he would never see Shannon again.

* * *

Burns dropped Shannon off in front of a storefront with garish red doors under gunmetal gray awnings with white script *Café en Seine* bracketed by Jameson logos.

"Sir Alistair will be on the upper level, front corner. Tell the hostess you are meeting 'Mr. Smith.'"

Shannon smirked. Mister Smith.

She strolled through the open French doors of the entrance, and felt as though she should be producing her passport at the French border. She wandered inside to a cacophony of bronze statues of half-naked women, big art-deco lamps looming overhead, casting a dim, gloomy light over everything. Palm trees and urns and pillars and plush chairs and leather sofas, small side tables, and along the wall opposite the bar, a long velvet bench with marble tables. A cross between a French museum and a New

Orleans brothel. It seemed an odd venue for afternoon tea, but judging from the sparse patronage, Shannon guessed why he had chosen it.

A hostess greeted her by the bar. "May I seat you?"

"I am meeting Mr. Smith."

"Of course, follow me." She followed the hostess along the polished-tiled aisle past the bar into a large solarium, where turquoise iron railings lined a tiled staircase up to the second, and then third, balcony, each one lined with small round tables and bent metal chairs along the outside walls, wrapped around the open space. More ice cream parlor than brothel. On her way, she was seized with a cynical streak that pulled her back to Savin Hill. Who was this smooth old man, and why should she believe he was doing her any favors. What did he want with her?

When she reached the top level, her heart pumping, she glanced around to find her bearings, and spotted Sir Alistair. Against the back wall, out of the direct sunlight, Alistair sat ramrod straight, bowler at his elbow. He wore a grey herringbone suit and black Church shoes, unrecognizable as a butler in any venue, the only occupant on the floor. He rose, gave her hand a formal shake, with only a brief eye-contact.

"Mrs. Forté," he said with a short bow.

"Mr. Connolly-Smith," she said.

"I have tea coming," he said. "I suppose you have not slept well, and have asked for a tray of light treats."

"Thank you, Alistair. This is quite a place for a meeting."

"Privacy in Dublin is purchased, Mrs. Forté."

"Do you mind calling me Shannon? I've never gotten used to being called Mrs."

"I beg your pardon," he said. "Shannon."

"And having Mr. Burns deliver me, in the Jag? That was some wake-up call."

Alistair bowed in apology. "Forgive me for all this secrecy. I only wanted to protect your privacy."

"You mean *our* privacy, don't you?" Shannon gave Alistair her very sweetest smile, so that he knew she was teasing him.

Alistair closed his eyes a moment, until his own mouth curled at one corner. "Yes, of course."

A round young woman with pale skin and orange hair delivered a pot of tea, cups, and a tray with scones and brown bread, jam and butter, and withdrew.

Alistair reached into the breast pocket of his blazer and produced a flash drive. "I believe Miss McGee will be able to use this in the days ahead." He slid it across the table.

Shannon picked it up, looked at it, put it in her jacket. "What's on it?"

Alistair peered at his hands. "As I cautioned you both in Waterville, the recording system is indiscriminate in what it picks up. I thought Mr. Fahey's publication of Miss McGee's folly was…deserving of turnabout."

"You have pictures of Fahey on this?"

Alistair nodded gravely.

"But you work for him, Alistair. Won't he know where it came from?"

"It's not important any longer," he said, and sipped his tea.

"What do you mean?"

"I think Miss McGee's work has taken its toll on Mr. Fahey. Your remarks this morning were quite damaging. That," he said, motioning to Shannon's pocket, "is the nail in the coffin."

"What about the murder of Eoin Ryan? Shouldn't he have that to worry about that?"

"That he may be able to evade, with proper counsel. That," he said, emphasizing Shannon's pocket, "he cannot survive."

"The dungeon," Shannon said. "You've got him in the dungeon."

"There is a dartboard in the dungeon, too, Shannon. He is not playing darts." Alistair reached for his hat. "I'm afraid I must be quite rude and leave you. These sorts of clandestine meetings make me nervous. Please make sure Miss McGee gets that."

"Why didn't you invite her instead of me?"

Alistair pushed away from the table and stood. "If one were to be seen with you, one could dissemble. Not so with her. Besides," he said, "you're so much more elegant than she. Thank you for your courage and your joie de vivre, Shannon. I'm sure I will see you in the future. Please know you and your husband are welcome at Castle Cormack any time."

"Thank you, Alistair." Shannon stood, Alistair gave her a prim handshake and glided toward the stairs.

Shannon sat back down to finish her tea. She surveyed the untouched tray, but did not feel any hunger. She pulled out her phone and Skyped Paul. No answer. She speed-dialed Finola.

"Finola McGee."

"It's Shannon. Are you still at your office?"

"Yes. Are you feeling like dinner?"

"I'm feeling better than that. I have something to show you."

"One-twenty Baggot Street Lower. Five minutes by taxi."

"Be right there."

In the taxi minutes later, she called Paul's cell, left a message, tried Skype again, texted and emailed.

She got nothing.

Chapter Fifteen

A liar and a sissy, four 'ayes,' and a viral photograph

The moment Finola walked into the office, a hassled Maureen shoved a pile of telephone messages at her.

"Get busy, girl."

She riffled through them, all from other journalists, asking for background information on Shannon and her role in the Fahey debacle.

"What are the online pages saying?"

"All over the map," Maureen said. "The publisher has called me three times in the past half hour. He doesn't know whether to pop a cork or a blood vessel."

"Well I think she was brilliant," Finola said with a firm nod.

"I agree. Come on, let's get back to work. Return those calls!"

Finola strode to her desk, opened her browser and clicked one-by-one through every online site in her "PRESS" folder.

She spent the afternoon with her ear glued to the telephone and her right index finger on a mouse pad. While she wrote-answered the same questions over and over, her finger clicked. A photo of Fahey with bandaged nose captioned "Can this man take a punch?" A grainy close-up of Shannon (not her best) under the headline, "**Finola McGee digs up surprise witness.** *The Times*, with a flattering photo of Shannon, blasting, **"Witness: Aidan Fahey is a liar and a sissy."**

Finola paused at this one to read the lead:

> An American woman has stunned the Dublin political establishment with the revelation that she witnessed Aidan Fahey assaulting Irish Telegraph political editor Finola McGee in her Castle Cormack hotel room, and punched him in the nose to thwart him.

Finola made a note to send the reporter a bottle of wine. She read on:

> The witness, Shannon McGonigle Forté of Boston, told a packed Merrion Hotel conference room that she and her husband, Boston lawyer Paul Forté, were on a brief holiday in Ireland when they were invited by Fahey himself to attend the recent business development festivities at the Waterville resort owned by Chiar-Tech.
>
> Mrs. Forté's account is dramatically different from that of TD Fahey, and lends credence to McGee's accusation that Mr. Fahey was in McGee's room to steal what she alleges are damaging documents contained on a flash drive that was in the possession of Eoin Ryan when he was murdered.
>
> Officials at the Ministry of Justice declined to comment on whether they plan to initiate any sort of investigation of the allegations.

Finola almost cried. When she clicked through to The Sun, she did. Their garish home page blared, "**It doesn't wash, Finola**," with the subtitle: *Finola McGee attempts to cover up with mystery girlfriend's wild scenario".*

"You'll want to take screenshots of *The Daily News* pieces," Maureen said from over her shoulder. "You'll surely be suing them."

Finola skimmed the article and saved a picture of it.

"You're either a heroine or a bum. Except in *The Daily News*, you're a lying bitch."

"I know." Finola suddenly giggled. "Sheila thinks she's on a roll. I can't wait to expose her tush on the front page."

"You'll have to be patient. I'm getting resistance from our publisher. There are *legal issues*. Liam's on the case, so I hope he'll have something for us soon."

"I bet Fahey's legal team are on overdrive trying to get him off the hook," Finola said with great glee.

"We'll have to make him squirm some more," Maureen suggested.

"I might have something else soon. Shannon is on her way here with something she said I had to see."

Maureen sat down on the edge of Finola's desk. "That girl is a real trooper. Maybe she'd like a job here? Or she could be our Boston correspondent."

"Why don't you ask her?" Finola looked at her watch. "She should be here any minute."

Maureen nodded. "Finola, she was brilliant at the press conference. A real star. And I might add, youthful middle-aged and beautiful. Prime target, especially for the tabloids."

"I know. I don't know what she's doing to dodge the press. They must be staking out the hotel."

"No question. I hope she'll be able to shake them. Not even dear old Bertie could do that when they were baying for his blood after the Mahon Tribunal. Not to mention Celia. She was

Full Irish | 203

more hunted than Princess Diana. I began to feel sorry for her in the end."

Finola laughed. "That's funny, coming from someone who told me to sit in my car outside Bertie's house for a whole night, in case she appeared."

Maureen grinned. "Yeah, but that was when he had been lying through his teeth. And we were the first to break the story. We'll do it again with this one."

"Hope so. I'd hate to disappoint you."

Maureen got up from the desk. "I have to go. Must catch up on my e-mails and write that editorial. Let me know what Shannon came up with."

"Will do."

Maureen wasn't gone two minutes, when a breathless Shannon arrived in Finola's office. Her face flushed and her eyes sparkling, she didn't even say hello, but simply pulled something from the pocket of her tweed jacket and threw it on Finola's desk. "Plug this in."

"What?" Finola took the flash drive and peered at it. "Not another one, for feck's sake."

"Hey, stop moaning and stick it into your computer. Haven't seen it myself, but I got it from a good source."

Finola looked at Shannon's glowing face and felt a surge of excitement.

"Source? What source?"

"You'll know as soon as you see it."

Finola's trembling hand stuck the flash drive into her USB port. They waited for the window to come up.

"Your computer's a fucking dinosaur," Shannon complained, peering at the screen over Finola's shoulder.

"It's not that bad. You're just so bloody impatient."

"I know, I know. But I can't wait for you to—hey, there it is. Click on it!"

Finola did as she was told.

The two of them froze as a picture suddenly filled the screen. Finola was the first to respond. "Jeeeesuuuus," she whispered, her heart beating like a hammer. "Wow… just… wow."

"Mother of God," Shannon gasped, eyes the size of saucers. She fished her iPhone out and punched up Paul on Skype. No answer.

Cell phone. No answer.

She texted, "Where are you? I'm worried!"

No reply.

Shannon tapped the phone on her thigh and frowned.

* * *

In vain, Shannon tried gamely to put the worry out of her head as she half-listened to Finola and Maureen chattering over their "celebratory" dinner. The picture of Fahey would whip an already delirious press corps to new heights, to say nothing of Liam's new piece on the chauffeur's connection to him. It was all over but the shouting!

Picking at her Irish stew, Shannon tried in vain to contact Paul via Skype and wireless. He never went dark for that long. He knew what she was up to. He'd wanted to know what was happening as soon as possible, and Bejesus, she had news! She'd sent him the photos from the press conference and hadn't received any reply. And the photo of Fahey, too. Something was wrong! Her distractedness was not lost on the journalists.

"Shannon darlin', I'm sure it's nothing to worry about. His battery must have died," Finola suggested.

"Or he left his phone in the office, or in the car," Maureen said.

"Or it was stolen," Finola added.

Nothing they said could dissolve Shannon's sense of dread. The smell of the stew turned her stomach, and she pushed it away.

"I'm sorry," she said, "I'm not feeling well. I'm going to call it a night and go back to the hotel. Maybe he's left a message with the concierge. I need to sleep. Maybe I can get an earlier flight home in the morning."

Finola and Maureen frowned in silence as they watched her push away from the table, but they did not argue.

Shannon gave them each a weak hug, they said their goodbyes, and she floated out of the restaurant as though she were under hypnosis.

Back at the hotel, the concierge had received no messages from Paul, but did succeed in helping her change her flight from 11:00 am to 9:30. She found her room, took a shower, packed her bags, laid out her travel clothes, and climbed naked into the comfort of her bed.

But sleep would not come. She kept the phone by her side, checked it repeatedly as she twisted and turned. Nothing.

At 4:13 am, Shannon punched in Rex Barkley's number, prepared for the peevishness certain to come from a gruff man who has been awakened in the middle of the night.

"Yes?" said the gruff voice.

"Rex, it's Shannon."

"What's wrong?"

"I can't get a hold of Paul. He hasn't responded to any of my attempts to contact him since yesterday morning."

Rex replayed his earlier conversation with Paul. "I'm on it. When are you leaving?"

"I moved my flight to 9:30. I'll be back in Boston by noon tomorrow."

"I'll call you back if I hear anything before you board. Don't worry."

Click.

Don't worry, she scoffed. Don't worry. She closed her eyes and fought for sleep, as her mind rolled through a catalogue of dire scenarios in which the love of her life had been snatched from her.

* * *

The headline screamed out the news across the top of the front page of *The Irish Telegraph*. Finola stopped at a newsstand on the way to the office and picked up a copy. Standing in the street, jostled by people rushing to work, she admired Liam's work.

MEMBER OF GOVERNMENT CONNECTED TO EOIN RYAN MURDER
Aidan Fahey escorted to Garda station for questioning
By Liam Connolly, crime correspondent.

Garda spokesman Daniel Murphy confirmed late last night that the Minister of Finance, Aidan Fahey, was invited to answer questions at the Phoenix Park Garda Headquarters in Dublin, after the discovery of his connection to a dead man who was identified by two citizens as Eoin Ryan's murderer.

The man, identified as Rodolfo Eduardo Silva, a Brazilian national, was seen by two eye-witnesses to push Eoin Ryan into the path of an oncoming train at Monasterevin Railway Station. He died at the scene. A week later, Silva was found shot dead in an alley in Dublin's Temple Bar. When his photo was published in the media, the eye witnesses said they were positive this was the man they had seen push Eoin Ryan. It was discovered recently that Silva had been employed as Fahey's chauffeur.

Mr. Fahey's connection with Rodolfo Silva was discovered by my colleague, *Telegraph* political editor Finola McGee, during research for a profile of Fahey. While searching the Telegraph photo archives, she found a photo of Silva, in chauffeur attire holding a limousine door open for Fahey and a female companion. Telegraph Editor-in-Chief Maureen Fitzgerald forwarded the photo to the police, who, after further investigation, asked Mr. Fahey to come down to headquarters to answer questions. Later in the day, Mr. Fahey appeared briefly outside headquarters in the company of his solicitor. Mr. Fahey had 'no comment', and pushed this reporter out of the way en route to his government-financed black Mercedes. Later, Mr. Fahey's solicitor said that his client would make a statement once he has been given the go-ahead by the police to speak about this matter.

"Fat chance," Finola said out loud and folded the newspaper. Pushing it into her bag, she noticed a long queue had formed at the newsstand and that everyone was buying *The Irish Telegraph*. She glanced at the headlines of rival newspapers and noticed none of them ran the story. Maureen would be ecstatic. Another first for *The Telegraph*. And it wouldn't be the last. She smiled to herself. They haven't seen anything yet, she thought. Fahey might be able to squirm himself out of this one but he'd by truly stitched up very soon.

The office was a great buzz of excitement. Phones rang nonstop, every reporter pitching in. Liam was talking to the RTÉ newsroom and, in her office, Maureen held her mobile in one hand and the hard line in the other. She paused briefly as Finola arrived. "Jesus, this is hot! We're the number one paper in the country right now."

Finola grinned. "I know. The news stand was mobbed."

"We're reprinting for the lunchtime crowd. And there'll be a special evening edition once Fahey makes his statement. But by then, everyone will have the story, of course. It will be yesterday's news very soon."

"Yeah but then we'll hit them with something even better; Alistair's little gem."

Maureen brightened. "That will be the cherry on the pie." She went back to the phones. "I'll call you back. I need to consult with my staff."

"Fahey's statement will be read out on RTÉ in a second," someone called from the main office.

Finola and Maureen raced to the big flat screen TV on the wall in the newsroom, where everyone, from the secretaries to the editors had gathered.

There was a hush as Fahey's solicitor, standing outside the Department of Finance, read from a piece of paper.

"After the revelations that a convicted felon and suspected murderer was in his employ, my client, Mr. Aidan Fahey has this to say: 'I officially support Ireland's immigration policies and also personally feel that immigrants to this country greatly improve our economy by working hard and contributing to the ever changing cultural landscape, making us a growing, multicultural society...'"

"What the feck does that mean?" one of the secretaries muttered.

"Nothing," Maureen said. "Just political gobbledygook."

"Shh," Finola said. "He's coming to the crunch."

The solicitor continued: "I was told that Mr. Silva, who had applied for a job as temporary chauffeur when my permanent driver was on leave, was not only an asylum seeker but also had a criminal record. Upon reflection, I felt it was my moral duty to support Ireland's generous immigration policies. Life is hard for immigrants, especially those who have been persecuted in their country, some of them having to resort to crime merely to feed their families. Adhering to those principles, I accepted Mr. Silva's application. He worked for me for over six months without any hint of bad behavior and I thought he would continue to respect the law and thus continue to live a good and honest life. The murder of Eoin Ryan shocked and deeply saddened me. The further revelations that my driver was responsible for his death is something I find very hard to deal with. It goes without saying that this has absolutely nothing to do with me."

There was a brief silence. The solicitor took off his glasses and added: "My client would be deeply grateful for some privacy at this very difficult moment."

The broadcast ended.

* * *

Rex Barkley knew his pal had an iPhone, he knew it would be registered, and he knew it would be on, as long as it still had power. He brought this information to the attention of the Boston Police. He had to tell a few fibs to convince them that their time and effort was essential. That there really was a concern for Paul Forté's wellbeing. He informed them that Paul had been threatened earlier, although he left out the part about who'd done the threatening.

After forty-five minutes of cajoling a recalcitrant desk sergeant, he was passed off to an Area C-6 detective, who ushered him back to a small office stuffed with far too many horizontal surfaces, all of which were stacked with manila files and loose papers.

Detective Walsh reviewed the information taken by the desk sergeant, sighing in the manner of one who had better things to do.

"You say he was threatened? By whom?"

"I'm not at liberty to say," Rex said.

"Look, Mr. Barton."

"It's Barkley. Rex Barkley. Data Quest Investigations. Former United States Treasury agent. Former Green Beret in Vietnam. I am professionally associated with this man. He is engaged in a legal proceeding in which a great deal is at stake. He was to meet me last night. He did not. In the ten years I have known him, he has never failed to keep an appointment. I would simply like you to contact iPhone legal, explain the circumstances and request that they initiate the 'Find my Phone' feature on his iPhone."

The Detective listened to Barkley with diminishing impatience. "Treasury agent?"

"Yes," Rex said. He removed his wallet and showed the detective his old ID.

"We may need a subpoena."

"An administrative subpoena will do it. If you don't have a form, I can type one up right now."

Detective Walsh didn't move. "I'd have to clear it with the captain."

"Then clear it with the captain."

Walsh's desk phone rang, the old fashion Ma Bell ring.

"Walsh," he said. He listened. He hung up.

"No need for a subpoena. We found your boy."

Rex bolted out of his seat. "Where is he?"

"He's on his way to Mass General Hospital."

Rex left the detective sitting at his desk. He did not bother to thank the man.

* * *

In a small conference room on the twelfth floor of One Ashburton Place, members of the Comptroller's Committee for the Procurement of Financial Management Software sat before a half-dozen spectators, all staffers wearing grim faces. Not one representative of any of the three bidders was present, because none of them had been notified of the meeting.

Nor had the press.

Teddy Price brought the meeting to order with a rap of the gavel on the laminated wood conference table.

"Do I have a motion, please."

The sour woman sat forward and read from a single sheet of paper. "I move that the committee recommend to the awarding authority that a contract be awarded to Chiar-Tech upon the terms specified on the bidder's price proposal."

"Second," said the pudgy one.

"Motion made and seconded. All those in favor."

"Aye."

"Aye."

"Aye."

"Aye," Price concluded. "Opposed?" He looked at the one member who hadn't voted.

"I abstain," he said.

Price stared at the abstainer. "One abstention," he said, not hiding his contempt. "The motion carries, four ayes, zero nays," glancing again at the lone hold-out, "and one abstention."

"Move to adjourn."

"Second."

"Motion to adjourn is made and seconded. All in favor?"

"Aye," all members chorused.

"The meeting is adjourned."

Within the hour, an execution copy of a 370-page contract was placed in front of Arthur Logan, properly "approved as to form" by his general counsel, although the general counsel had not, in fact, reviewed it. Logan flicked through the pages without seeing the words until he arrived at the signature page.

He picked up his pen, signed his name, handed the document back to the deliverer, and permanently altered the arc of his political fortune.

* * *

No story of Finola McGee's had ever gone viral. She had dreamed about it enough, wondered how it would feel, one of those silly dreams, where you made that acceptance speech at the Oscars, or received the Nobel Prize or won the Euro Millions, the Nobel dream being her particular favorite.

But here it was, a mere few days after her own bit of humiliation, she seemed to have turned the tide. The eyes were off her cleavage and onto someone else. The Telegraph had gone ahead with the publication of Alistair's precious gift.

A photo of Aidan Fahey, to be precise, on the front page of *The Irish Telegraph*, wearing nothing but a pair of Jockey y-fronts, trussed up like a Christmas turkey, looking balefully at a leather corset–clad woman standing above him with a bull whip. Nothing was left to the imagination, even though only the back of the woman could be seen. But they were obviously not playing bridge.

Once the first edition was out, Dublin went wild. This was even more of a sensation than the revelation that Fahey had been questioned by the Garda. Not only was it on the early morning news on all radio and TV stations, the photo also went viral on YouTube, Twitter and Facebook within twenty minutes, downloaded, shared and retweeted over a half-million times. It was beyond Finola's wildest dreams.

Maureen had hesitated for only half a minute when she saw the photo and the short piece Finola had written, with the headline: **Fit to be Tied**. *Aidan Fahey reveals all. This photo was obtained from a surveillance camera in an underground lair of Castle Cormack, owned by Irish software giant, Chiar-Tech*, Finola wrote. I will leave it to the photo's subject to explain.

Liam joined Finola at her desk, chewing on a pizza crust from yesterday's take-away meal. "Fahey shows a little less than more, don't you think? Not what you'd call well endowed, is he?"

"Always knew he was a miserable little prick," Finola said. "Despite his posturing and harassing innocent young interns."

Maureen joined them. "What young interns? Are we going back to his misspent youth? Or yours?"

Finola felt the old anger well up. "Both, I'm afraid. He harassed me when I was a press aid at his party's headquarters. Election campaign in 2001. I was twenty-four. Cornering me in the back office when no one else was around. Grabbing for my boobs, saying filthy things, trying to put my hand—" She choked off the end.

Liam stopped chewing. "What did you do?"

Finola glared at him. "What would you do?"

"I'd knee him in the balls."

"I was too scared. I cried. I told the press secretary, then the campaign manager but they did nothing. Fahey jeered at me for ratting on him. So I left. Fahey won the Kerry seat then, remember?"

Maureen nodded. "That's right. And that's also when you came to work here. Seems like yesterday."

"Thirteen years ago," Finola said.

Liam swallowed his mouthful. "And now you've finally gotten payback. Must be a good feeling."

Finola grinned. "The best. But it's not over yet."

Liam raised an eyebrow. "What other surprises do you have in store?"

Finola waved her hand in the air. "Nothing. He'll do it all himself from now on." She copied the article link and emailed it to Paul Forté. Odd, she hadn't received so much as an acknowledgement of her previous missives.

* * *

Jackie McDonough picked up the iPad from the two hundred year old desk and hurled it against the mahogany paneled wall behind him. With that, the photographs and articles from the Irish press vaporized.

Charlie Sligo and Dennis Boyle sat rigid and stone-faced in front of him.

"What the *fuck* are you morons doing to me?" he hollered.

Sligo and Boyle glanced at each other.

Boyle volunteered. "Mr. President, there was absolutely no reason for us to suspect anything like this."

"Like *this*," McDonough mocked. "Like fucking what? A pansy member of the Irish Parliament in a ball gag implicated in the murder of one of his fucking colleagues? The guy who owns the fucking company we're shilling for?" He spread his arms out, palms up. "You can't make this shit up!"

"Boss," Sligo began.

McDonough exploded anew. "Don't give me that 'boss' shit, you fat fuck! You brought me this deal. You and your fucking buddy here," nodding derisively at Boyle. 'It's a great opportunity,' you said. 'Nobody understands this software shit,' you said."

He strode from behind his desk and across the broad expanse of his office, throwing himself into one of the many expensively restored antique chairs to which he was a mere custodian, then rising again, pacing the floor, finally coming to rest looming over them.

"Okay, here's the deal. If one falls, we all fall." He locked eyes with each of them, back and forth, pointing his finger as he shifted. "If one falls, we all fall." He stepped closer to Sligo, extending his arm straight out at his chest. "If you fold, we're all fucked." He switched to Boyle. "If you fold, we're all fucked."

McDonough reeled backward until he was half-sitting on the front of his desk, and crossed his arms. "If either of you so much as squeak a syllable of our involvement in this cluster fuck, I will personally put you through a wood chipper. Do you understand?"

Boyle and Sligo were as pale and still as marble statues.

"I said, do you understand!"

"Yes."

"Yes."

McDonough's feverish intensity waned a fraction. "Okay." He pointed at Boyle. "You are going to visit this Price guy as soon as possible, and you are going to get him to rescind the vote that that fucking committee took the day that Forté bitch shot her mouth off in Dublin. You," he said, pointing at Sligo, "are going to call Arthur Logan immediately and make sure he doesn't sign that contract."

"I think he already did," Sligo muttered, ducking like a beaten dog.

"Well get him to fucking unsign it! Get the fuck out of my office! Make this shit go away!"

Boyle and Sligo sat three seconds too long.

"Get out!" McDonough hollered as he put his hands under the lip of the desk and flipped it over toward the fleeing solons.

Chapter Sixteen

A dumpster, the undead, and a rat

Through a gauzy hydrocodone haze, Paul imagined an angel, disguised as his wife, swiftly descending on him. As the angel got closer, the features of her face clarified, and for a terrifying moment, he saw Shannon as a marionette.

"Your cheek looks like an eggplant," Shannon the puppet said, gliding to Paul's side, patting him gently with its tiny hands.

"You look like Pinocchio with tits," Paul said, totally serious.

The floor nurse poked her head in. "Mrs. Forté, your husband has just had a fresh dose of pain killer, so I would give him a wide berth on whatever he says."

"What do you mean? He talks to me like that all the time." She patted Paul's hand. "Don't you, sweetie?"

"Just don't get him excited. He needs rest."

Shannon gave the nurse a mock glare. "I beg your pardon?"

The nurse tittered and retreated.

"Where's Rex?"

"He went to get something to eat."

"You see him?"

"Yes. He told me what happened. The Senate President had a bunch of hoods jump you in Southie? In a fuckin' alley next to a *dumpstah?* That's so trite."

Paul stared at the woman holding his hand, the smirk buried in her delicate lips, the fire in those dark eyes. "You're not a puppet," he crooned, thinking she'd come to life like in a fairy tale.

Three sharp raps echoed in Paul's head.

"Good morning, good morning," said a large man in a white coat.

Oh, it was Doctor Wise.

Dr. Wise introduced himself to Shannon.

"She was a puppet just a minute ago," Paul said.

Dr. Wise smirked.

"How's my warrior doing, doc?"

Paul felt Shannon's grip tighten on his hand.

"Your husband was very lucky. Some contusions, abrasions. A slightly bruised kidney, a few bruised ribs. No missing teeth or broken bones, although the blow to the head here," he pointed out the purple area around Paul's left cheek and eye socket, "came very close to damaging the zygomatic bone."

"Funny," Paul said, chuckling weakly.

"What's that," the doctor asked.

"The zygomatic bone. I was gonna meet Rex later at Les Zygomates."

Dr. Wise exchanged a bemused look with Shannon. "He'll be sore and a little wobbly for a week or two, but he has no evidence of concussion, although we should keep an eye on that."

"When can I get out of here?" Paul asked.

"You can be home by dinner time, if you play your cards right."

"What are we playing? Cribbage? I haven't played cribbage in years."

"We're playing she takes off, you get some sleep, and we take another look at that kidney. If all's clear, she can feed you at home."

"Okay, doc. I'm in. Can my wife and I have a few minutes

before you kick her out? I miss her like crazy, since she's been punching TeeDees in Ireland all week."

Dr. Wise looked at Shannon. She shook her head and waved him off.

"It's his standard humor. He's not delirious."

"But she did punch a member of the Irish Dáil," Paul affirmed.

"She did?"

"I did."

Dr. Wise smiled and shook his head. "You folks lead interesting lives." He shook Shannon's hand. "Pleasure to meet you. I'll be in to see him again mid-afternoon. We'll know more then."

"I'll be back by four."

"That should work. Goodbye." He pointed at Paul. "Get some rest," he said, and was gone.

Paul watched Shannon staring at him as she fondled his hand. "You look full of pity," he said.

"You look pitiful." Her face wavered between adoration and fright. "I was so terrified when I couldn't reach you on the phone. Promise me you'll never not respond again."

"I promise to avoid dumpsters as best I can." He locked fingers with her and pulled her to him. She rested her head on his good shoulder.

"You did great," he said.

"But you haven't seen the latest."

Shannon tapped her iPhone a few times and held the screen a few inches from Paul's face. The picture was blurry.

"Can't see it."

Rex walked in with newspapers under his arm. "Look what I found at Out of Town News." He tossed them onto Paul's lap. Paul held one up, then the other. Two of the Dublin dailies, both with Fahey's trussing in full display on page one.

Paul began laughing, then wincing from the pain in his ribs. "Don't make me laugh."

"Okay, I'll make you cry," Rex said. "I'm going back to Hawaii."

My work is done."

Shannon frowned. "I barely got to see you."

"I'm not dying, I'm just going home. Come and see me when he gets out of here. He can convalesce in Oahu."

Paul knew he was right. Rex had performed his role, there was nothing of excitement left for him except as a spectator. "Thanks, pal."

Rex shook Paul's hand, accepted a hug from Shannon. "Come see us as soon as you want."

And he left the two of them to resume mooning at each other.

* * *

Fahey did his best to stay underground, limiting the press jackals to the occasional long-range telephoto shot of him exiting the back of Leinster House. He once let his guard down and was buttonholed by a young female journalist who stuck a mike under his nose as he attempted to sneak out a side exit. Her videographer caught it all, and Fahey led the news again, as he had for the past five days.

"That photo was taken during a Halloween party," he said, wiping his brow with a handkerchief. "Nothing to do with Castle Cormack at all. That McGee woman is committing criminal libel. I'm surprised that it isn't obvious to you."

"Odd that the background in the picture was exactly the same as the one taken of Finola, then, isn't it?" The journalist asked.

Fahey looked at her, even more flustered than before. "Well, I... I don't have time for this nonsense," he snapped, his face turning bright red. "I'm appalled at the time and energy you people waste on trivial rubbish like this." He turned and walked away, his raincoat flapping in the wind.

The journalist trotted after him. "Is there a sex dungeon in the basement of Castle Cormack? What does the Irish government pay Chiar-Tech for the use of that facility? Did you have anything to do with the murder of Eoin Ryan?"

Fahey quickened his pace, but she stayed with him, badgering away until he got into his car and slammed the door on her and her microphone.

"Seriously rattled," Maureen remarked as they watched the news clip. "Only a matter of time now."

"I wouldn't hold my breath," Finola said. "He's still in office. I've heard him being called 'the undead' by the opposition. He might be able to ride it out."

"Not for long," Liam said. "The Taoiseach became oddly silent after the Garda questioned him. And some TDs are demanding that he should be expelled from the party and forced to resign. The debate is continuing after lunch if you'd like to go watch."

"No, thank you. I just find it hard to believe he'll finally get kicked out. Dreams don't often come true."

"This one will," Maureen said. "The shit has well and truly hit the fan, and he is standing in front of it all by himself. And we made it happen."

She was right. That afternoon, the Dáil debate took off after lunch and very soon turned into a shouting match between the opposition and Fahey's few remaining supporters, until the Speaker called for order and the Taoiseach rose to make a brief statement.

"I take no pleasure whatsoever in doing so, but it is my duty to ask Mr. Fahey to resign as Minister for Finance. I discourage my friends and colleagues all not to rush to judgment in these matters. Mr. Fahey has yet been charged with no crime. Yet I must insure that our people have confidence in their government, and confidence at the moment is no more important anywhere than at the Ministry of Finance."

His remarks were met with a moment of somber deference, followed by the growing din of partisan bickering, although Fahey's party colleagues were not so much defending him as throwing him under the bus. Before the close of the session, party officials emerged from the Speaker's office to announce that Aidan Fahey had been expelled from the party. Thus, he was no longer eligible to remain as TD for South Kerry.

The silence in the Dáil after the announcement was deafening. Finola sank down on a chair in the newsroom as the broadcast ended. "Someone pinch me," she said. "I must be dreaming." She held up a hand as Liam stepped forward. "No, on second thought, I want this dream to go on forever. And I want to wake up when the little prick is arrested for Eoin's murder and also gets done for fraud."

"You can't have everything," Liam said.

"If there is any justice in this world, I will," Finola muttered. "But I suppose Kerry will have to freeze over first."

"I wonder who the new Minister will be?" Maureen pondered.

"And who'll represent South Kerry?" Liam remarked. "There has to be another by-election. Nearly at the same time as the one for Eoin's seat. Interesting."

"This election is going to be very interesting," Finola remarked. "Who's going to take over the Fahey reign?"

* * *

During his brief convalescence at home, Paul read and assembled all of the stories Finola had forwarded into an impressive compendium, placed them on a thumb drive, and invited his old friend, Corey Fitzpatrick, to join him for a beer. The former Boston Phoenix reporter had moved up in the world, now running the State House News Bureau, a wire service that supplied political news to the rest of the ink-stained wretches who were too lazy to find their own news.

Corey was seated at a bar stool, flicking his finger across the touch pad of a laptop, when Paul arrived at The Barking Crab.

He smiled at Corey, but somehow he still felt his face was bent.

"Holy shit, what happened to you?"

"I kissed the broad side of a dumpster."

Corey looked sceptical. "Looks to me like you got the shit kicked out of you."

"Closer to the truth," Paul said. He received a sympathetic smile from a lovely bartender and asked for a pint of Harpoon.

"What's going on, Paul? Haven't seen you for a long time."

"I have a good story for you," Paul said. He pulled the thumb drive from his pocket and handed it to Corey. "Go ahead, take a look."

Corey plugged the drive in, tapped a few times and scanned the material for a minute or two. Paul used the time to swallow a pain killer with his beer.

"This have anything to do with your facial arrangement?"

Paul nodded and sipped.

"How about Massachusetts politics?"

"It does."

Corey perched his fingers above the laptop's keys. "I'm listening."

Corey's fingers flew as Paul told him about the Chiar-Tech bidding, Boyle and Sligo, his trip to Ireland, Castle Cormack, the grudge match with Fahey, the murders, all of it. He capped it off with the conversation with McDonough and the surprise meeting with the South Boston fight club. When he finished, Corey was smiling at him.

"Jesus Christ, you lead an interesting life."

Paul smiled, feeling the tightness in his cheek.

"Is this for attribution?"

"Every word of it," Paul said.

"McDonough will deny it."

"So what. It's word against word, and I've got the bruises to show."

Corey was scanning the stories while they talked. "Shannon

really clocked the guy, huh?"

"Yes, she most certainly did." He chuckled, and received a stab of pain from a bruised rib.

"Who's this Irish reporter, McGee?"

"She's a pistol."

"Balls the size of watermelons," Corey said with admiration as he inspected the picture of her at the stripper pole.

"True, true. So how fast you think you can get this on the wire?"

Corey glanced at Paul's glass. "Before you finish that beer. It'll be in the news by 11:00 tonight." He tapped some more, scrolled, tapped, scanned it over and hit *send*. "My editor'll look it over and call me in a few minutes."

"Okay, I'm grabbing a cab back to my place. I need a nap."

"One more question before you go."

"Shoot."

"How was the golf course?"

"Fabulous. We'll go back."

"Yah, right."

Paul took a cab back to Farragut Street. The beer made his head swim. He wanted to go up to the roof to relax, but he didn't feel good about the climb up the ladder. So he rolled the futon out in front of the big window and conked out.

He awoke to the sound of the door opening, then heard footsteps, then opened his eyes to see Shannon standing over him, pointing the television remote at the flat screen on the wall.

"What's going on?

"Shhh!"

The screen blinked on and filled with the face of a local reporter in mid-sentence.

"Police said Senator McDonough was alone when the attack occurred, and he did not see who assaulted him. Doctors declined to comment, but a spokesman from the Senate President's office said he suffered from a fracture of the zygomatic bone."

Paul stared at Shannon. Her wicked smile grew.

"Aloha, Rex," she said.

* * *

At 3:42 am, Charlie Sligo sat at the desk in his home office, twisting an elastic band around his fingers. His first shot at a life-changing score. No more worries about private school tuitions, three weddings, maybe a vacation house in Ireland. All fucked to a fare-thee-well because some faggot Irish prick Boyle had brought to him couldn't figure out how to muzzle one fucking reporter.

Well it was all coming apart now, wasn't it?

And what did he have to show for it?

Boyle got the dough, and he shared it, but not with his old pal Charlie. No, Charlie was told he had to wait for his cut, while the Big Man got his tithe just for letting it all go down.

Well, Charlie Sligo wasn't going to make Janice and the girls visit fucking Danbury instead of him visiting Dartmouth. No fucking way.

Charlie Sligo was nobody's patsy. He wasn't going to do what he was told so Jackie McDonough and Dennis Boyle could skate. Besides, who's to say they weren't already throwing *him* under the bus?

He went back to bed, but didn't sleep much while the darkness of his bedroom waned and the birds began to chirp and his wife murmured in a dream. But in that time, he made a decision.

And after he'd dragged his ass out of bed, ate the eggs and sausage Janice cooked for him, and donned a crisp white shirt and chocolate brown suit, he left his home, drove to John Joseph Moakley Federal Courthouse, took the elevator to the ninth floor, and entered the reception area for the United States Attorney's Office.

"Can I help you?" asked an immaculate woman with a short hair and glasses.

"I'd like to see the head of the Public Corruption Unit, please," he said, and finally began to relax.

Chapter Seventeen

An arrest, a brother, and another pint

Three days after Aidan Fahey had been questioned by the Garda, the chickens arrived home to roost.

Finola had taken a few well-earned days off to rest, catch up on her sleep, and begin the outline of a book she planned to write, a book she would dedicate to Eoin and Orla Ryan. She lounged on her couch in front of a muted television, a glass of wine by her side, tapping notes on her laptop. She glanced up to notice the news had begun. Nothing left to report, unless they'd finally gotten the bastard to confess. She'd had such high hopes when the Garda had brought him in for questioning. Surely they would find some tie to the murderous chauffeur. Who else would have hired the man, Margaret Thatcher? No, as each day passed by, Finola's hope and belief in justice ebbed.

She watched the mouth of the pretty newsreader move as a picture of a bus crashed loomed over her shoulder. The mouth stopped moving, then a picture of Fahey appeared as her lips began moving again. Finola lurched for the remote and unmuted the television. "…week after he hosted VIPs at the Castle Cormack, Former Minister for Finance Aidan Fahey was arrested just half an hour ago and taken to the Bridewell Garda station in

Dublin, where he was charged with murder for hire in the death of his colleague, TD Eoin Ryan. No bail was set."

Finola jumped up from the couch and punched the air. "YES!" she yelled. "Yes, yes, yes!" She laughed out loud while she watched two guards escort a handcuffed Fahey to a squad car. He stood with a stiff bearing, his face empty and emotionless, as a guard opened the door and pushed him inside.

She grabbed the phone and punched Liam's number. "They got him!" she shouted when he answered. "They arrested the bastard!"

"Yes," Liam laughed. "Stop shouting, woman!"

"This is big!"

"No kidding. Maureen's going crazy. Everyone's going crazy, actually. You have to come in. We're all going out for a pint in a minute."

"Did you see his face?" Finola chortled. "He looked like shit. Oh, wow, this is a day to remember. It's like…like winning a zillion euros in the Lotto. Or like… I don't know. Words fail me."

"That's a first. But yes, it feels good that he finally got what he deserved. I was worried The Guards wouldn't find anything to connect him to the murder. I wonder what they finally found?"

Finola calmed down. "Yeah, you're right. That's a little strange all right. Is there any way you could find out before the others? You're on a roll, Liam."

"Not sure. I suspect they'll keep such details well under wraps at the moment." Liam was quiet for a moment. "But I'll see what I can do."

"Let me know if you find out anything. We have to make sure The Telegraph stays ahead of the posse and breaks yet another story before anyone else." Finola switched on her laptop. "I'm on my way. I'll just have to e-mail the news to a friend."

"Please give Mrs. Forté my best wishes."

* * *

Finola arranged to meet her colleague, RTÉ news anchor Paula Donnelly, for a celebratory glass of Guinness at Temple Bar. Paula had asked Finola if she'd want to do an on-camera interview about her role in the crime of the decade. Finola wasn't sure about that, but it was a good excuse to get back out and do something with her night life.

After they'd exhausted the gossip on Fahey, they moved on to the coming by-elections and who might take the vacancies left by Ryan and Fahey.

"Have you seen today's issue of *The Kerryman*?"

Finola looked up from her phone. "Oh gosh, I'm afraid I am so far behind on the local rags. I've only read the evening dailies. They're still full of Fahey's arrest and the evidence and the speculations about the cabinet reshuffle that will be announced tomorrow. What about *The Kerryman*?"

Paula wiped Guinness foam from her upper lip. "Yeah, me too. There are so many of them. But my mother rang me this morning from Tralee and said there was an item about the upcoming by-election that could be interesting. So I took a look and…" she paused and looked at Finola with a little smirk.

"—and?" Finola urged. "Spit it out, woman."

"Take a look at their website."

Finola typed *The Kerryman's* website address into her iPhone. "Okay. Here it is…" She stared at the front page. "Fahey vacancy… three candidates…."

Paula nodded. "Yes. All quite well known."

"Sean Fahey," Finola said with disgust. "That's Aidan's nephew. I wouldn't bet any money on him. Can't understand how that family would have the brass neck to put forward a candidate."

"They're just having a go to make sure they keep their name in the pot, I suppose."

Finola scowled. "That boy's as thick as two short planks. And the Faheys are finished." She continued reading. "Ronan Murphy, nice guy but no track record. He might get the younger voters though…" She continued to skim.

"Oh! A Duggan!"

Paula grinned. "The one we should watch out for?"

"Conor Duggan," Finola read, "Former counsellor of Kerry County Council... went to Clongowes Wood College, then law at Trinity and then local politics…Quietly working for the good of the community…also part-owner of a software company in Boston with his older brother, Francis." Finola looked up and stared at Paula. "Boston?" She tapped the link through to Paul with a "???" message.

"What?"

Finola shrugged. "Probably nothing… Never mind." She went back to the item on her phone. "Aww, listen to this. His older brother, the one in Boston, was adopted by an uncle in the States when their dad died. The mum couldn't afford to support the two boys, so the uncle brought the older one to America - and then he bought the uncle's business and put his little brother, Conor through university."

"Sweet story," Paula said. "The voters will love it. And so will the press."

"I know," Finola replied, her eyes on the photo of Conor Duggan. "And he's really good looking, too."

"He's a hunk." Paula winked. "I wouldn't mind interviewing him."

"I have a feeling you'll get your wish. It says here that this Duggan guy is starting to surge and has plenty of money and grassroots support."

Paula nodded. "My mum saw them in action in Cahersiveen at the weekend. Talk about pressing the flesh and kissing babies. They were trumping up the honesty card and dancing on Fahey's grave, she said. They've been talking about this boy taking on Fahey for a while now. I'd never heard the story before, but the Duggans and the Faheys have fought over that seat for four generations."

"You don't say," Finola replied, musing over Paula's words.

"I know, how is this not known? So, mum said the Duggans are descendants of-

"Ciaran Ó Dubhagáinn. I know that part."

"Well, two hundred years after Ciaran was done raiding castles, his descendant, Padraig, got elected to the South Kerry seat. He held the seat for twenty years before he got beat in a bruiser of a campaign fight to Aidan Fahey's father. He used the dark history of the name in the campaign, as Padraig still used the Ó Dubhagáinn name."

Finola finished the story like she knew it all along. "…and while Aidan Fahey was being groomed for his father's seat and keeping it warm, the Duggans were biding their time, until Sean came along. Jesus, this is amazing," Finola said, pausing for a generous gulp of Guinness. "The Duggans rise again. Funny, though…"

"What?" Paula frowned.

"You don't think it's possible that the Duggans were behind all this, do you?"

Paula stared at her near empty pint in silence. She leaned forward and flagged the bartender. "Could I have another pint, please?"

Chapter Eighteen

Two confessions, attorney-client privilege, and a referral

Finola's phone pinged beside her bed at six o'clock. She scrambled for it in a groggy haze and barked, "Yes?"

Seamus Nolan's voice. "Finola," he said. "I have to talk to you. It's urgent."

She glanced at the clock. "It had better be." Whatever he wanted, she suspected the answer was "no," but Fahey's arrest and the looming Chiar-Tech collapse were still big news, and Nolan was in the middle of it. Maybe he could still be useful.

"Can you meet me at Sandymount in an hour?"

"I'll be there."

The vast, flat beach was empty, except for a man walking his dog. Finola pulled her jacket tighter against the wind and walked to the water's edge, watching the dark hull of a ship at sea. The tide was out and the sky merged with the horizon in the grey light of the early morning.

"Am I walking into eternity along Sandymount strand?" a voice said behind her.

Finola stopped and turned. "Have you come here to quote Joyce at me?"

"Not really," Nolan said, his blond hair ruffled by the wind.

"And I won't expect you to lift your skirts like Gertie either."

"If I was wearing skirts, I wouldn't lift them," Finola said.

"The wind would do it for you." Nolan smiled, then looked at her, a bleak expression in his baby-blue eyes. "Never mind. I didn't ask you to come here to exchange pleasantries."

"I certainly hope not. It'd be a lot of work for me."

"No." He fell silent while they walked on. "I appreciate you coming here."

"Why here?"

"I didn't want witnesses. Or eavesdroppers."

Finola stopped walking and faced him. "Protecting yourself, again. Right, okay. So talk."

Nolan stared out toward the horizon and cleared his throat. "I'm turning state's evidence in the Aidan Fahey murder case."

She nodded. "I'm not surprised. Was it you that got him charged?"

"Yes."

"And I assume you've arranged some sort of deal that will guarantee you don't go to jail."

"Well yes, there is that. But truthfully, my only crime involved not speaking up."

Finola scoffed. "You've had that problem your whole career. Besides, I don't believe you. Your reaction in the conservatory was more than that. You knew what I had, and you threatened me."

"You're right. I did know what you had. And I knew what you'd do with it. But I was working on fixing that, and-"

"What do you mean, 'fixing it'?"

"I was going to get that money back where it belonged. It was a short-term cash management problem. I had a handle on it."

The anger in Finola boiled over. "A short-term cash management problem? Do you hear yourself, Seamus? Do you know how ridiculous you sound?"

"I have investors I'm responsible to-"

"And you think the investors of Chiar-Tech are served by your diverting government funds to your private company?"

"It did not go to the company. It went into a long-term maintenance fund for the castle. To fund the government's share of the expense."

"Oh, that sounds so innocent and plausible, doesn't it?" Finola glared at Nolan and stabbed her finger at his chest. "Eoin was *killed* because of that money going astray. A life was lost and a family was devastated."

"I know, Finola. I'm just as horrified by what Aidan did as you. That's why I decided to turn him in. He has to pay for what he did. He panicked, plain and simple."

"How did you know it was him?"

Nolan's shoulders slumped. "He told me."

"Why on earth would he think killing Eoin would fix things?"

Nolan shrugged. "He was terrified his career would be destroyed."

"And now it truly is."

"As is mine. Not much chance the new Minister's going to want to keep me around."

"I should say not." Finola sighed. "What a mess."

"Yes." They walked on in silence for a while. "I don't suppose you'd be inclined to cover my side of this scandal with some degree of sympathy?" Nolan said.

Finola felt the hair on her neck rise, and stopped short. "Why, you conniving, gutless weasel! You didn't come here to confess or apologize, you came here looking for me to help bail you out." She sneered. "I'm leaving. I can't stand the sight of you."

"I have a family, too, Finola."

"Yes, well it's a damn shame you didn't give that more thought before."

She started to walk away toward the car park, and then turned around. "I have a confession too," she called across the stretch of sand.

"What's that?"

"I never read Ulysses. Didn't even get through the first chapter."

* * *

Paul finished reading the material Finola had emailed him. *The Kerryman* story about Conor Duggan and his brother in the States. Old stories about the political feuds and election battles between Faheys and Duggans. Finola's notes of conversations she'd had with various locals in Killarney and Kenmare.

He called the corporate office of BosTech. Duggan's secretary told him her boss was attending the annual meeting of the Ancient Order of Hibernians, Boston Chapter, where he was to receive the award for Humanitarian of the Year.

"How exciting, June," he said. "Where do they hold that meeting, anyway?"

"It's down at Dooley's in Jamaica Plain. They take over the whole place. It'll be like St. Patric's Day, jammed to the rafters. Do you want me to text him you're coming?"

"That's okay, June, I'm not sure I'll make it. Thanks a million."

"No problem, Mr. Forté. And congratulations! That was quite a feat you pulled off for us."

"All in a day's work," he said. "Bye, June."

He sat in his office chair, festering, ruminating over just what the hell he would do and if it would do any good. He concluded that he didn't care. People had been murdered, careers destroyed. And he had been played like an Irish harp.

He checked his watch, guessed the drive time to Jamaica Plain at mid-day, and took the stairs down to the back exit into the alley, careful to insure the absence of thugs before he closed the door behind him. The purple on his face had faded to a dull yellow. He wasted no time getting into the Saab and leaving the alley.

Fifteen minutes later, he parked the Saab at a hydrant in front of Dooley's Tavern, the only spot within blocks, both sides of Washington Street stacked with parked cars.

He opened the door. The heat of male bodies blasted him. Two broad, meaty backs clad in off-the-rack suits blocked the vestibule. Both turned to look at Paul, and turned back.

"Can I get in?" he asked.

One of them turned again. "Not humanly possible."

He stood at the open door, one foot on the stoop, one on the sidewalk. Deep inside the tavern, a man spoke. The voice was faint, but he recognized it.

"…there is nothing more important to me than the welfare of our people, and the vibrancy of our homeland. Long live Ireland!"

A riot of clapping, whistling and *huzzahs* ensued. The two broad backs turned to exit. Paul moved aside as they spilled out the door, followed by a procession of other men. Faces were flushed, eyes glassy, smiles slack. It had been a long and liquid lunch.

He waited for the first human wave to slake, saw an opening and squeezed through. Dozens had left, and still every table was occupied. A lot of small-nosed fellas stood around, one hand in a pocket, the other around a pint. He spotted a gap in the shoulder-to-shoulder line at the bar, and filled it.

"What can I get youze," a sweating bartender asked, stuffing empty pint glasses into a dishwasher.

"Guinness and Paddy's." He turned his back to the bar and surveyed the crowd. Duggan stood by a table in the middle of the room, taking the shoulder claps and handshakes from a river of fellow Hibernians. Duggan's eyes shifted from man to man, over their shoulders, scanning the room, plastered smile, a lot of nods. Just like a politician.

His eyes finally landed on Paul, and the plastered smile cracked. He nodded toward the front door.

Paul turned to the bar, tossed down the Paddy's, glugged half the Guinness, threw a twenty on the bar, and worked his way out to the sidewalk. A few boisterous boyos stood by the wall, smoking and gassing with their soft "R"s. *Chah*-lie, how *ah* ya? Paul considered bumming a cigarette, fought it off, crossed the street and leaned against the wall of a Mexican tapas place, watching the door.

Duggan stepped out a few minutes later, nodded and waved to the fellas, spied Paul and crossed the street. His sleek blue suit swayed with him.

"What're you doing here, Paul?" The soft eyes Paul had been introduced to were gone.

Paul pulled a copy of *The Kerryman* from the breast pocket of his blazer and handed it to his client.

"I've been conditioned to expect that my clients aren't telling me the whole truth, but you are one hell of a liar."

Duggan glanced at the paper and waved it away. "Would you have agreed to represent me if I'd told you the truth?"

Hibernians trickled out the door, calling out to Duggan, who waved them off.

Paul wanted to punch himself. "You knew I despised Boyle."

"Yes, I did."

"Talon Group isn't just your cousins."

"No, it's not."

"It's going to take over Chiar-Tech now."

"That's the plan."

"Its agreement with the company allows it to acquire the majority's interest if certain things occur, such as the arrest of its managing director."

"A standard provision."

"At a strike price far below what it would have been if these contracts had been signed."

"That's the nature of valuation."

Paul stared at Duggan's tie clip. "Did Fahey know the Duggans were involved?"

Francis Duggan paused. "Not until the very end."

Paul took some perverse pleasure in that. He watched a T bus dump off a half dozen citizens of JP at the corner. "You didn't *need* me. You didn't need to send me to Ireland."

"I didn't send you to Ireland. You invited yourself. Then you called your State Department contact, who hooked you up with the American consulate, and *they* got you right into the middle of it."

Dammit, he was right. The whole trip had been Paul's idea. "I saw your cousins, right on the street."

"Yes, you did."

"You didn't think us going to Castle Cormack was a little risky?"

"We didn't expect your wife to punch Fahey in the nose. We also didn't expect Fahey to have Eoin Ryan killed."

Paul's mouth fell open. "*You* gave Ryan that information."

Francis gave his lawyer an embarrassed smile. "This is not how I prefer to do business, Paul. My cousins are different people, and Ireland is not America. They handle their business over there the way they know, the way that's worked for them. It's not how I do business here."

Paul's insides itched. "You knew that Fahey was fallible."

"It wasn't a well-kept secret, Paul. Irish politicians tend to have a taste for the…unusual."

Paul watched the clutch of Hibernians across the street, smoking and eyeing him and Duggan. "But you've got a rival business in competition with them. You must have spent millions developing your state of the art."

"We did, and none of it is on the Chiar-Tech books. We've purchased a company with ongoing contracts and an international presence."

"You didn't purchase it, you stole it."

Duggan smiled weakly, closed his eyes, and shrugged. "The

method was aggressive, I admit. But we didn't do anything except set in motion what was sure to occur."

"Except three murders."

Duggan winced. "I don't think anyone expected Fahey to be so ruthless. A greedy liar and a cheat, sure."

"And a widow and two children pay for your miscalculation." Paul stared at Duggan. "What about Brooks Kelly? Why did he get a bullet in the head? He wasn't even after Fahey."

"I do not know anything about that, Paul."

"He got killed asking around about your hedge fund."

"It's not my hedge fund. I put money in it. I don't manage it. It's just holding my share of Chiar-Tech."

"I don't believe you. Your cousins are barmen, not software venture capitalists. You set it up, and you brought them in. And now I know why."

"Don't tell me about the Duggan-Fahey rivalry."

Paul laughed. "No, although that makes a good story. You did it to make it right with your cousins. Their father brought *you*, not them, to the States. He made you rich, and left them in Kerry to pour Guinness."

Duggan watched the traffic on Washington Street. "It makes quite a story, doesn't it? Confirms everyone's worst opinions of the Irish. Never forget a grudge, better in a barroom than a boardroom, all that."

"Your cousins are not bar owners, they're murderers."

Duggan didn't have a reply.

Paul scrambled it around inside his head, every little detail, trying to understand why he didn't see the whole picture as it had unfolded before him. He'd been called gullible before, but not since his narrow escape from the hands of Bernard Kilroy. Perhaps he hadn't learned as much as he'd thought.

Then it came to him. "Did Fahey know Ryan had the thumb drive with him?"

Francis Duggan would not meet Paul's eyes. He stared at a

point over Paul's head, as though the words he searched for would appear in air. "Paul, my part of this plan occurred over here. I did not involve myself in the dirty details involving my cousins."

"And as a reward for your wilful ignorance, you will soon have a brother in the Dáil."

Francis Duggan's eyes shifted from apologetic to defiant, and in that second, Paul saw the glint of the cousins' angry eyes from their glare in Cahersiveen. "I make no apologies for my roots. Nor for the way our people, or the Irish people in general, conduct their politics. You of all people should know it's a goddamn dirty business. All the more for a guy like you to clean up," the last crack all sarcasm.

"You're comfortable with that? Your cousins chummed the water with an honest man and then pointed the shark at him?"

"I didn't say I approved of it," he protested. "I said it wasn't my responsibility."

A temper Paul didn't remember having crawled from his chest. "Quite a distinction for the Humanitarian of the Year." He stepped close to Duggan and stuck a finger in his chest. "I'm going back to my home to take a shower. Our relationship has concluded. I will preserve confidentiality insofar as it relates to my client, BosTech. Just remember, I have no duty of loyalty or confidentiality to Chiar-Tech or to the Duggan clan." He started towards his car.

"Are you sure, Paul? Once the transfer is complete, the business here in the States is going to be robust. I'd like to make you our principal outside general counsel. You could deal off the procurement work in the other states to whoever you wanted, keep a piece for yourself."

He squelched the urge to go back to Duggan and throw a punch. The boyos across the street would be on him in a flash. He turned and shouted, "You'll pay for this."

* * *

Paul sat at his desk in the same foul mood he'd nursed the day before. He thought of all the things he would like to have said to Duggan, each line better than the last, all of them unutterable. A lawyer takes his client as he finds him, and everyone is entitled to competent counsel. Even scum in a five thousand dollar suit. That was a truth that made him think of doing something different with his life.

The receptionist appeared in his doorway. "There's a detective from the Boston Police here to see you." She raised her eyebrows.

"Well, bring him back. Never keep a law man waiting."

She returned a moment later and ushered the man in. "Mr. Forté, good morning. Detective Cane, Divison E-13."

Paul stood and shook the detective's hand. "Good morning, detective. Have a seat, please."

"Thanks." Cane was a wiry man, thinning dark hair, a creased face. Gray slacks, an ill-fitting blazer, a polyester tie.

"What can I do for you, detective?"

"Can you tell me where you were last night between 7:00 pm and midnight?"

Paul's heart skipped. Prickles crept up the back of his scalp. "I took my wife to dinner at The Chop House, then we went home. What's this about?"

"Did you spend the entire evening with her?"

"Yes. What is this about, detective?"

"Where can we find her to corroborate?"

"She's in her studio at home, Farragut Street, Southie. What the hell is going on?"

Cane's demeanor did not change. "Are you acquainted with Francis Duggan?"

"Yes, he was my client. Until yesterday."

"We have witnesses who saw you and Mr. Duggan arguing outside of Dooley's Tavern in Jamaica Plain."

"I don't know if I'd call it arguing, but yes, we did have a conversation, at about 2:30 in the afternoon."

"What was it about?"

Paul's neck hair rose. "I am not free to disclose confidential attorney-client communications, detective. You know that, I'm sure."

Cane's eyes never left Paul's. "There was one part of the conversation that wasn't confidential. Where you stated," he consulted his notebook, "*you'll pay for this.* Did you say that to Mr. Duggan?"

Paul's heart hammered to get out. "I guess I did, yes. Why are you asking me this? Get to your point, please."

Cane didn't flinch. "Mr. Duggan is presently in the Intensive Care Unit at Mass General Hospital. He was nearly beaten to death last night, approximately 10:30pm."

Paul stared at Cane as the hissing in his ears began.

"You don't know anything about that, do you, Mr. Forté?"

This was unbelievable. A cop asking him if he'd arranged to have his own client pummeled. It was all he could do not to laugh. "Of course not, detective. Do I seem like the type of guy who'd hire thugs to beat up a client?"

"More likely to hire someone than do it yourself, sir." Cane's eyes dropped to the notebook for a second and returned to Paul's face. "To be fair, no, you don't. But you understand we have to ask. We do have a person of interest who was seen leaving the area shortly before Mr. Duggan was discovered."

"What does he say?"

"He's not talking. But his knuckles are awfully raw."

"Who is he?"

"His name is…" Cane consulted his book. "Fahey. Sean Fahey."

Pins and needles crawled down Paul's arms as the wheels in his head spun.

"Know anyone by that name, Mr. Forté?"

Paul calculated the edge of his ethical duty. He pulled *The Kerryman* story out of his breast pocket once more. Cane was more receptive to it than Duggan had been. He scanned it and looked back to Paul. Paul handed him a copy of another story. Finola McGee's last piece.

"I think you might want to call this woman."

EPILOGUE

The courtroom reporters and talk show hosts licked their chops inside Courtroom 13 of the Moakley Federal Courthouse, awaiting the verdict of the thirteen ordinary citizens who were far from "peers" of the now powerless former President of the Massachusetts Senate. The most notable of those reporters had been covering political corruption in Boston politics for thirty years, witnessed three consecutive House Speakers convicted of felonious acts while in office, and written multiple best-selling books on organized crime. But he'd yet to have the pleasure of seeing a Senate President indicted, tried and convicted – something he would readily acknowledge was at the top of his bucket list.

John Fitzgerald McDonough sat at one defense table next to his lawyer, elbows planted on the table, the broad expanse of pinstripes tugging against his back. His lawyer, one Alan Croston, reclined in a swivel chair doodling on a legal pad in his lap.

At another table, Dennis Boyle busied himself with anything but acknowledging the presence of his co-defendant, while his lawyer read on his phone. Despite his lawyer's ardent effort, Boyle had failed to have his trial severed from that of McDonough. The result had been catastrophic, as each sought to point the blame at the other. The jury couldn't help but despise both of them.

Seven seasons had passed since news of Aidan Fahey's treachery had first landed in Paul Forté's inbox. Corey Fitzpatrick's partnership with *Irish Telegraph* political editor Finola McGee had produced a magnificent series of stories that gave New England a stark look at Dublin's political underbelly. Together, they collected thirteen awards, and their hardcover account, The Black Heart, had been sold to Penguin Random House for what Publishers Marketplace called a "very nice deal."

Starting with Ciaran Ò Dubhagáinn's castle plundering during the days of the nine years war in the seventeenth century, Fitzpatrick and McGee traced the history of the Duggan-Fahey rivalry, climaxing with the duplicitous scheme in which the Duggan brothers lured the rapacious and gullible Fahey to sell them a minority interest in Chiar-Tech, and then set him up, knocked him down, and bought him out for a sum that barely covered his legal fees. And the elegant denouement, that ubiquitous device of Irish justice: Fahey's revenge on the long lost cousin in Boston. In between, there was flattering coverage of Sir Alistair Connolly-Smith, the new Lord and Master of Castle Cormack. As the Boston trial ground to a close, Penguin Random House announced that the movie rights had been sold to Paramount.

During the research and writing of the book, Finola McGee rented a flat in the South End of Boston, and Corey Fitzpatrick borrowed a cousin's couch in Dublin. Paul and Shannon speculated as to the true extent of their collaboration.

Charles Sligo had been the government's star witness, and although he would not be remembered for his elocution, his wardrobe or his physique, he did stand up well enough to Alan Croston's blistering cross-examination that he didn't need a recess to change his underwear. Assisting him on the list of government witnesses were Arthur Logan (who came across successfully – and truthfully – as the ignorant dupe) and Teddy Price (who testified under a grant of immunity in a deal that avoided jail time).

One of the lesser charges against McDonough was a criminal civil rights violation, relating to McDonough's threat against Paul

Forté, and subsequent battery upon his person by unknown persons. Paul had begged his brother-in-law, U.S. Attorney William Hartfield, not to make that charge, but Will threatened Paul with obstruction of justice if he did not agree to appear as a witness to describe his successful efforts to prevent the conspiracy and save the taxpayers millions. It wouldn't hurt his legal business.

During Paul's cross-examination, McDonough's counsel asked , "Mr. Forté, are you aware that, the day after you were discharged from Mass General Hospital, Mr. McDonough was viciously battered by an unknown assailant?"

"I heard something about that on the news, yes."

"Are you aware that Mr. McDonough suffered a fracture of the very same facial bone as you nearly suffered?"

"I don't recall the details, but if that is what was reported, I have no reason to disagree."

"Did you have anything to do with the attack on Mr. McDonough?"

"I'm sorry to say I did not."

Neither Paul nor Alan Croston was ever asked if they had a prior relationship.

Francis Duggan's strategy to take over Chiar-Tech might have worked out well, were it not for the Fitzpatrick-McGee exposé. In Dublin, the company was sued by the government over the theft of the money from the Liffey Water Project, the Duggan brothers were stripped of their pub owners' licenses for unsavory conduct, and young Conor Duggan's first term in the Dáil was beset by the lingering animosity of the deposed party (the Labour party lost 13 seats in the by-election) and the distrust of his own party, tied as he was to his cousins. Conor was a good looking young man, but he was as guileless as his cousins were shrewd. The Kerryman had him ten points down going into his first re-election.

Despite the challenges besetting Chiar-Tech, Sir Alistair's deed to Castle Cormack was inviolate.

Shortly after 3:00 pm, all stood as the federal jury filed back into the courtroom and resumed their seats before delivering a verdict that would surprise no one.

Five thousand miles away, Paul and Shannon Forté snuggled in a rope hammock under a thatched roof lanai in Oahu; and in Dublin, Finola McGee chose a Mini Cooper Roadster over the vulgar Porsche Cayman GTS.

An Deireadh

About the Authors

Pete Morin is a former politician, bureaucrat and lobbyist, now trial lawyer, blues guitarist and crime novelist.

When he is not writing crime fiction or legal mumbo jumbo, Pete plays blues guitar in Boston bars, and on rare occasion, plays a round of golf or two. He lives in a money pit on the seacoast south of Boston, in an area once known as the Irish Riviera.

Pete is represented by Christine Witthohn of Book Cents Literary Agency.

Visit Pete at his website, www.petemorin.com or his blog, www.petemorin.wordpress.com. Find him on Facebook, https://www.facebook.com/pete.morin2, and on Twitter, @petermorin.

Visit Pete's Amazon author page to check out ***Diary of a Small Fish*** and a variety of short fiction:

http://www.amazon.com/Pete-Morin/e/B006YXIAKY/

Susanne O'Leary has been the wife of a diplomat (still is), a fitness teacher and a translator. She now writes full-time from either of two locations, in a ramshackle house just outside Cahir, County Tipperary or in a little cottage overlooking the Atlantic in Dingle, County Kerry. When she is not scaling the mountains of said counties (including MacGillycuddy's Reeks, featured in this novel), or keeps fit in the local gym, she writes books in a number of genres; contemporary romance, romantic comedy, historical fiction and, recently, detective.

Visit Susanne at her website, www.susanne-oleary.com or her blog, www.susannefromsweden.wordpress.com/ Find her on Facebook, https://www.facebook.com/authoroleary and on Twitter, @susl

Visit Susanne's Amazon author page to check out all of her previous thirteen titles in various genres. http://www.amazon.com/Susanne-OLeary/e/B001JOXAJO/